She was his ~~enemy~~...

But the things he'd learned set his heart racing and made him feel more alive than he had in ages.

Bold. Headstrong. Foolish. Curious. All the things that would chase away boredom and keep his long days filled with intrigue.

Wanton. Fearless. Willing. All the things that would make his dreams unbelievably lush and keep the short nights filled with passion.

A scuffing sound behind him should have been enough warning, but he'd tried to ignore her tossing and turning. So when she threw the tunic across him and curled up beneath it against his back, then slipped her arm over his waist, Bryce tensed in surprise.

"There is no reason for either of us to freeze to death."

Her whispered words against his neck assured him that this would be the longest night of his life.

* * *

Falcon's Heart
Harlequin® Historical #833—January 2007

FALCON'S HEART

DENISE LYNN

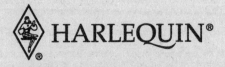

HARLEQUIN®

TORONTO • NEW YORK • LONDON
AMSTERDAM • PARIS • SYDNEY • HAMBURG
STOCKHOLM • ATHENS • TOKYO • MILAN • MADRID
PRAGUE • WARSAW • BUDAPEST • AUCKLAND

ISBN-13: 978-0-373-29433-6
ISBN-10: 0-373-29433-6

FALCON'S HEART

Prologue

Ashforde Keep, Devon, England
Early summer 1143

Bryce of Ashforde squinted through the billowing smoke at the charred remains of Ashforde Keep. Nothing had been safe from the fire set to lay waste to his newly granted land.

He'd been gone seven short days. Long enough to meet his intended betrothed and her family, and to begin the marriage arrangements with Empress Matilda and her husband Comte Geoffrey of Anjou. A sennight ago, when he'd first come to claim Ashforde Keep as the new lord, it had been sound. Now...now it lay in smoldering ruins.

Much would be required to rebuild; men, more gold than he possessed and a great deal of time. But half of his men were missing. The majority of his gold now filled Empress Matilda's coffers. Time was sparse.

The final betrothal agreement was in his saddlebag,

waiting only for his signature. Once it was signed, they would set a date to exchange their promises of the future. Then they would wed, a necessity for any lord of the realm. He needed a chatelaine for the keep and children—both requirements that could be filled by marriage. But he was to bring his new wife, Cecily of Glynnson, home to what?

He would have to hire someone to oversee the rebuilding of his keep. Because he would be gone, using those weeks…or months…hunting those responsible for this devastating act.

His nose burned. His chest tightened, protesting the dense, acrid smoke that made his eyes water and brought a harsh raspy cough tearing up his throat.

He'd counted seven bodies—apparently villagers by their obvious lack of weapons and chain mail. *Why were his men not among the dead?* It appeared they'd been removed from the keep. Or, that they'd run at the first sign of attack. He refused to believe they'd run. When Empress Matilda granted him the title and the land, she'd also granted him twenty men. Each one of them had willingly sworn their allegiance to him. He'd been assured they were faithful, honorable and brave men.

So, where were they?

The wind gathered speed, threatening to pull his hooded cloak from around his shoulders. It blew the smoke across the scorched field.

Bright summer sun sparkled off an object sticking out of the rubble. Bryce kicked the smoldering wooden beams away from what appeared to be a sword. After wrapping the edge of his thick woolen cloak around his hand, he pulled the weapon from the smoking pile.

Even though his heart felt as heavy as a boulder in his chest, and his throat ached from choking back a scream of rage, a bitter smile turned up the corners of his mouth.

A falcon was etched on the blade. The raptor's wings were spread, as if hovering over an unsuspecting prey.

Only one man would mark his weapon in such a manner—Comte Rhys of Faucon. While he'd never crossed swords with Faucon, he'd spoken to men who had. Each of them mentioned the etched falcon.

One question was answered—he knew the party responsible. He stared out toward the forest, now to find his missing men.

Bryce returned to his tethered horse and secured his own sword in a leather loop dangling from the saddle. With great care, he wiped the ashes from the sword he'd found, then held the weapon up toward the blazing sun and vowed, "I promise you, Faucon, I will return your sword and repay you in kind."

Chapter One

Faucon Keep, Normandy
October 15, 1143

Every autumn, for as long as Marianne of Faucon could remember, the Comte of Faucon hosted a grand tournament and faire. First her father's father had hosted the event, then her own father. The task now fell to the current Comte of Faucon, her brother Rhys. It had been taking place for so long, that it was an expected celebration.

The only difference this year was in the number of attendees. A devastating famine swept England, bringing more and more people to Normandy, France and other far-flung locations.

An imposing assembly of troubadours, jugglers, dancers and musicians came to entertain the masses gathered while lining their purses with coin. Knights and warriors, tired of earnest battle and seeking to fill their empty coffers with gold or the spoils of those less fortunate at combat, came to test their prowess on the tourney field. Merchants, desperate to profit from the throng and lighten their load of goods before winter set in, flocked to the keep.

It was a festival of merriment and necessity attended by many—evident by the multitude of gaily colored tents dotting the open area between the forest and the keep. Brilliant multihued pennants fluttered in the warm autumn breeze.

Surrounded by more people than she could count, Marianne could not dispel the restlessness coiling tight in her belly. It rested there all day, growing stronger with the setting sun.

Neither the clang of sword meeting sword, nor the excited shouts and laughter of spectators in the stands broke the unsettling gloom cloaking her like a dark, suffocating shroud.

An unhurried stroll amongst the vendors produced nothing to lighten her mood. No bright hair ribbons, exotic scents from the East, nor carefully crafted jewelry caught her eye. It was truly a sad day when she could find nothing new to purchase that would lift her spirits.

Marianne sighed before moving away from the crowd attending this day's events. The annual festivities used to send a thrill through her body. She'd looked forward to the excitement for months in advance. Over the last two years, the thrill had steadily begun to pall.

"Surely you are not leaving so soon?"

An arm draped across her shoulders slowed her departure. She knew by his simple act of lightly caressing her shoulder, which of her three brothers sought to prevent her leaving.

Her eldest brother Rhys would not have taken the time to approach her. With so many armed men about, he was far too busy keeping them in check.

Darius, the youngest brother, would never think to be so familiar with her. He'd not lived at Faucon while she was growing from child to young woman. Their relationship was more formal than the one she shared with her middle brother Gareth.

Marianne lowered her shoulder and sidestepped Gareth's touch. "Yes. I am. The day has been long. My head aches and the noise worsens the pain. Perhaps a few quiet moments in my chamber will help lessen the throbbing." The lie was a small one, surely not of a size worth an eternity in hell.

He grasped her wrist and tugged her back to his side, bringing her escape to a halt. "It is heartening to discover you have not lost the ability to fabricate tales with a straight face."

Marianne smiled up at him. "I learned from the best, did I not?"

His eyes widened briefly before his lips turned up into a crooked, answering smile. "I suppose you did." He released her wrist and ran a hand through his sweat-dampened hair. "But maybe it is time to refrain from following in your brothers' footsteps. After all, you are a girl."

"Girl?" Oddly enough, Marianne's temper sprang to life at his innocent statement. Her blood ran hot and her heart quickened its pace in her chest. She had not been a *girl* for many years. It was doubtful if anyone outside of her family would mistake the roundness of her hips, or the fullness of her breasts for a girl.

Gareth raked her from head to toe with a slow, piercing stare. The sort of studied perusal a man used when uncertain of what he saw before him. A frown creased his forehead. He rubbed the bridge of his nose, before shaking his head. "Nay. You are a girl no longer, are you?" He sounded surprised. "When did this happen?"

His sudden realization of the obvious banished her ire. "Oh, I am fairly certain it occurred just last week." She could no more refrain from teasing Gareth than she could cease breathing.

He ignored her banter and glanced briefly toward the lists, obviously eager to return to the last of the day's action provided in the tourney ring. With a resigned sigh, he brought his attention back to her. "Why is it that you are unwed?"

Unrestrained laughter burst from her lips and worked its way through her whole body. She wiped the tears from her eyes, shook her head, then gesturing toward the men waiting their turn to joust, she asked, "And who among those gathered would Comte Faucon find suitable? Which man would be worthy of my hand in marriage?"

"What are you saying?"

"Simple, my dear brother, of late I have encouraged more than one eager man to seek Rhys's approval, to no avail."

"Were his reasons not sound?"

"To him, perhaps. But to me they seemed minor." Marianne recited them. "Too old, or not old enough. Not wealthy enough, or strong enough. Too arrogant, or not arrogant enough. One was even deemed not intelligent enough to become related by marriage to the great Faucon family."

Gareth stared at her. "Why did you never complain until now?"

"I never felt that anything was missing in my life until now."

"What do you wish me to do?"

Marianne shrugged. "Perhaps you could talk to our brother, the Comte, and convince him that my heart, too, is deserving of love."

"It may not help, but I promise to try."

Certain Gareth would indeed talk to Rhys, she resumed her escape of the crowd. The short jaunt to the keep was uneventful in an annoying sort of way. She would give anything if some brutish lout would think enough of her to take advantage of the fact she walked alone.

No maid accompanied her. When she'd left the keep earlier, they'd been too busy attending to the numerous honored guests. A blessing as far as she was concerned. It was rather enjoyable to have the freedom of movement without her every step being watched.

Although, if Rhys or his wife Lyonesse discovered her outside the keep without a maid or guard in attendance, Marianne's ears would burn from their words of censure.

Both of them acted as if she was some great prize who needed to be protected at all costs. It might make sense to her if she was of royal blood, but she wasn't. The only thing of value, besides the land from her mother's family, was her virginity. And at the moment she'd give that useless treasure away to anyone bold enough to ask for the honor.

Marianne's face heated at her wicked thought. Her family would be horrified, worse, they'd be ashamed to know what vileness ran rampant in her mind of late.

Was it normal to have these unexplained urges, these frustrating feelings of need that kept her awake at night and surly most of the day?

Or, was this unquenchable yearning the Lord's retribution for carrying the name Marianne? Nay. Surely, she could not be held responsible for her sire's anger at the Church. An anger so great that he burdened his only daughter with a bastardized version of the Blessed Virgin's name. It was no wonder the Church had excommunicated him.

Thankfully, that dire decree had not been extended to the entire family. While her sire might reside in the devil's realm for an eternity, at least she and her brothers still had a chance for salvation.

That is, if she could find a way to rid herself of the uneasiness threatening to rule her.

Is this why most girls were married at a young age? So that by the time they started having this odd, irritating bodily awareness, they'd already be safely ensconced in their husband's bed?

Now her head truly did pound. All of this thinking, wondering and longing for something she'd yet to experience would soon make her senses take leave. As she drew closer to the keep, she mingled with a group of people. If anyone from her family saw her entering Faucon, she could then say she'd not been out alone.

Before heading to her pallet for an early night, Marianne detoured toward the family's private sitting area. Maybe a brief visit with her nephews would take her worries off things she could not change.

"Who do you think Marianne should be given to?" Lyonesse's voice drifted out of the chamber.

Marianne came to a rocking halt just outside the archway. She ducked out of sight and pressed tightly against the wall, listening to her sisters-by-marriage discuss her future.

"I thought Lord Markam's son looked promising," Rhian, Gareth's wife offered.

Marianne bit the inside of her mouth to keep from snorting aloud. Markam's son? Only over her dead body would they convince her to wed that pompous ass.

"Markam?" Rhys's wife laughed before thankfully dousing any continued discussion of that suggestion. "Lord Markam's son has not enough gold, strength or wit to protect his own pretty face let alone Marianne's."

"It is well past time for her to marry. Soon, she will be too old for any to consider. Marianne has seventeen years on her and is not getting any younger. She must wed with haste."

Oh, bless you for that observation. Marianne wanted nothing more than to wrap her hands around Marguerite's neck and squeeze tightly. How Darius could have married this woman was completely beyond her comprehension.

"Rhys is well aware of his sister's age." Marianne cringed at Lyonesse's sharp tone. When the Lady of Faucon spoke in that manner, most people gave her a wide berth. "He is doing his best to find someone suitable."

"Yes, well, Rhys needs to quicken his search before some knave recognizes the unquenched lust sparking from those eyes of hers." Marguerite's observation brought the heat of embarrassment back to Marianne's cheeks.

"Ah, you've noticed that, too? Then perhaps to hasten the matter along, maybe the three of us should offer to assist him." Rhian's calming tone eased some of the tension from Marianne's neck and shoulders. "After all, we are more able to know what would make another woman content."

Content? Marianne shook her head as the tension returned. She wished not to be content. Not wanting to be seen, or heard, she backed silently away from the chamber. Not one of them would have settled for being content, why did they assume she would?

She was no different, she wanted the same things they had. There was little privacy in a keep, even one as large as Faucon. Marianne knew what these women shared with their husbands. She'd heard the throaty laughter of the chase, the breathless sighs of pleasure and the lingering moans of fulfillment.

She needed that, too. She craved desire, a fierce all-consuming passion that would drive her mad, while at the same time leave her completely fulfilled.

But never content.

Dear Lord, please, never let her live in so boring a manner as content. She'd sooner die.

Marianne physically shook the thought from her mind and body with a heartfelt shrug before heading below stairs. But the overheard conversation had left her more restless than before. A restlessness now laced with urgency. Perhaps, instead of seeking her bed she could find some type of entertainment in the great hall.

She paused at the bottom of the narrow stairs, sweeping her attention across the hall. In preparation for the festival the walls had been recently white-washed. Lyonesse and Marguerite had painted wildflowers and herbs on them. When Gareth and his wife had arrived, Rhian had added trailing vines to the colorful foliage.

The floor had been cleared of the old rushes and new ones had been spread. Sweet woodruff had been scattered liberally to aid in keeping the smells as pleasant as possible.

Since the great hall was used mostly for eating right now, the trestle tables were left in place most of the day, instead of being taken down after the meals. Extra benches had been brought in and lined the walls.

The far end of the hall was left open, giving the entertainers a place to perform. It also provided room for those guests wanting to take part in dancing.

To the right side of the hall, shallow alcoves had been cut into stone walls. These tiny, cavelike rooms were used for private conversations…or stolen moments alone.

The one alcove at the farthest end was curtained and used only by her brothers. Two guards stood just outside that alcove, letting her and everyone else know that two of her brothers were inside the private room and wished not to be disturbed.

Marianne drew her attention back to the overcrowded hall. Very few of the men still gathered had not succumbed to the heady intoxication of Faucon's wine. Those who still possessed their wits were either very old, or very young. Neither group attracted her interest.

She headed toward the large double doors leading out of the keep. If she couldn't count on her family to find her a man worth having, perhaps it was time to count on herself. With the number of men gathered for the tourney, there had to be at least one who would quicken her pulse and make her knees weak with longing.

After dismissing the guards at the door with a nod, she stepped outside the keep. Thankfully, none of her brothers' captains were present. They never would have let her pass so easily.

The wind lifted her ebony hair and sent a chill down her spine. A slight nip in the evening's breeze bore promise of the coming winter. She pulled the hood of her woolen mantle over her head.

The sound of people enjoying themselves drifted on the wind. Hoots of laughter, voices raised in song and good-natured shouts of dare sailed over the keep's walls.

Marianne glanced briefly over her shoulder. If none of the family saw her leave, they couldn't stop her. She would pay dearly when they discovered her missing, but right now, she needed this freedom.

Never in all her life had she been permitted outside the walls at night without one of her brothers in attendance. But since their marriages, they'd seldom seen fit to escort her into the village to attend any of the celebrations. She'd spent many a night sitting beneath the narrow slit of a window in her chamber listening to others' merriment and growing more frustrated with each beat of her heart.

She was tired of being obedient, sick unto death of being the good Faucon sister. If she was well beyond her prime age for marriage, then surely she was of an age to take care of herself while seeking just a measure of entertainment.

With a quick check of the small sheath hanging from her belted waist, she made certain her dagger was at hand before passing through a postern gate at the rear of the keep.

She soon caught up with a group of tradesmen and

their families who were headed toward the faire grounds set up off to the side of the clearing. If there was truly safety in numbers, then she'd be more than happy to follow right behind them on the short walk.

The moon shone brightly in the cloudless, star-studded sky. A fine night for a faire. Perhaps a night so fine she might forget the nagging unease clawing at her belly.

The succulent aroma of pig roasting on an open spit set her mouth to water. If Faucon's cook had anything to do with this feast, the meat would be basted and served in a rich raisin and wine sauce. A pinch of cumin would be added to lend just the right bite to the flavor. If done correctly, the diner's stomach would trip with joyous anticipation before the first mouthful even reached his waiting lips.

Marianne followed her nose. With winter fast approaching it was her duty to pad her flesh with a little extra fat for warmth. She chuckled at her reasoning— extra padding was something she didn't need, but she was out here this night to make merry. And if making merry couldn't include a man, then food would have to suffice.

"Are ye all alone?" A man grabbed her arm, stopping her abruptly. "No lass should be by herself on a night such as this. Let me and my friends keep you company."

Even though being detained by a man was something she'd recently wished for, this one was not what she had in mind. He reeked. Neither he, nor his clothing had been washed in many moons. She glanced at his friends. They, too, appeared to be just as unkempt. Not quite what she sought.

"Thank you, nay." She tried to shake him off to no avail. To keep from pulling out her dagger and causing a scene that would bring unwanted attention her way, she grasped for a lie he might believe. "My husband awaits my return."

To her amazement the fabrication worked. The man released his hold. "I beg your pardon, milady. I meant no harm."

She wanted to assure him that no harm had been done, but feared any further conversation would only encourage him. So, she simply nodded and continued through the crowd, toward the food.

Close enough to see the cooks around the spit, Marianne stopped. To her dismay, her nose had been right—Faucon's cooks were in charge. She had been the chatelaine at Faucon until Rhys married Lyonesse. The cooks would recognize her instantly.

She quickly assessed the others waiting their turn to purchase a share of the food, then stepped up to an unfamiliar child. The boy nearly drooled at the smells wafting across his nose. From the looks of his dirty and tattered clothing, Marianne doubted if he had enough coin to buy anything to eat. Then again, he could simply be a typical young boy—tattered and dirty clothing would not be out of the ordinary for him.

No matter. He was still a boy and from what she'd observed through the years, they had bottomless stomachs always begging to be filled. She pulled some money out of her pouch, then touched his shoulder. "Lad, would you be kind enough to do me a great favor? I will pay you well."

His eyes lit when he glanced at the coins in her hand.

She held out enough to purchase for her and at least ten others. "Oh, aye, milady."

After dropping the money into his cupped hands, she nodded toward the spit. "All I desire is a portion of that pig. The rest is yours." She resisted the urge to put a finger under his chin and close his open mouth. "I will await you here."

Without a word, he scampered away to do her bidding. Marianne's stomach growled in anticipation. She'd skipped the noon meal because she hadn't been hungry. When the evening meal was served, she'd been too busy feeling sorry for herself to join the others. So, this guilty pleasure was as much a necessity as a desire.

The lad rushed toward her with his purchases hugged tightly in his arms. Halfway to her, he stopped. His eyes grew large and he opened his mouth. She saw his lips move, but with all the other noise, couldn't hear his words.

Marianne took a step toward him. At the same instant she heard, "There she is." Before she could react a hand clamped over her mouth, choking off her scream. Another laced around her neck, jerking her backward into the shadows.

Bryce of Ashforde watched in stunned silence as four strangers plucked Marianne of Faucon nearly from his own grasp.

For two days he and his men had prowled the faire waiting for the opportunity to snatch Faucon's sister. And now someone had beaten him to his prey.

If not for the unwanted attention it would draw, Bryce would have shouted in rage. The same threat of unwanted attention kept him from attacking the men who unwittingly thought to best him at his own game.

"My lord?" Sir John's tone echoed the same stunned surprise. "Shall I order the men to overtake the rogues?"

Rogues? Bryce nearly laughed at his captain's description. If the poorly dressed louts were rogues, what was he? Had he not come here to Faucon seeking to do the very same thing?

Perhaps not *exactly* the same thing. His men were to kidnap Faucon's sister, blindfold her and cart her toward Ashforde. There he, Comte Bryce of Ashforde, would bravely rescue the maiden, see to her comfort and safety, then return her unharmed to her brother's care. Thus earning himself the undying gratitude of Comte Faucon.

Faucon's gratitude was but the first step toward the revenge he sought. Revenge and the whereabouts of his still missing men.

Unfortunately, he was in enemy territory. Otherwise, he'd not have thought twice about rescuing the lady immediately. If he did so now, there would be too many questions he couldn't answer. He could think of no good explanation for being at Faucon in the first place.

Granted, the festival drew many to Faucon, but it was highly doubtful if any of those in attendance were loyal supporters of Empress Matilda.

"No. Do nothing to give away our presence." Bryce shook his head. "Follow them, closely. Intercede on the lady's behalf only if circumstances seem dire. All may yet fall into place as planned."

Chapter Two

Faucon Keep, Normandy
October 16, 1143

Lyonesse of Faucon absently ran a wide-toothed comb through her hair as she stared out the arched second-story window opening. Early morning sunlight streamed into the chamber she shared with her husband Rhys. Dust motes seemingly danced in the shimmering light.

Since it was still early, the baileys were quieter than they had been in days. Even the keep was reasonably quiet. A blessing to be sure. While the faire was a grandly looked forward to event, it was also more tiring than she could have imagined. Thankfully, it only lasted a fortnight.

The chamber door slammed against the wall, breaking the quiet she'd been enjoying. Only one person could force the door to swing so solidly on its hinges.

She turned away from the window, her welcoming smile fading as she stared at her husband.

Rhys, the Comte of Faucon, her own devil comte looked the part. The scowl on his face boded the coming of a disastrous thunderstorm. She'd not seen his jaw so tight, or the tic pulsing in his cheek for many months.

She glanced quickly out the arrow slit, studying the landscape intently. Were they under siege? Did an army approach Faucon?

"Marianne is gone."

Lyonesse swung around so fast at his stark pronouncement that her head spun. "What do you mean gone?" She tried to wipe the questioning frown from her face as she walked quickly toward her husband.

"Gone. Her bed was not slept in last night. She is not to be found in the keep, the baileys, or the village."

"Oh, Rhys, nay." Lyonesse placed her hand against his chest.

He pulled her into his embrace and buried his face in her hair. She rested her cheek against him. The need for action battled with the need to give her husband what little comfort she could.

Finally, he released her. The gold flecks in his eyes shimmered. His raven eyebrows met like wings over them. A slight smile crossed her mouth at the image before her. Ah, yes, this was her devil comte, ready to battle any who'd dare stand in his way.

He drew back his shoulders and fisted his hands. Movements that forced a laugh from her. A laugh that only intensified when he turned his fierce scowl toward her.

"Rhys, my love. Before you gather your army, should you not perhaps look for her again? Then wait a day or so before going to war against an unknown opponent?"

"Of course I will keep looking for her."

She stroked his fist. "Without destroying every building in the village?"

While he unclenched his fingers, his expression did not change. "She cannot be far. She was just here yesterday…." He paused, his eyebrows winging up in question. "Wasn't she?"

With so many strangers gathered at Faucon, Lyonesse knew that he'd been distracted from his family. His focus had been on the men taking part in the many games of war held in the open fields. The tourney drew nearly as many people as the faire itself, except those here for the tournaments were armed.

"Yes, fear not, she was here yesterday…." Now Lyonesse paused. When had she seen Marianne last? The girl hadn't appeared at the evening meal. Nor had she gathered with the family in the solar afterward.

"What?" Rhys looked down at her, his scowl quickly turning to a frown of worry. "When did you see her last?"

Lyonesse turned yesterday's events over in her mind. Had she seen Marianne after the morning meal? Not that she could remember. "Yesterday morning. But I saw her maid before retiring last night."

His eyes widened. "Alone?"

"Yes. The maid had helped out in the keep yesterday. I assumed Marianne would know enough to remain close by."

Rhys groaned. "What sort of mood was Marianne in last you saw her?"

Lyonesse glanced toward the ceiling. "The usual. Moody. Distracted. Frustrated."

While he appeared to toss that information around, she asked, "Do you think she would have taken it into her head to run away?"

Rhys paused before answering. Finally, he shook his head. "Nay. She might be willful, and might on occasion slip away from her maid for a ride across the demesne lands, but no, she would not run away."

"Then that can only mean—" Lyonesse gasped. "That someone took her."

"Aye. 'Tis what I fear."

"Perhaps a ransom note will soon arrive?"

"If the people who took her wish to live, a demand for ransom better arrive quickly."

"Have you told the others?"

Rhys shook his head. "No, I wanted to speak to you first."

Lyonesse suggested, "Perhaps you'd better tell them now."

"I will locate Gareth and Darius, while you find their wives."

"Of course. Shall we meet in the solar? It would provide more privacy than the hall."

After Rhys left she turned her full attention to the task at hand. Lyonesse prayed that those who'd taken Marianne knew who they had captured. The girl was ripe for a smooth-talking man to turn her thoughts from honor.

If her identity was known, it was highly doubtful any man would be stupid enough to dishonor the Faucons' little sister.

While she worried for Marianne, she knew that Rhys

and his brothers would do everything in their power to find their sister.

And once they did, she'd see to it that the girl found herself a husband posthaste.

Chapter Three

Hampshire, England
October 19, 1143

It took nearly four days before anything fell into place for Bryce of Ashforde. From the start, luck had seemingly gone against him. The men who'd kidnapped Faucon's sister joined up with a caravan heading north. Then they'd crossed the channel, and traveled toward Hampshire.

Bryce had sent two of his men ahead, to ferret out what they could. The kidnapping of Faucon's sister was a daring act. One that would set the tongues of rumor and gossipmongers wagging at a furious pace. He wanted to know what word was being bandied about.

Then, with little more than the blink of one eye, the Good Lord saw fit to be kind—an occurrence that did not happen much of late. Bryce wiped the smile from his face before rejoining the circle of men.

For the first time in months he felt that luck was on

his side—he could feel it pulse through his veins like warm honey, and could taste its sweetness.

The men gathered in a circle diced for a rare prize—one that would be his. A prize that would gain him the opportunity to make Comte Rhys of Faucon experience just a measure of the revenge due him.

Faucon thought he could destroy Ashforde Keep without suffering the consequences. The coward and his men had attacked while Bryce was attending Empress Matilda. He'd returned to his demesne lands to find his keep in ruins, his crops destroyed, seven villagers dead and his men gone.

War was war, and while Faucon may have been the victor on that particular day, he would soon taste defeat. In the end, Ashforde would prove victorious.

Just this morning his men had brought word of a rumor from Baldwin de Redvers the Earl of Devon. The band of thieves who had kidnapped Faucon's sister held her outside of Hampshire.

After lightening his purse of coin to grease a few palms, Bryce discovered the merit behind Baldwin's tip. He'd learned the kidnappers were horrified to discover who they'd taken. Too afraid to demand ransom, they'd left Normandy and crossed the channel into England. Perhaps they weren't complete idiots—they'd immediately realized that Faucon would kill them in lieu of paying ransom.

To relieve themselves of what they now deemed an unprofitable burden, the thieves were going to offer her as a prize in a game of chance. A prize Bryce would gladly accept.

The game was to take place this day. He'd made certain

to be at the prearranged site behind the smithy's early. Bryce would not chance missing this blessed opportunity.

"Your toss, milord."

He took the pair of dice and warmed them in his hand. It all came down to this final toss. Silence fell heavy upon the circle. He could nearly hear the thrumming of pounding hearts as the others watched…and waited.

He shook the dice, willing the smooth carved bones to do his bidding one more time, then released them into the circle.

A lifetime passed before his mind's eye as the dice tumbled and rolled across the crude circle etched into uneven dirt, before coming to a rocking stop.

All of the other men shouted—some in despair for their own loss, others in congratulations for Ashforde.

He rose, accepting the hearty congratulations in silence. But inwardly his shouts of victory bounced against his chest. A toss of the dice not only won him the prize he sought, it saved him from ordering his men to take Faucon's sister by force.

The man in charge of the game waved morosely toward a multicolored tent. "Your prize is in there, milord."

Before the man finished speaking, Bryce had crossed half the distance to the tent pitched at the edge of the clearing. He paused for a moment, savoring his win and the taste of long-awaited revenge, before stepping through the flap.

A small metal brazier dimly lit the inside of the tent, chasing away the shadowed darkness and illuminating his winnings in the far corner of the tent.

Even bedraggled and dirt-streaked, Faucon's sister made him wish circumstances were different. As dark-haired as her brothers, she was taller than most women, but taking the height of her siblings into consideration, her family most likely found her stature unremarkable.

The sudden desire to see those long limbs stripped bare for his perusal made his heart pound erratically in his chest. A happening he was certain his intended would not find acceptable in the least.

He'd only been in Cecily's company a few short days, but he'd seen her temper flare often enough to know she'd not take kindly to the thoughts running through his mind over another woman. To calm his racing pulse, Bryce lifted his gaze to her face.

But staring into her brilliant green eyes did little to ease his growing discomfort. By the saints above, what was wrong with him? Not only was he sworn to another, this beguiling woman was his enemy's sister.

Yet, she was guiltless. His revenge was not directed toward her, nor should it be. She was simply a means to an end, an unwitting pawn in a game not of her choosing.

He approached her slowly, wishing not to cause her more fright than what she surely must already have suffered.

Marianne kept her unwavering attention on this new stranger as she took a long, steady breath, then turned sideways, making her body a smaller target by putting her left shoulder toward the man.

With a great deal of anger toward herself and the men who'd taken her from Faucon, she'd already accepted the fact that she might not survive this twist of fate. But she'd not breathe her last without putting her brothers' lessons to good use. If this man moving steadily toward her thought to attack her and come away unscathed, he was in for quite a surprise.

She tightened her grasp on the knife she kept hidden in the folds of her torn and dirty gown. While the small blade might not kill him, Marianne hoped he'd be taken aback by her action long enough to give her time to escape.

Her kidnappers had been careful so far. They'd disarmed her the first day. But this morning, when one of them had brought food to break her fast, their carefulness had gone astray. A small eating knife had been left behind.

The man took another step closer. By shifting her weight back to her right foot, she'd be in the correct stance for a quick lunge. Marianne extended her left hand, palm out as if to ward him off. "Stop. Come no closer."

His flaxen eyebrows rose, nearly disappearing beneath unruly waves of wheat-colored hair. But he stopped and stared at her a moment before saying, "Fear not Marianne of Faucon, I seek only to make certain you have suffered no harm before returning you to your brother."

Such concern from a stranger surprised her. His deep voice floated across her ears as smooth and steady as a calm summer breeze. She tightened her suddenly lax grip on the knife. "We are not acquainted, who are you?"

She stole another glance at her rescuer—if that's what he truly was. The stomach-clenching fear she'd experienced over and over the last few days returned full force. He'd said that he posed no threat. Could she believe him? While he didn't appear as ruthless as the men who'd originally captured her, he was still a stranger. A stranger whose unwarranted familiarity sent a sharp stab of warning to her very bones.

With a brief half bow, accompanied by a devastating

smile, he introduced himself. "Bryce of Ashforde at your service, my lady."

His name made something in the back of her mind twitch. Thankfully, that odd twitch prevented his flashing smile from taking her breath away.

"Ashforde...Ashforde...I know that name."

A dark frown replaced his smile. Instead of explaining why she might have heard his name before, he stepped within reach. "We must leave here quickly."

Something was dreadfully wrong. She tensed her muscles in preparation to defend herself if need be. While he'd done nothing so far to cause her harm, Marianne had no reason to trust him any more than she did those who'd taken her in the first place.

She nodded down toward her tattered dress. "I, too, would like to leave this place—for good reason. Pray tell, what is your haste, my lord?"

"I would hate to lose my winnings so soon." Ashforde glanced over his shoulder toward the tent flap before adding, "Unless of course you would prefer their company to mine."

Marianne did her best not to gape. "Winnings?" She quickly surveyed the tent before narrowing her eyes at him. "I see no bags of gold or other riches."

Without a trace of humor on his face or in his voice, Ashforde cleared her confusion. "You were the prize."

She blinked, certain she'd not heard him correctly. "*I* am the prize? You *won* me?"

"Yes. In a game of dice."

"A game of dice?" She couldn't decide if she wanted to laugh or cry. She'd been offered up like a cache of gold, or a piece of horseflesh.

Obviously hoping to catch her off guard, Ashforde moved a hair's breadth closer. Marianne shook her head. "No. Stay where you are." He only shrugged before moving back.

"So, instead of seeking ransom, these imbeciles took it into their lack-witted minds to offer me up in a game of chance?"

"'Tis likely they wanted someone of less importance than Comte Faucon's sister and feared demanding ransom from him."

She chewed on her lower lip. *And who was the bigger imbecile?* "They learned that bit of information from me."

Ashforde laughed, then said, "Perhaps your most unwise move."

"Debatable." A flush of embarrassment at the lack of decorum responsible for her being in this position in the first place heated her cheeks. She admitted, "I am fairly certain that cavorting about the village, at night, without an escort could be considered my most unwise move."

His soft whistle surprised her. She thought for certain he would laugh, belittle, or lecture her.

Instead, he asked, "Have your brothers lost their senses?"

"They are not to blame. I took advantage of an overcrowded keep to slip away unseen."

At that, he did laugh. "Quite the handful to control, are you?"

His question, asked in a tone one would use with someone much younger than she, nicked at her pride. She lifted her chin a notch before seeking to set him right. "I am not a child to be controlled by my family."

Ashforde met her stare for a moment before letting it trail pointedly down the length of her body. His eyes shimmered and a soft half smile played at his lips as he drew his gaze ever so slowly back up to hers. "No, Marianne of Faucon, you are no child."

The growing hunger in his eyes sent her heart stuttering madly in her chest. Good Lord above, what had she done?

Silence fell heavily inside the tent. The walls seemed to inch closer, suffocating her. She licked her suddenly dry lips. Ashforde's sharp intake of air echoed in the confined space.

To her amazement and dismay her body reacted not with fear, but with anticipation. It was apparent, to her body at least, that this man, this tall blond stranger could fulfill the longing that'd battered at her day and night for countless months.

When she'd gone looking for excitement to quench her frustration, this is what she'd been seeking—but not in this manner.

Not as a prisoner needing rescue.

And most certainly not as a prize offered in a game of dice.

She wanted to step back, to move away from the desire wafting from him, beckoning her to surrender to her own hunger. She needed to run before she did something extremely unwise—like bolt right into his arms.

Voices from outside the tent distracted her. Ashforde lunged and she instinctively threw her weight forward, while at the same time swinging her right hand, blade extended.

Bryce saw the knife coming and twisted his body just

enough to catch the blade on his side, not directly into his stomach.

After knocking the knife from her grip, he jerked her against his chest with one hand, threaded the fingers of his other hand through the snarls at the back of her head and ordered against her lax lips, "Fight me, you little fool."

When she did nothing except stare blankly at him in shock, he slid his hand down her back, cupped the soft roundness below and brought her roughly against his groin. "If you wish to leave here in one piece, fight me, Marianne."

Once she started struggling in his arms, Bryce swung her around so he could face the intruder who'd entered the tent. Just before lifting his mouth from hers, he whispered, "Scream."

He glared over her shoulder at the man standing before the tent flap. "Something you want?" He curled his lips, hoping the man took it as a feral snarl and not a grimace of pain.

"Let me go," Marianne shouted. "Release me."

The man laughed. "Nothing, my lord. I only wished to make certain you were enjoying your prize."

Marianne gasped and strengthened her struggles.

Bryce hung on to her, laughing harshly. "I was, until you interrupted me."

The man tipped his head and before leaving said, "Forgive me, my lord. I leave you to your sport."

"Sport?" Marianne's voice rose. "Rhys will see you all dead!"

Once Bryce was certain the man was truly gone, he released Marianne.

"You pig!" She swung an open palm at his face striking him against the cheek.

He ignored his stinging face and grabbed her wrist. "Try anything that stupid again and you will regret it."

"Me?" Anger suffused her face with a deep blush. She bent over and picked up the small eating knife, then pointed it at him. "If you touch me again, I will kill you."

When he'd mulled over all the difficulties that could occur with this plan, he'd not expected her to pose a problem. As brash and bold as her brothers, Marianne of Faucon could end up being his biggest difficulty—unless he could quickly gain the upper hand.

Bryce grasped her wrist and shook it until she dropped the knife. The small but lethal weapon thudded onto the dirt floor of the tent. He tried to intimidate her with a glare and suddenly wished she were a bit shorter. He gritted his teeth against the pain in his side, then said, "The next time you seek to kill me, I suggest you complete the task."

"Or you'll do what?"

By the saints above, what would he do? He furrowed his brows as he tugged her closer. "I could kiss you into submission." He paused, giving the light in her eyes time to go from shock to outrage before adding, "Perhaps it would be safer for both of us if I were to simply truss you like a stag."

"You would not dare." She tried backing away.

A sleeve of her gown hung in tatters. While securing her with one hand, he tore a strip of fabric free, wrapped it around her wrists, then tied it off and smiled. "I would dare much more, but this will suffice—for now."

Marianne stared at her wrists as if trying to make sense of what had just happened. She twisted her hands to no avail, succeeding only in chafing her flesh. Then she tried plucking at the bindings with her teeth. Again, her efforts were futile.

Finally, she hung her head and held out her arms. "Please, my lord, I will cease tormenting you, if you will but free my hands."

He wanted to believe her, but Bryce had an inkling she was simply lying to get her own way. The sound of booted feet walking by the tent quickly made him choose. He took his dagger out of its sheath and slid the shiny blade through the cloth. "I cannot help but wonder what this stupidity will cost me."

As soon as she was free, Marianne tried shoving him away. It was comforting to know his suspicions were still functioning well. She pushed at him again, catching his wound with the heel of her palm. He gasped at the sharp jab of pain.

She stepped back and stared at him for a heartbeat before nearly crying, "Oh, my lord, you are bleeding."

"For the life of me I can hardly imagine why." Sarcasm was not his usual way of dealing with inane comments of the obvious, but there was nothing usual about this day thus far.

"That is where I stabbed you."

He quelled the urge to nod in agreement and at the same time swallowed his retort. Instead of making her appear the fool, he pointed at a jug by the cot. "What is in there?"

Marianne crossed the floor and retrieved the jug. "'Tis the most bitter wine to ever exist, but it will serve the purpose." On the way back, she picked up the eating knife from the floor. At his loud sigh, she quickly assured him, "To cut bindings from my gown." Once she returned to his side, she pushed his cloak from his shoulders. "Undress."

"Such an inviting offer, my lady." Bryce took the knife and jug from her hands. "After you."

Chapter Four

Marianne nearly choked on her sudden gasp for air. "After me?" Her rescuer was beginning to prove more dangerous than her captors.

Ashforde shook his head. "I apologize. That was unwarranted." He studied the tent flap. "As much as I truly appreciate your offer to bind the wound you made, we have not the leisure."

Her own glance toward the flap assured her that no one was in the entryway. "There appears to be no lurking danger." She hacked off a strip of her gown and held it out to him. "This will not take long."

He grasped her wrist and pulled her toward the back of the tent. "They are pacing before the flap. Now that you have told them your brother will see them dead, they cannot risk letting you return to Faucon." After slitting the tent wall, he held it open. "If you wish to leave here in one piece, head straight toward the forest. I will be right behind you."

She hesitated, not certain whether to believe him or not.

The shuffling sound of footsteps near the front flap hastened her decision. Marianne ducked out of the opening and as quickly as her tired body would move, dashed for the cover offered in the dense growth of the forest.

"Here, this way." Ashforde strode past her, leading them off to the right and to a waiting horse.

He pushed her unceremoniously up onto the saddle and guided her hands to the beast's mane. "Hang on." Without sparing her little more than a glance, he took the reins and led them deeper into the woods.

Marianne gripped the coarse hair with all her might. Now that she was finally off her feet and not quite as worried about her immediate safety, she could feel the exhaustion of her body. The parts of her body that did not ache, burned. She couldn't remember the last time she'd eaten, drank or even slept for more than a few hours.

When he slowed down to assess his bearings, Marianne licked her dry lips. "Do you think I could have a drink?"

He looked up at her. "There's a stream just a short way from here. We will be there shortly."

Sunlight broke through the foliage. The shimmering brightness rippled across his ruggedly handsome face, creating an unworldly glow from his eyes.

She stared into the ice-blue depths and searched her suddenly empty head for an answer. The combination of anger and fear had partly clouded her vision in the tent. But now, without the blinding need for bravado, she could clearly see him. And what she saw took the breath from her body and all logical thought from her mind.

His blue eyes were the shade of a winter pond's frozen surface—and just as transparent. Ashy-colored lashes created a frame that made the spellbinding gaze only more intense, more piercing.

He didn't just look at her—he seemed to peer into her very heart and soul. In that instant, she felt as unkempt, vulnerable and exhausted as she must appear.

"I…um…very well." In an attempt to coax her tongue to form coherent words, she dropped her gaze. "I can wait." Never in her life had she felt so ill at ease and inept around a man. And with the number of men coming and going from Faucon, she had been around a great many. She wished for the earth below her to somehow open and swallow her whole.

"Are you all right?" Concern laced his words.

Good Lord above, the man would soon think she was addled. Not that she blamed him after her senseless response. But a little worry on his part might be just what he deserved for the way he'd handled her in the tent.

If she answered him, he would hear the amusement in her voice, so she merely nodded. When he turned and adjusted the reins in his hands, Marianne did her best to swallow the laughter bubbling in her throat, but some of it escaped.

He looked at her over his shoulder, his soul-searching eyes narrowed. "You are amused?"

"A little." Marianne shrugged. So much for hiding her laughter.

He resumed their journey with a smothered curse. It was cruel to let him believe she was not whole and hearty. He had threatened to truss her like a gutted stag. It would serve him right to live with his worries and thoughts for a time. But she was unable to be that deceitful.

"I am not addled."

"So you say."

"I beg your pardon?"

Without halting their progress, he said, "I find it interesting that someone in your position would consider this amusing."

"You said you posed no threat."

"And you believed a complete stranger? Do you not find that a mite foolish?"

She found it more than a mite foolish—and before he had the opportunity to realize what she was about to do, she unclamped her fingers from the horse's mane, sent a quick silent prayer to God, then threw herself sideways from the saddle.

Marianne hit the ground with a thud, rolling immediately to her knees. Her heart racing, she scrambled blindly to her feet and ran into a solid wall of masculine flesh and muscle encased in chain mail.

Before she could back away, he grasped her shoulders and pulled her close. "While I fully expected you to seek your freedom, I thought you would at least wait until we were gone from this area."

Marianne said nothing. She only tugged sharply at his hold, trying to get him to release her.

He slid a knife from its sheath and held it between them. Her stomach flipped with dread. Her head spun wildly. She'd been right not to trust him. She would die here in the middle of nowhere and her family would never know.

Frantic, she kicked at him while trying to pull free from the hold he now had on her one wrist.

"Stop it." He jerked hard, slamming her body against his. "Cease this stupidity."

Before she could gasp for another breath, he pulled her wrist up, slapped the handle of the knife into her palm and forced her fingers to curl around it. He then stepped back and pointed toward the denseness of the forest. "You are free to go."

No sooner had she spun in the direction he'd suggested, he added, "Be warned, the men who took you to begin with are right behind us."

Marianne froze.

"You need make a choice right now. Either get moving into the forest, or get back on the horse and let us be gone from here."

The distant sound of men's voices ended her mental debate. She bid freedom farewell—for now—and turned back toward the horse. Without saying anything, he assisted her into the saddle, grabbed the reins and took off at a run, leading the horse behind him.

Marianne clung to the horse's mane. "You cannot keep up this pace. I can ride pillion behind you."

"I thank you, no. My camp is but a short ways from here."

"Perhaps, but would it not be faster—" Shouts from the men chasing them cut her argument short.

Marianne turned in the saddle and saw four men racing toward them on foot. All of them were from the group who had kidnapped her at Faucon. And all of them held their swords before them, ready to do battle.

Her rescuer drew his weapon, while urging, "Go. My men are camped straight down this path at the first clearing."

"I cannot leave you here alone."

His eyebrows rose at her statement, but he only tossed her the reins and smacked the horse's rump. The animal bolted, nearly throwing her from the saddle.

The effort to bring the beast under control nearly drained her of what life she had left. But she quickly dragged the horse's head around, slowed its pace and headed back to where Ashforde fought the other men.

She had to give him credit—he fought well. He had already dispatched one man by the time she returned to the clearing. With a sudden burst of renewed energy, Marianne slid from the saddle and led the horse into the forest where she wrapped the reins around a small tree trunk. She then picked her way from tree to tree and retrieved the dead man's weapon. Before anyone saw her, she raced back to the horse and mounted with the aid of a fallen log.

While being harbingers of death came easily to her brothers, she'd never killed a man. But there was a first time for everything and that time seemed to be now.

Two of the men attacked Ashforde. The third had spotted her and rushed in her direction. The expression of glee on his faced boded ill will. Marianne sent a quick, silent prayer for strength and kicked the horse into movement.

Her enemy did not appear to be afraid of her. In fact, he appeared to be laughing at her. She tested the balance of the sword in her hand. Poorly made, it did not swing evenly. She held the blade low, parallel to the ground, resting the flat of the blade against her leg and charged toward the man.

Caught off guard by the mere idea that a female would bring him injury, the man left his chest unprotected, making it a perfect target.

When she swung the blade straight ahead, the open target was one she did not miss.

The expression of complete surprise on his face just before he fell would have amused her, had she not been overwhelmed with the sudden urge to vomit. Marianne blinked away the tears threatening to blur her vision and urged the horse toward Ashforde.

With her borrowed sword still lodged in the chest of the man she'd just killed, the only thing she could think to do was to run one of the men over with the horse.

She chose the one farthest from the forest, leaned low over the beast and urged the horse toward the man. Flesh and bone were little protection beneath the heavy hooves of a full-grown warhorse.

Her tactic gave Ashforde the chance to dispatch the man still standing. He spun around, knocked the last man to the ground and then pressed the tip of his sword to the hollow at the base of the man's neck.

Fear tightened the muscles in the kidnapper's neck. He swallowed hard, unwittingly pushing his throat up against the tip of the blade.

As she dismounted, Marianne heard Ashforde ask, "Why would you think to go into battle against a knight without wearing your armor?"

She joined the men and realized he had asked a valid question, considering her kidnapper wore only a padded gambeson. The heavily quilted short tunic offered no safety against the thrust of a sword.

"We thought the odds were in our favor."

Ashforde stepped back and ordered, "Get up." After the man rose, he knocked the sword from the lout's hand. "Tell your master this game is finished. Leave Marianne of Faucon alone." He placed the edge of his weapon across the man's throat for emphasis, adding, "You won't be as fortunate the next time."

When the sword lowered, the man took off at a dead run. But it wasn't that man who captured her attention. It was the one who'd remained. Ashforde.

The sheen of sweat coated his face. His overlong hair, damp from his exertion, curled about his neck. Ice-blue eyes glimmered with rage.

Warmth flowed through her veins. Her heart lurched before settling into an uneven rhythm. It made little logical sense. But she'd learned long ago that logic sometimes got in the way. She swallowed a gasp and bit back a smile.

His clothing, chain mail and weapons were of excellent quality, so apparently he had wealth enough. She'd just seen him in battle and knew without a doubt that he was strong and brave enough. While his rugged good looks made her heart beat faster, he seemed not to notice them, so he obviously was not vain. His speech was refined, so he would be considered intelligent enough.

There were many unanswered questions regarding Ashforde and she wasn't at all certain she could completely trust him. But she could not deny the simple truth her entire being screamed—this was the man.

Rhys would not be able to find anything wrong with him. And if he did, well, she'd go over his head. It would be easy to throw herself on the mercy of her sisters by marriage.

The biggest obstacle would be Ashforde himself. How was she to convince him that a match between them would be well served? He seemed honorable, a man of his word…another smile twitched at her lips.

Had he not himself threatened to kiss her into submission? What would it take for him to make good that threat?

He turned to look down the path and flinched. Worried about the wound she'd given him earlier, Marianne touched his arm. "Have you suffered further injury?"

Bryce couldn't help himself. He laughed in disbelief. The woman had disobeyed a direct order. Yet she stood there inquiring about *his* welfare? She should be concerned with her own. Had the ordeal of killing a man left her in a state of shock?

"You were told to go join my men."

"I know, but you were outnumbered."

"Those men were inexperienced knaves. I was in little danger of losing life or limb."

"How could you be certain of that? I only thought to help."

Oh, aye, it was comforting to know that this woman, barely more than a girl, thought he needed her help in a fight. In truth, it was nearly more galling than he could bear. "While your brothers may require your assistance, I do not."

When she finished laughing, a sound that set him more on edge than he already was, she said, "My brothers do not require assistance from anyone."

Her laughing statement drew bile to his throat. To think, he'd once felt a moment's guilt for using her as a pawn in his revenge.

He'd earned his title and lands by his prowess on the battlefield. He'd not become one of Matilda's trusted men by any means other than the use of his sword arm. As much as he wanted to throw that fact in this woman's face, he bit his tongue, adding the taste of his own blood to the bile.

By divulging that information he would only give away his plans. That was something he was not yet ready to do.

He could not prolong this discussion. If he did, he would end up losing what little control of his temper remained. "Get on the horse."

"You are angry."

If nothing else, she excelled at stating the obvious. "I would be concerned for any man who would not be angry."

"I fail to understand. Why?"

Bryce felt that last thread holding his rage intact snap. He turned to face her. "Why?" To keep his hands from doing something he'd only regret, he tightened his grip on his sword until he thought his knuckles would break. "I do not require any more assistance from you than any of your brothers would. I have not lived this long by not knowing how to defend myself."

"But—"

"Cease." He lifted his free hand. Her shocked expression led him to realize that his fingers were curled into a fist. After unclenching his fingers, he said, "No. Do not say a word. I am a man, I know and understand my duties. And I perform them quite well. You, on the other hand, are a woman and it is obvious you do not know your duties. So, let me explain exactly what I wish you to do."

She crossed her arms against her chest. "Oh, please, do."

He ignored the sarcasm in her tone. "You will do as you are ordered, without question. When danger strikes you will take yourself to safety and stay there until I tell you otherwise."

"You will, of course, let me know when to eat, drink, sleep and relieve myself?"

It wasn't her question that added to his anger, it was her sickly oversweet tone and the brightly false smile she pasted on her face.

Bryce reached over and grabbed the reins of the horse. Before he was able to stop himself, he picked Marianne up and nearly threw her onto the saddle.

"We will be at my camp soon. Once there, you will keep your mouth shut."

"If I choose not to?"

What was she looking for him to do? Did her brothers truly permit her this much free will? Did they never seek to restrain her mouth or manners?

It was no wonder that Marianne of Faucon was still unwed. What man in his right mind would wish for a wife so contrary and stubborn?

If anyone was foolish enough to marry her and later discovered her willfulness, what could he do? He would likely be risking his own life if he so much as raised a hand to her. If she did not kill the man in his sleep, her brothers would take care of the deed for her. And Bryce doubted if they would make it a quick or relatively painless death.

He closed his eyes and inhaled deeply, silently praying for the strength to deal with this woman.

As if through a thick fog he again heard her laughter. For some odd reason it brushed soft and warm against his ear.

"You did not answer me, Ashforde. What will you do if I refuse to follow your high-handed orders?"

He opened his eyes and looked up at her. Marianne

was leaning closer to him, smiling as if she had not a worry in the world. Perhaps it was time the woman learned that her brothers could not always protect her.

Before she could stop him, he pulled her off the horse and into his arms. Bryce fought to ignore the sudden heat rushing through his veins. He pretended he didn't hear the loud, rapid tattoo of his heart in his ears.

With what he hoped was his most stern and commanding look, he glared down at her. The sparkle in her eyes and the half smile flitting at the corners of her parted lips was his first clue that he'd made a grave error in judgment.

Marianne reached up, ran her fingers through his hair and gently drew his head closer. "That took you long enough, my lord." She brushed her lips against his, before pulling back to ask, "How much further do I need to go before you kiss me into submission?"

He closed his eyes and groaned. Dear Lord above, his enemy's sister was out to seduce him.

And God help him, he rather enjoyed the thought.

Chapter Five

Marianne looked away from the shimmer of high emotions racing across his eyes. Had she made a grievous mistake with her boldness? The queasy churn of nervousness fought with the butterflies in her stomach.

Surely his ragged groan and stark expression spoke of his horror at her actions. But when she tried to pull free, he tightened his hold.

"Forgive my boldness, my lord. Let me go." The bands of steel surrounding her only strengthened at her plea.

Ashforde dipped his head, brushing his lips across her cheek. "Let you go? I thought you wanted me to kiss you into submission?"

His raspy tone of voice bid her do what she must to gain her freedom. "Yes—I mean no." At this moment she wanted to run. "Please, I rashly spoke out of turn. I did not mean to sound so wanton."

A low, soft laugh was his response. Before she could

say anything else, he cupped her face. Strong fingers held her still.

He did nothing more than stare down at her. A mind-robbing look that kept her rooted to the ground. His hand on her face seemed to burn her flesh. Far from hurting her, his touch made her want to lean into the warmth.

Some wild, uncontrollable part of her wondered what his lips would feel like against her own, but ingrained self-preservation warned this was not the time, nor the place to make that discovery. Long-suffered caution urged her to be rational. To think of her safety at this moment and not of her wants.

Before his soul-searching gaze could cast any more of a spell about her, Marianne pushed hard against his chest. "For the love of God, please, let me go."

For a moment longer he held her, an odd half smile curving his lips. To her relief he relaxed his hold. "You need not fear me."

"Fear you?" Without thought, she admitted, "I fear myself more."

Ashforde stepped away and glanced at the dead men on the ground. "With good reason." He'd spoken more to himself than to her, so she remained silent. The last thing she wished to do was repeat the argument that had led her to act so foolishly in the first place.

"Let us go." He grabbed the reins to the horse and helped her mount. "My camp is nearby."

True to his word, Ashforde's men were camped a short distance down the path. Though Marianne wouldn't quite call it a camp. It was nothing more than a clearing with half a dozen men gathered around a crackling fire. Their horses were tied to nearby bushes. Beyond that, she heard the rushing of a stream. A small, hastily erected tent leaned toward the trees at the right side of the clearing.

And at the moment, it was the most wondrous sight she could envision.

She slid from the saddle and could not decide what she wanted to do first—seek much-needed slumber in the tent, slake her thirst with water from the stream, or fill her belly with the unidentifiable meat roasting over the fire.

The wildest-looking man she had ever seen in her life rose from his seat by the fire and approached, ending any thought of sleep, water or food. Marianne instinctively stepped behind Ashforde.

An ill-healed scar twisted one side of the man's face, giving him a permanent sneer. White and gray streaks in his untrimmed, brownish-hued hair lent him the appearance of a wild animal.

"Jared!" Ashforde quickly stepped forward, meeting the man halfway across the clearing and grasping his forearms in greeting. "When did you arrive?"

"While you were out gaming." The man nodded toward Marianne. "I see you won."

"That's debatable," Ashforde mumbled before waving her forward. "Marianne of Faucon, this unkempt dog is Jared of Warehaven."

The Dragon? He looked more like a war-scarred wolf than a dragon. She looked from Warehaven to Ashforde uncertain what to think, or what to say. As far as she knew, Warehaven was her brothers' enemy. So, what did that make Ashforde?

Yet, Jared bowed slightly before fixing his off-colored green gaze on her and said, "Your brother Darius is well-known to me. He is an interesting man."

The raspy timbre of his deep voice was intriguing. Pleasing to the ear, it invited one to listen, just to hear him talk. Marianne blinked. Obviously, too tired for clear thinking, she simply agreed, "Yes. That he is." She then touched Ashforde's arm. "Will we remain in camp for the night?"

"Aye." He motioned two of his men forward before continuing, "The tent is for your use, and there is a stream a short distance down the footpath. Sir John and Eustace will guard you."

She hesitated. While his men did not appear intent on harming her, they were strangers. The older white-haired man looked as unyielding as a giant oak tree, while the younger red-cheeked one appeared to be overly fond of his drink.

All of these men were strangers. And she wasn't at all certain whether they were friend or foe. The rapid pounding of her heart made breathing difficult. Sweat beaded on her forehead.

Marianne glanced at the horses. None of them were saddled. Even Ashforde's was being groomed by one of his men. She could ride a palfrey bareback, but wasn't certain she could control one of the larger destriers without the proper equipment.

"Chase those thoughts from your mind, my lady." Ashforde stared hard at her.

How did he know what was on her mind? After closing her eyes and taking a long, deep breath, she looked up at him. "I was thinking nothing. I just…"

When her words trailed off, he provided, "You wondered what would be your best method of escape."

"I am your prisoner then?"

"You are my prize—won by a lucky toss of the dice." His softly spoken admission sent another sliver of fear rippling down her spine. "You are in my care. Until I reunite you with your brothers, I will see to your safety whether you like the idea or not."

"I can see to my own safety."

"Without coin or weapon at hand, how safe will you be?" He stepped closer, tipping his head and lowering his voice. "Your clothing is torn. You are disheveled. What will other travelers see when they look at you?" His eyebrows shot up in question. "A lady from Faucon?"

To her chagrin, she realized the truth in his words. "So I am forced to remain under your protection? A prisoner by necessity if not by deed."

"You choose to look at it that way because you are tired. A decent meal and a good night's sleep will put a different light on the situation."

His presumption to know what she thought or how she viewed anything rankled. Did he think her stupid? He'd called her his prize more than once now. He ordered men to guard her—not to *protect,* but to *guard* her. As angry as she was becoming, she knew enough to keep her opinions to herself. Instead of arguing, she nodded. "Perhaps you are right."

He stepped away with a laugh. "My men will take you to the stream, then bring you back to the tent."

Marianne crossed her arms against her chest and nodded.

Ashforde sighed and shook his head. "I need to speak to Jared. When I am finished, I will bring you something to eat."

He watched her walk with his men to the stream's path and wondered momentarily if he had indeed made a mistake in not warning his men to be careful. But she was unarmed, and her steps were slow, her movements stiff and sluggish. If she did take it into her head to attempt an escape, it was doubtful she'd succeed.

Marianne wearily trudged down the path to the stream. The guard in front of her was young—close to her in age. His ruddy complexion and unsteady footsteps confirmed her first impression of his fondness for drink.

The older man behind her remained silent. His silence was not an oddity, but something about him spoke of danger. It could have been the deadly glare in his eyes when he waved her and the younger man forward. Or maybe it was the way he held his sword at the ready for no apparent reason—unless he considered her dangerous.

The only thing she knew for certain was that his steady, overly heavy steps behind her did not suggest a man who might be easily misled.

Once they reached the stream, they gave her a few moments of privacy before the younger one called out, "My lady, we need return to camp."

She had no wish to return. But Marianne realized she didn't have an option. At least not a reasonable option. She stared down the stream. Even if she could elude her guards where would she go? It would soon be dark and she feared the men who'd diced her away would not give up their quest to steal her back.

And Ashforde was correct—she did not have the appearance of a lady. Unkempt was a kind description of how she must look. She raised a hand to her hair. The braids had come undone days ago and she'd given up trying to untangle the snarled knots. She'd simply torn another strip from the skirt of her gown and tied the ebony mess behind her head.

Both her gown and undergown were filthy and torn. Each step she took exposed her legs clear up to her thighs. The sleeves of the gown weren't any better. They hung like tattered ribbons about her arms.

If she somehow escaped, the first man she'd come across would think he'd found himself a well-used harlot. It would be impossible to make her way to Faucon without coming upon any men.

For now, she'd have to remain Ashforde's *prize*.

She shuddered at the thought. While this situation was entirely her own fault, every fiber of her being rebelled at being considered someone's prize.

Not more than a few hours ago she'd considered Ashforde a man Rhys would permit her to marry. Bah, she'd not plight her troth with a man who humiliated her so.

She understood none of it—he'd claimed to have rescued her and said he'd deliver her safely to her brothers. So, why was she now nothing more than winnings from a game of chance? And why was she under guard?

Dead leaves crunching underfoot let her know Ashforde's men were coming to escort her back to camp. Marianne knelt by the stream. She splashed the icy water on her face. It would do little for her appearance, but perhaps the chill would help chase away the heat of useless anger.

"Come. It is time to return."

She didn't move. It was one thing to be ordered about by Ashforde. But he and his men needed to learn she'd not be ordered about by everyone at whim. The least thing the guards could do was to wait until *she* was ready to return.

Footsteps drew closer. "Did you hear me, my lady?"

She momentarily ignored the younger man and splashed some more water on her face before answering, "Yes."

He poked her shoulder. "Then do as I ask."

He'd not *asked* anything of her and if he so much as touched her again, he'd soon regret doing so. "In a few moments."

"Now would be better."

Marianne smiled to herself. Without moving, she lazily stirred the water with her fingertips. "Do you have a name?"

"I am called John—Sir John."

She blinked. Never would she have picked him as the knight of the pair. "Sir John, I will be ready soon."

A twig snapped beneath the feet of the older man as he moved closer, too. He cleared his throat before asking, "What is taking so long?"

Marianne shrugged. "I lost a bauble in the water." Realizing her tone of voice needed a little more urgency to sound convincing, she swished the water again and quickly added, "It was given to me by my brother. I must find it."

The older man sighed heavily. "Oh, for the love of— let us be gone from here."

"It is very special to me." She glanced between the two men and added, "I think he said it was an heirloom."

"It will not hurt to help her." Sir John's tone was sharp. He knelt beside her and peered into the stream. "I see nothing."

Marianne pointed to a spot just beyond her reach. "I think it is right there. See? Something is dangling between those two larger rocks."

The instant Sir John reached out, she pretended to lose her balance and bumped into him, knocking the man into the ice-cold stream.

She jumped up in a rush. "Oh, forgive me. I am sorry." Marianne looked to the older guard. The scowl on his face deepened. But he moved forward to help his partner out of the water.

When he leaned forward to grasp John's outstretched hand, Marianne placed the bottom of her booted foot against his arse and put all of her weight into the shove.

She stooped to grasp a large rock and hid it in the folds of her gown. Without waiting for the unsuspecting guards to come after her, she took off for the camp at a run.

After Marianne and his men left the camp, Bryce took a seat on a fallen log.

Jared joined him, asking, "Was it wise to send her off with only two men?"

Bryce shrugged. "If she tries anything foolish it will be two men against one tired woman."

Instead of responding, Jared grunted. A noise that from the time they fostered at Redvers had made Bryce want to gnash his teeth together.

"I hope your hunt for me was not too strenuous."

Jared admitted, "One of Redvers's men pointed me

toward Hampshire. Once there, it took nothing more than the promise of coin to discover the direction you took upon leaving there this morning. I simply followed the road until I found the men."

"Then I assume you came here for some reason other than to grunt at me."

"Curiosity drew me here. I wanted to see if you won the prize you sought."

"And now that your curiosity has been satisfied, you will be departing on the morn?"

"Not alone. I'm to escort you and your…charge…to Baldwin."

Bryce's breath left him in a rush. The Earl of Devon, Baldwin de Redvers had taught him much. Even though Baldwin had had to give Carisbrooke over to Stephen, or lose his head, he still respected the man. But he also knew that when a notion struck Baldwin, there was no swaying him.

Bryce should have known the earl was up to something when he was sent the information on Marianne's whereabouts. Because of Carisbrooke, Baldwin wanted revenge against King Stephen, or one of Stephen's men. Taking possession of Faucon's sister would serve the earl's thirst for vengeance.

An event he should have foreseen. But he'd been too intent on righting his own thwarted plans to give the earl's fortuitous help any thought. "I am to take refuge with the earl?"

"Nay. You, my friend, are to give custody of Faucon's sister over to Redvers' wife. And since I knew you would not be agreeable to that plan, I volunteered to bring you the news."

"The earl will not take custody himself?"

"No. He has joined up with Gloucester and Anjou in Normandy."

"And after I hand over Faucon's sister?" Bryce assumed they would also join the battle for Anjou's conquest of Normandy.

"We are to head toward Cambridge." Jared attempted a halfhearted laugh before adding, "Just to see if we can convince the Earl of Essex not to destroy all of England."

"And who issued those orders?"

"It was not precisely an order." Jared shrugged. "It came as a *request* from the empress."

Both men were intelligent enough to know a request from Empress Matilda was a rare, albeit nicely worded order. Bryce shuddered. "Has Mandeville run out of new methods of torture, or has he just run out of victims?"

"I am of the opinion he has only begun. True or not, I do know we will be unable to locate him."

"Agreed." The last thing Bryce wanted to do before he died was to get anywhere close to where Geoffrey de Mandeville might be. No one had ever called Bryce a coward, but Mandeville had become inhuman.

The man had lost all reason when King Stephen forced him to surrender the Tower of London along with two of his other castles. Since then, the earl had taken to burning, pillaging, raping and torturing not only those men who opposed him, but women and children. Not even men of God were safe from Mandeville's wrath.

"I thought perhaps you would like to make use of my lair until you are able to rebuild your keep."

Jared's lair, as he called it since his dubbing of The Dragon, was a fortified stone keep on the Isle of Wight.

It would be near Carisbrooke, but not close enough that any of Stephen's men would happen upon them unseen. So far, as long as Jared did nothing to boldly provoke those currently holding Carisbrooke, he'd been left alone.

"Nay, thank you, but we are only a day's ride from Ashforde. I would like to see how much progress has been completed on the building and I need to ensure there are supplies enough to last through the winter. Then I will escort Marianne to her brothers."

"I understand, but Isabella and Beatrice were looking forward to enjoying your company."

Bryce groaned. Jared's sisters dabbled in herbal remedies. Their disagreeable-tasting concoctions were supposed to help them find husbands—providing their brews didn't kill the men first. Thankfully, even though he had been on the receiving end of their potions more than once, he still breathed.

"So." Jared stretched out his legs and nudged Bryce. "Tell me about your lady."

Bryce wondered where to start. Marianne of Faucon was like no other woman he'd ever met. In the short span of time he'd been in her company, he'd come to realize that she could cause him more trouble than imaginable. And it would be trouble of the worst sort—the kind that would involve not only his heart and mind, but also his soul.

"Other than the fact she can use a blade, there isn't much to tell." Feeling Jared's questioning stare, he grasped for an explanation at first. "She stabbed me, but 'tis nothing more than a flesh wound."

When his friend remained silent, Bryce continued, his

thoughts easily flowing into words. "She's too old to be unwed. But too young, too inexperienced to know much about men outside of her family." He shrugged. "A instructional task that might prove interesting for the right man, if they could get by her brothers. Of course, then the greater problem would be Marianne herself."

His friend stared at him with such an odd expression that prompted Bryce to add, "She is willful, outspoken, daring and curious. A combination as intriguing as it is irritating."

After a moment's pause, Jared sputtered. "Good Lord, man." His bark of laughter seemed to bounce off the surrounding trees. When he finally spent his mirth, he said, "While your explanation is enlightening, I was asking about Cecily of Glynnson—your intended wife."

Bryce silently cursed his own rampant stupidity. With any luck, the flesh wound on his side would fester until it eventually killed him. That would be the only relief he'd ever have against what would surely become Jared's constant reminders about this conversation.

Even though it was far too late to save his dignity, Bryce ground out, "Lady Cecily is well."

"But obviously not as memorable as Marianne of Faucon."

No one would be as memorable as Faucon's sister. He didn't voice that opinion. Instead, Bryce offered, "Cecily is a lady in every sense of the word." That much was true. She'd been raised to fill her position in life as some man's wife. There was no doubt that she could easily oversee any domestic aspect of a keep, or castle. For the most part, not counting her bouts of whining, complaining, or her short temper, she knew her place.

"I am not at all certain I would want that type of lady for my wife." Jared slid him a look that Bryce recognized as a coming challenge. "Would not someone bold and curious be of more...comfort...than someone who always knew their place?"

"Comfort?" Sometimes acting dull-witted could prove useful. Bryce was certain this was one of those times. "I would think that having a wife capable of overseeing the day-to-day running of my keep would be quite a comfort."

"If you had a keep to oversee." Jared snorted at his unnecessary reminder of the total destruction at Ashforde. "Perhaps *comfort* was the wrong word, but you know full well I was not referring to domestic duties."

"Aye." It wasn't as if Bryce hadn't wondered the same thing—would Lady Cecily's strict upbringing allow her to experience passion or desire?

An unfair question to be sure, one he hadn't given a thought until this day. They'd not been permitted so much as a heartbeat alone. Although, some of the blame for that lack lay at his feet. After he'd witnessed her screaming at a servant for spilling a drop of wine on the linen table cover, he'd not pursued any time alone with Cecily. For all he knew, she could be the most passionate woman alive. But he doubted if that'd prove true.

As far as he could tell, when servants weren't involved, Cecily was well-mannered and controlled to the point of boredom. The only time he saw any passion flicker behind her eyes was when they'd discussed his holdings. Never once did she turn a look of desire, or even simple interest toward him.

At least not in the way Marianne of Faucon looked at him. Bryce's pulse quickened. While he hadn't bedded countless women, he had enough experience to recognize what he saw in Marianne's eyes. He'd seen the interest, the curiosity and the thoughtful measuring of his worth.

He'd also witnessed the change from initial attraction to a nearly spellbinding desire. And that is where the danger lay—in acknowledging that unbidden desire. It would be an easy thing to use her inexperience and desire against her. It would also be less than honorable. But had Faucon thought of honor when he'd set fires to Ashforde?

Jared shook his head. "'Tis obvious this Faucon woman has already cast her wiles about you. Perhaps you should consider delivering her to Carisbrooke before it's too late."

"She has cast nothing about me and I'll not give her over to Baldwin's care."

"So that's the way of it? Have you signed the betrothal document yet?"

"No. I will. Soon."

Jared rolled his eyes. "You best make a decision before permanently tying yourself to Glynnson."

"The two are not related. Faucon's sister is nothing more than a means for revenge. She has no influence on my coming betrothal to Cecily." Bryce shrugged. "Even if she did, Empress Matilda will never permit me to back out of this marriage."

Jared rose, then looked down at him. "Enough gold will send Empress Matilda hunting another husband for Lady Cecily before your unpledged betrothal is forgotten."

"And what of the lady herself? Does she not deserve a measure of honor from her intended?"

"What do you deserve?" Jared nodded toward the path leading to the stream. "What better revenge than to steal this woman's heart and loyalty away from her brother?"

"She is little more than an untried girl."

"Girl?" Another irritating grunt punctuated Jared's question. "Have you gone blind as well as daft? She is certainly no slip of a girl. Untried perhaps, but she is a woman full-grown. Unless she plans to take the Church's vow, the day will soon come when she leaves her family for a husband. Why not be that man?"

"I…" There were countless reasons why he could not be that man. The most obvious one rose to the fore in his mind. "When she discovers who I am and what I plan, she will kill me herself."

"Not if her heart is securely tied to yours."

The more thought he gave this idea the more sense it made. The desire for revenge bade him to follow through with what would be the most complete method possible. But honor warned of the danger involved.

"There is no need to make a decision this instant." Jared lowered his voice. "Just think about it, Bryce. Think about that woman sharing your life and your bed. And think about how angry it would make the man who destroyed your keep and lands."

A commotion from the forest snared both men's attention. Bryce rose, drawing his sword, instantly on the alert. Then he spotted Marianne racing out of the forest before she ducked inside the tent.

Jared laughed. "I see she's still well guarded." He walked away adding, "I'll join the others around the fire and leave you to your *prize*."

What did she do with his men? Bryce started toward the tent when Sir John burst out of the forest.

"My Lord Ashforde!" John raced toward him, shouting. Eustace followed a little slower. Sir John had the wild-eyed look of surprise on his face. Eustace appeared more embarrassed than surprised. Both men were dripping with water.

Bryce groaned. He knew what the news was going to be before either man said another word. Somehow she'd managed to toss both men into the ice-cold water. This was his fault. He should have seen to her himself. At least she'd not taken it into her head to escape.

"My Lord, I—"

Bryce cut off Sir John's explanation. "I will deal with this. Both of you go dry off by the fire."

Chapter Six

Marianne awoke with a start. Something had pulled her from her dreams. She couldn't believe she'd fallen asleep, not when she'd been waiting for Ashforde to appear. When she'd run into the tent earlier, she'd expected Ashforde to charge in after her demanding to know what had happened at the stream.

He'd come as far as the flap. She heard his steps falter, then he turned and walked away. Immediately after that she heard more steps approach the tent. Nobody entered, but the men had taken up positions surrounding the tent.

After that, the last thing she remembered was stretching out on the pallet to await Ashforde and his rage.

Now, making as little sound as possible, she inched her hand along the hard pallet made of covers folded on the ground and wrapped her fingers around a rock she'd found at the stream. Not much of a weapon, but the smooth round rock fit her palm and would stun a man if she hit him hard enough.

She could see nothing in the blackness of the night, but she listened carefully for anything out of the ordinary. The sounds were familiar; murmurs of the men around the crackling fire—meaning they no longer guarded the tent—the evening breeze shaking the leaves on the trees, the stream in the distance, the sound of her own breath…and someone else's.

She listened closer. Soft clinks of the small metal links that made up chain mail fell against each other, confirming her fear—she was not alone. Marianne tightened her grip on the rock.

"Perhaps I should have checked for weapons." Ashforde's voice curiously calmed the fearful stuttering of her pulse. "What are you reaching for?"

How did he know? The tent was cloaked in darkness. She no longer believed in things unworldly. Had she made some small sound that had alerted him to her movements? Or was he instinctively that perceptive?

"Nothing." She relaxed her fingers, but left the rock hidden beneath her side. "I was just stretching. This pallet is not the most comfortable I have slept upon."

"I tried not to wake you." He laughed lightly and she heard him move closer along the ground.

"I thought you would be in here earlier to discuss your men. Did they make it back to camp?"

He ignored her question and said, "I was. But you wouldn't have heard me over the rumbling of your stomach. You are hungry."

Yes, she was hungry. But again, his assumption of her state of being rankled. No matter how much she wanted to rail against his unusually well-honed intuition, she was truly famished. So much so that the mere thought of food took her mind off the questions and complaints bouncing around in her head. He could shout and rage all he wanted, if only he gave her food to eat first.

Something thudded on the ground, bringing a curse from Ashforde before he said, "Wait a moment. Let me see if we can get some light."

When he left, Marianne sat up and patted her hands around on the ground until she located a small bundle. She'd not eaten yesterday. And had barely touched the food her captors had brought her this morning. Her fingers shook as she unwrapped something that felt as greasy as a spitted hog.

She was hungry enough to care little about what food he'd brought. The meat smelled like heaven and no matter how badly it might have been prepared, would taste as good as anything from the Faucon kitchens.

Marianne took a bite and sighed. She'd been correct. The cold, tough, greasy, unseasoned fare was fit for a feast.

Ashforde returned and tied back one of the tent flaps. "This tent is too small to build a fire inside and we have no brazier for light. I moved a torch closer to the tent, but if you like, we could sit outside around the fire."

Between bites, she mumbled. "Nay. This is fine." She could see the campfire through the open tent flap. The glare from that fire and the torches situated throughout the clearing provided enough light for her to see Ashforde's shadowy form inside the tent.

When he dropped down beside her, light from the fires flickered across his face. Ah, yes, no matter how hard he tried to hide it she could read his angry expression. It took no intuition on her part to know that the thinned lips, clenched jaw and thunderous scowl spoke of only one emotion—tightly reined ire.

There was a time to goad a man into spilling what real or imagined transgression had fueled his rage, and a time to wait for him to do so without provocation. A lifetime of living with three strong-willed brothers had taught her to recognize the difference.

She was alone with Ashforde, in an enclosed space. Like the men she knew, he would think his anger was justified. Marianne didn't know him well enough yet to determine how well he controlled his rage.

Ashforde nodded toward the bundle. "I see you found what passes for food."

"It is wonderful." She held the hunk of meat out to him. "Would you care for a bite?"

"No." He waved it off. "I've had my men's cooking before."

"You lived, so it must not be too bad."

"True." Bryce lifted a wineskin. "I attribute that miracle to the wine. It seems to negate the poison."

Marianne finished off the last bite before plucking the wineskin from his hands. She lifted the flask toward him briefly, then she brought it to her lips. "Just in case you are correct." Nearly choking on the bitter wine, she quickly handed the wineskin back to him.

His fingertips grazed hers. The brief contact of flesh reminded her of her complete vulnerability in the company of strange men.

Ashforde was not one of her brothers. Nor did she want him to be.

To her utter disgust, she wanted him as a woman wants a man. Perhaps even as a husband. She needed to know more about him first—who he was, where he came from, why he treated her like a prisoner and most of all why his name seemed familiar.

Yet, for no apparent reason she suddenly felt shy around him. Just his presence made her feel not quite uncomfortable, but on edge…more aware of things she'd normally not notice.

Things like the quickening of her pulse, the heaviness of her breathing, the unanswered longing in her chest, the way the slight breeze brushed cool across her heated cheeks. To take her mind off her tumbling thoughts, Marianne folded her hands in her lap and stared into the darkened corner of the tent.

Ashforde touched her shoulder. "You have had your fill?"

"Aye." Her mouth went dry, but the bitter wine would only make it worse. She swallowed hard, waiting for his tirade.

"To answer your earlier question, yes, my men made it back to camp."

She'd not had to wait long. But his method of delivery surprised her. She'd expected him to rage or shout, to sound as cold and unyielding as his expression promised. Instead, he kept his deep voice low and even. As if he spoke to a lover, the near-husky whisper caressed her, lulled her into a sense of safety she should not feel—but could not ignore.

He rubbed the back of his fingers across her cheek. The gentle touch trailed a blaze against her skin. She jerked away from his disturbing touch. "Do not."

An exaggerated sigh lifted the wisps of hair hanging over her ear. "Do not what, Marianne?"

"Do not try to soothe me as if I am a skittish colt, or your favorite hunting dog."

"You are nothing like a colt, or a hunting dog."

"No. I am nothing more than a prize you won dicing. A captive who not only tested her blade on your flesh, but who also refused to obey orders and humiliated your men." Goodness, what was wrong with her? If he said the sky was blue, she was certain she would argue that it was green simply to goad him…to do what?

The hand he slid along the back of her neck trembled slightly. "You are wrong again." He drew her closer and whispered against her ear, "You are a desirable woman who I wish to know better."

"I do not believe you." Marianne's heart thudded to an abrupt halt as a sudden realization chilled her fevered body. "You seek only to humiliate me. To make me pay for tricking your men in a way only a woman can."

He removed his hand from her neck, leaned away and stared at her. The confusion dancing across his face made her wonder if perhaps she had judged him unfairly.

Bryce glanced away. What caused her to think such a thing of him? Even if he did decide to take Jared's suggestion, he would proceed slowly, with great care. Aye, he was angry at what she'd done, but raping Marianne of Faucon would in no way tie her heart to his—in fact, it would sicken him to do so and would likely get him killed. There was little question that facing three Faucons intent on defending their sister's honor would be a quick or painless death.

He shook his head. "Where did you get such a notion?"

"You hold me as prisoner."

"I do no such thing."

"Yet, you set guards to escort me to the stream—"

"Oh, aye and they performed their orders so well, did they not? I should not have to remind you that the forest is home to brigands who would do you more harm than you seem to think I will." At least she had the grace to look away.

If Bryce was to be honest with himself, he did find it amusing that two of the empress's men had been bested by a woman. Clenching his jaw to suppress a smile she was sure to notice, he asked, "How did you manage to get both of them in the water?"

She snorted. He could not believe it. Marianne of Faucon actually snorted in what sounded to him like amusement.

"It was not hard considering the younger man is more interested in his drink than his duty."

"And you find that amusing?"

She turned back to face him. "Amusing? Nay. I find it rather odd that not only can your men not cook, but you see fit to have a drunkard among them. It seems to me they do not serve their lord with any competence."

Up until a few months ago he'd been nothing more than a mercenary, plying his trade for Empress Matilda. It was only happenstance that he'd been the one close enough to save her from a well-aimed arrow while out hunting. A happening that earned him a title and a small keep. Ashforde, now a ransacked burned-out pile of ash that was, as he spoke, scattering on the autumn winds, was the first piece of property he could call his own.

How was he to explain that these men Marianne thought were his, were in truth only on loan from the empress? He'd not yet had the opportunity to replace them with men of his own choosing. Which was why it was so imperative that he locate the rest of the men—so he could return them to their true liege.

"I am not a mighty Faucon with seemingly unlimited resources." He grasped at a half truth. "Perhaps these men do not appear to serve their lord with any competence, but circumstances have been quite dire of late."

"'Tis no excuse. You deserve to be better served."

"You need to concern yourself with things that relate to you. I can see how you managed to trick Sir John into the water, but Eustace could not have been as easy."

"Actually, he was." She shrugged. "When he bent over to assist your Sir John, I simply booted him into the stream."

For some odd reason Bryce wanted to laugh. But that would only encourage her. So, instead he swallowed his laughter, gritted his teeth and declared, "You should be whipped for acting like such a willful child."

"Whipped?" Her eyes wide, Marianne leaned away. "And who do you think would be...foolish enough to try?"

Her hesitation made him wonder if she'd wanted to ask who would be man enough to try. At least she'd been quick and smart enough not to tempt him that far. But the wideness of her eyes and the slight tremble of her chin made him regret his choice of words.

"Marianne, you will someday come to rue such bold recklessness."

She jumped to her feet and paced the small confines of the tent. "It is not reckless to want freedom."

Bryce leaned back, resting on his elbows. "You are not a prisoner." He needed to banish that idea from her mind. Regardless what plan he eventually decided to use, it would never work if she considered herself his captive.

"No?" She stopped her pacing and faced him. "Then what am I? Besides your booty in a game of chance."

Ah, and what booty she was. Bryce kept his smile to himself. No man could ask for a greater prize than the one standing before him now. Sister to the enemy or not, she'd sweeten his revenge.

"I thought I'd rescued you from kidnappers." He shrugged. "If that is not the case, I will gladly return you to their tender care upon the morrow."

Marianne stepped toward him. "You would do that?"

He frowned. Only while drawing his last breath. "If that is what you truly wish."

"I am not certain what I wish." She tossed her arms in the air before crossing them against her chest. "It might be better for all if you did just that."

He blinked, then narrowed his eyes. She was but toying with him. Two could play that game. He rose, went to the tent flap and called out to his men, "Sir John. Eustace. We will be traveling to Ashforde by way of Hampshire. Make certain every man is armed and their weapons fit for battle."

Both men gawked at him as if he had lost his ability to reason. Thankfully, neither of them argued.

Marianne gasped. "You would give me back to those men?" Her pitiful-sounding voice wavered.

He turned away from the flap, strode the three paces across the tent and returned to his seat on the pallet. "'Tis what you wanted."

With hesitant steps, she walked toward him. She

stopped within arm's length and extended her hands as if to plead her case. Bryce grasped one cold hand and pulled her down beside him. Marianne landed on her knees with a dull thud.

Before she could react, he came up on his knees and pulled her against his chest. With one hand, Bryce held both of her wrists behind her back. He nudged her chin up with his free hand.

The faint light from the torches shimmered off the moisture in her eyes. He shook his head. "Do not even consider crying. You started this little game. Do not feign remorse simply because I decided to play along."

She tried to pull her chin out of his grasp. When she couldn't, Marianne narrowed her eyes. "I don't know what you're talking about."

"Like hell, you don't."

To her credit she met his stare with an unwavering one of her own. "You are angry."

"I have been angry since my men came back from the stream dripping with water and without the woman they were to keep safe."

"Safe?"

"Do not be a fool, Marianne. You are not my prisoner. I have every intention of returning, you to Faucon, unharmed and whole." He released her chin and freed her wrists. "But you seem to have a habit of taking unnecessary risks."

She turned her face away from the hunger shimmering in his eyes. "I only take risks I feel are needed."

"So, disobeying my orders and then assaulting my men were required risks?"

"I never disobeyed…." She stopped, remembering his

order to ride to camp when they'd been attacked on the path.

"Good, I see you remembered."

Marianne chewed on her bottom lip. Better to remain silent than argue with a man who held her so closely.

"You have nothing else to say in your defense?"

She shook her head.

"Then you agree—you took risks that were not needed."

An odd unsteadiness overtook her. She grasped his shoulders, wondering when he'd released his hold on her wrists.

Both of his arms were now around her, holding her firmly in place. "Are you going to answer me?"

His chin brushed against her temple when he spoke. She stared at his stubble-covered square-shaped jaw. When had he last had a shave?

"Marianne."

She gasped in surprise when his breath against her ear sent an icy flash of fire down her spine.

"Promise me you'll take no more risks with your safety until you are back at Faucon."

She swallowed hard and lowered her gaze to his throat. It was a promise she could not make. Not when the greatest risk to her safety held her against his rocklike chest.

He held her so tightly that the metal links of his chain mail pressed through the layers of his tunic and her gown to press into her flesh. Their bodies were so close she could feel the pounding of his heart against her chest. A strong, steady rapid pounding that matched the rhythm of her own wayward heart.

She closed her eyes against the ache coming to life in her chest.

"Look at me, Marianne."

"No. I cannot." If she foolishly did so, she would be lost in his gaze. She would willingly agree to anything he said…or suggested. Her will would flee in the face of the hunger she'd heard in his voice.

He wanted her to not take any more risks. Yet, if she but turned her face up toward him their lips would meet and no risk would seem too great.

He placed his mouth against the tender flesh of her neck and trailed kisses down to her shoulder.

Unable to stop the moan from escaping, Marianne let it slip free.

The sound emboldened him. Ashforde drew her chin up so she faced him. She closed her eyes tighter against the onslaught of emotions and feelings enveloping her senses.

He kissed the corner of her mouth, then stopped to whisper, "Just a kiss, Marianne, no more. I will not harm you."

She wasn't afraid of him harming her. He'd made it quite obvious that even when he was angry with her that he'd not cause her injury.

No, her worry was the kiss itself. What if a kiss was not enough to quench her fire? What if it only led to wanting more?

But this all felt so right. His arms around her seemed to offer safety. His beating heart silently beckoned her to believe a kiss would be enough.

Marianne sighed, then parted her lips. She felt the warmth of his breath and let her eyes close, preparing for—

"Bryce!" Warehaven's shout broke the spell surrounding her. Her eyes snapped open and she pulled away.

"To arms!" One of Ashforde's men raced by the tent yelling of an attack.

Bryce leapt up from the makeshift pallet, unsheathed his sword and pulled Marianne to her feet.

He headed toward the tent flap, ordering over his shoulder, "Do nothing rash. Stay behind me." Since he had no idea what he'd find outside the tent, and was even less certain of what she'd do, he grabbed her wrist.

Keeping behind the still-closed flap, he peered out the one he'd tied open. In the glare of the torches, he could see the shambles being made of the camp. At least ten mounted men attacked his smaller group. Unable to contain their horses in such a small area, most of the enemy had dismounted and were engaged in combat with his men. There was no telling if more hid in the woods.

Jared fought alongside the men guarding the tent. Bryce could hesitate no longer; his men were in good hands and as much as he'd like to join the fray, his main priority was clear. He tightened his grips on both his sword and Marianne's wrist. "Stay close."

All sides of the tent faced the clearing. While it made guarding the tent more efficient, it also made surrounding it just as easy.

The intruders were not a motley group of thieves looking to lighten Bryce of gold. They were well-armed, mounted knights who probably sought one prize— Marianne of Faucon.

Had this group come from Faucon to rescue Marianne, they'd have made themselves known. Since they hadn't, their reasons for wanting her could not bode well. The only way he'd relinquish her to them is if they killed him first.

He wasn't about to let either event happen.

Over the din of men shouting and blades clanging against blades, he told her, "As soon as we leave this tent, they will be upon us. Jared and my men will guard our backs for as long as they can. We must move quickly."

She responded, "You need not drag me about, I will stay by your side."

He didn't have time to determine if she told the truth or not. It would be safer to keep his hold in place.

When Jared moved within earshot, Bryce mimicked his friend's grunt, a signal that he was about to move. Jared acknowledged the grunt with a barely perceptible nod before forcing his opponent away from the tent.

Bryce ducked out of the opening, dragging Marianne behind him. They kept their backs to the tent and moved around to the side.

One of the intruders rushed at them, sword raised over his head. Bryce shoved Marianne behind him before he dispatched the man with a solid thrust of his sword through a gap between the man's coif and hauberk into his neck.

Lest any one else rush them, Bryce raced for the shelter of the woods. Not that he'd given her a choice, but Marianne kept up with his quick pace. When he moved behind a thick tree, released her wrist and drew an arm around her, she readily accepted his protection.

"Where do we go now?" Her breathless question gave him pause. His horse was gone with the rest. While they wouldn't go far, it was too dark to look for them now. The riderless beasts of the enemy were wild-eyed and unmanageable.

"We must find a place to rest until morning. Then we'll make our way to the main road." The forest was pitch-black in the moonless night. It would provide adequate cover, if he could find his way through the thickets in the dark. Before he talked himself out of it, Bryce took her hand and headed into the woods.

Unable to see, he felt his way with his sword. They slowly but surely moved away from the camp and the din of battle. Marianne's soft gasp and sudden intake of breath brought him to a stop.

"Are you all right?" His whispered question seemed to echo through the trees.

"I just wrenched my ankle tripping over that last log."

"Can you walk?"

"Is that not what I have been doing?"

"Marianne." He took a breath to calm his voice, "Do not start snapping at me now."

"I am not snapping." Her tightly spoken words gave lie to her statement. "When I snap at you, be assured you will know it."

Bryce inhaled deeply to steady his nerves. He reached up to cup her cheek and tried to reassure her. "We will be safe."

"Of course we will. But not if we stand here and discuss it."

It was impossible for her to see him, so Bryce let his smile curve his lips. He'd already learned that she was no simpering maiden, ready to faint at the least sign of trouble. Now he realized that anger was her way of dealing with danger.

"Then by all means, let us be off again." He dropped his hand back to hers and clasped her fingers in his.

"Are you laughing at me?"

She had no idea how much he wanted to do just that.

"No, my lady, I am simply gladdened that you face danger with rage instead of fear."

The breeze caught her sigh, but he heard the soft sound before it floated away. "I will be afraid later…when it is safe to be so."

Bryce tucked that whispered piece of information away. He would be there to soothe her fear when *later* arrived.

Chapter Seven

Bryce followed the stream by keeping the sound of the rushing water to his right. Eventually, the stream would cut across the road.

By leading with his sword, he was able to clear a path as best as possible. When he struck a boulder, he tapped around, ensuring there were no animals about.

As far as he could discern, what he'd discovered was an overhang of boulders. That outcrop along with the surrounding boulders formed a cave of sorts and would provide shelter for the night.

He released Marianne's hand. "Stay right here. Do not move."

She grasped the sleeve of his tunic. "Where are you going?"

"I think I have found us shelter for the night. I want to make certain it's safe." He pulled free of her hold. "I will be right here."

He dropped to his knees and crawled into the cave-like outcropping of rock. After clearing away stones, dead branches and other debris, he called out to her, "Come down on your knees and crawl straight ahead."

She did as he suggested and took a seat next to him. "Are you sure this is not some animal's den?"

"No, I am not sure. But I found nothing resembling a nest or bedding, so we should probably be safe for this night."

"Probably? How reassuring."

Her voice shook. She wasn't laughing, nor did the sound ring of fear or worry. He could only assume she was tired. "Enough talk. Rest until morning."

Marianne didn't argue. It would require too much effort to keep her teeth from clattering together. She couldn't remember ever having been so cold before. The night air was damp with the promise of a coming frost. Her tattered gown offered no protection against the chill.

She wanted to burrow into the warmth of the man seated beside her, but feared he'd take her action as a sign she wanted more than just the heat of his body. Another bout of shivers racked her.

Ashforde put one arm around her, drawing her close. He reached across them and briskly rubbed her arm. "You are freezing."

Unable to answer through the chattering of her teeth, she drew her arms over her chest and huddled against him to soak in his offered warmth. She nodded in agreement. He wore chain mail beneath his woolen tunic. The metal links permitted little of his warmth to seep through.

He unwound his arms from about her, jerked his tunic over his head and then dropped it over her. "'Tis not much, but put this on."

She tried to tug the garment off. "The air is too damp, your armor—"

"Put it on." He cut off her words. "It will give my squire something to do besides complain of his boredom."

Once she dragged the near gown-length tunic beneath her, she curled her legs so they could share in the added protection.

Ashforde pulled her tighter against his side, keeping his arms around her. "Try to get some sleep."

Marianne rested her head against his chest. She heard his heart pounding through the chain mail and wondered if the rapid pace was from their hike through the forest, or if it could be for the same reason hers now hammered so quickly.

He told her to sleep. But now that she was getting warm, sleep was not what she wanted. They were alone. It was dark. She wanted that kiss. But if she instigated the act, would he let her cry off if she changed her mind?

Marianne squeezed her eyes closed. Not again. She swallowed her groan of disgust at herself. This back-and-forth wanting, then not wanting wore thin on her patience. What in the name of all that was holy was wrong with her?

Never in her life had she been so indecisive…so uncertain…of her own warring emotions. If her confusion unsettled her, how did it make him feel? It would be too much to ask that he somehow understood—he was a man and her experience had taught her that men were not indecisive. He had to be near to throttling her.

It was time to end this torment. After all, it was just a kiss. She took a slow measured breath, seeking courage for what was surely a most bold, wanton move.

Marianne tipped her face up toward his and rested a palm against his cheek.

He grasped her wrist. "No."

"No what?"

"You were going to kiss me."

She was suddenly grateful for the blackness of the night. At least he couldn't see the heat of embarrassment that must be reddening her face. Since he knew the truth, it would be useless to lie. "Yes, I was."

"Do not."

Marianne sighed before folding her hands in her lap and placed her cheek against his chest once more. It was her own fault. She couldn't be angry with him. She was the one who'd missed the chance.

He rubbed his chin against the top of her head. "I would enjoy nothing more than kissing you. It just becomes rather—bothersome to keep trying to kiss you."

She turned her gaze toward him. "Kissing me is bothersome?"

"Aye, love. Either you change your mind, or we are interrupted."

Love? Did he realize he'd spoken such an endearment to her? That and the uneven beat of his heart made her question if perhaps there was still a chance to change his mind. She had to try. "We are alone now. There is no one about to interrupt us this time."

When he said nothing, she rose up on her knees until she felt his breath against her lips. "And I will not change my mind."

He groaned before whispering, "You do not understand the fire you seek to play with."

"Then it will be my own fault if I get burned."

He hesitated and she thought he would be the one to cry off. "Ashforde, kiss me."

"My name is Bryce. You address me as any other man would. Calling me Ashforde does little to make me want to kiss you."

She trailed a finger along his jawbone, before repeating her request, "Kiss me…Bryce."

Like a wild animal scenting its prey, he slowly inhaled, then just as slowly exhaled. Suddenly afraid he would devour her whole, Marianne closed her eyes.

His warm breath caressed her ear. A shiver raced from her scalp to her toes, chasing away the uncertainty along with her ability to form coherent thought.

He placed a quick, fleeting kiss just below her ear, and then whispered, "Is this what you wanted?"

She'd expected a kiss on the lips, not this odd touch on her neck that made her shiver for more. She didn't know what she wanted. She wanted him to cease touching her. Then, in the same heartbeat, she wanted him to continue. Instead of answering, Marianne pressed her cheek against his hand.

The next feathery touch of his lips fell partway down the side of her neck, before he trailed the tip of his tongue back to the spot beneath her ear. Marianne swore this unfamiliar onslaught had melted all the bones in her body.

He held her closer, gently nipping the line of her jaw, then soothed the spot with his mouth. His lips moved against hers as he again asked, "Is this what you wanted?"

Fighting to find her breath, Marianne said, "I don't know. I…"

He suckled her lower lip, then traced the outline of her mouth with the tip of his tongue, before asking his whispered question yet again, "Perhaps this is what you wanted?"

Once she caught her breath, she shook her head and nearly panted in frustration, "Yes. No. I—just kiss me."

He finally placed his lips against hers. Her mouth tingled. The steady pounding inside her chest faltered before fluttering in an uneven beat. When the ground beneath her seemed to waver, she grasped his shoulders.

The shock of his initial contact faded quickly and Marianne questioned her lack of fulfillment. *This* was what she'd longed to experience? This prolonged kiss was little more than a greeting of welcome or farewell she'd shared with a member of her family. Disappointment cooled what had been the beginnings of desire and she loosened her hold on him.

Bryce's lips twitched beneath hers as if he held back a laugh. She'd hoped for so much more than this from a man's kiss. The joyous ruckus she'd overheard from her brothers and their wives had led her to believe there'd be something wondrous, something that would make her lose the ability to think and would create some burning flare of desire.

With her nose pressed against his cheek and his mouth over hers, Marianne realized she could hardly breathe. She pulled her head back to take a breath.

At that instant, Bryce slid his hand from her cheek to the nape of her neck. Before she could finish drawing in air, he tumbled her onto his lap, slanted his mouth over her parted lips and teased her tongue with his own.

She froze. The earth shifted. When she tentatively returned the odd caress, his grew bolder, firmer, more de-manding…much more compelling.

This time when the earth rocked, she wrapped her arms around his neck. He nearly crushed her to him. Marianne gave in to the rush of feelings assaulting her and his hands stroking the length of her spine to hip.

Everyplace their bodies connected tingled—lips, mouth, even her scalp beneath his other hand. Her breasts, pressed impossibly tight against the hardness of his chest, seemed to burn for his touch. What had previously been a churning in her stomach, turned to fire— one that sent flames much lower than her belly.

Now she knew what made her sisters-by-marriage sigh and moan in their beds. She understood the heavily lidded looks they directed toward their husbands when they thought no one else noticed.

But she also knew without a doubt that there was something else. Something grander. Something more to be experienced.

There had to be—otherwise why would her body burn so with a hunger she could not name?

A soft moan of longing trailed up her chest and throat. It escaped only to be trapped by Bryce's relentless kiss.

He broke the contact and pulled her cheek to rest against his shoulder. Marianne felt a shudder ripple down his body. Was it possible that he felt the same emotions she had just experienced?

Still wanting more, she brushed her lips against the hard line of his square jaw. She could not resist the impish urge to nip his stubble-covered flesh.

Bryce knew if he held her on his lap any longer, he'd lower Marianne of Faucon to the ground and make her his.

She'd not fight him. This untried woman was desire embodied in living form.

A kiss was all she wanted. And a kiss was all he'd planned to give her. A gentle, nonthreatening lips pressed to lips kiss. One that would do nothing more than permit her to get used to the feel of his mouth on hers.

Instead, he felt her frown, had sensed her disappointed frustration. She'd been ready for more than a simple friendly kiss. He'd been ready to supply the answers to the questions tumbling about in her mind.

And now his eager willingness had guaranteed he'd be the one frustrated.

He tilted her face up toward his and rubbed his cheek against hers. "There. You have had your kiss."

She toyed with the hair curling about his ear. "Aye. And it was wonderful. I would have more of them."

Bryce grasped her hand. "No. I am not made of stone, Marianne. I cannot kiss you without having more."

"I would gladly—"

"Do not say it." He placed a finger over her lips. "Desire and longing make you wish for things you should not want. In the light of the morning you would be ashamed."

She drew away from him. As much as he wanted to pull her back into his embrace, it was safer to let go for a time.

He patted the ground. "This den is wide enough for us to lie down. You sleep in the rear and I'll rest across the entrance."

Without another word, Marianne slid off his lap and stretched out on the dirt floor. He waited until her breathing evened out, before he, too, joined her on the ground.

Turning over onto his side, facing the opening, he rested his head on his bent arm and stared out into the dark.

Was Jared right this time?

The relationship he shared with his friend was an odd one. From the day they met, they'd engaged in a game of dares. Who could climb to the highest branch, who could catch the most fish, kill the most hares, anger the most people while escaping unscathed. As they'd got older their dares remained, but changed, becoming bolder.

If one man was having trouble, the other would offer a suggestion…one meant to get the first man in more trouble if he was foolish enough to take the advice.

Silly? Yes. Immature? Undoubtedly. But they'd known each other long enough to realize when the advice was in earnest, or just another dare.

Jared's most recent advice to use Marianne of Faucon as a method of complete revenge was meant as a dare. Bryce knew that. But it'd started the thoughts swirling in his mind. Fanned the flames of longing building in his chest. And he realized how willing he was to take the risk.

His attraction to her made little sense. In fact, it made no sense whatsoever. Not only was she his enemy's sister, he'd known her but a day.

Ah, but the things he'd learned in those few hours set his heart racing and made him feel more alive than he had in ages.

Bold. Headstrong. Foolish. Curious. All the things that would chase away boredom and keep his long days filled with intrigue.

Wanton. Fearless. Willing. All the things that would make his dreams unbelievably lush and keep the short nights filled with passion.

A scuffing sound behind him should have been enough warning, but he'd tried to ignore her tossing and turning. So, when she threw the tunic across him and curled up beneath it against his back and slipped her arm over his waist Bryce tensed in surprise.

"There is no reason for either of us to freeze to death."

Her whispered words against his neck assured him that this would be the longest night of his life.

A finely honed awareness dragged him from sleep. Bryce remained motionless with his eyes closed, trying to ascertain the reason for his pounding heart. He listened closely, but heard no sound that would warn of danger.

Confused, because it wasn't normal for his senses to jolt him from sleep without cause, he opened his eyes. And stared into a pair of unblinking emerald orbs.

His physical awareness hit him with the force of a boulder flying from a well-aimed trebuchet. Not only did he face Marianne, but her head rested in the crook of his arm. His other arm…other hand…rested on her…oh, Lord, he hadn't been dreaming.

Bryce's breathing hitched as his pulse kicked into an erratic race. The urge to gently knead the breast beneath his hand was strong. But from the wideness of her eyes, he had the sinking feeling that he had already been doing just that.

Marianne closed her eyes and sighed heavily.

Upon hearing her sultry, passion-laden sigh, he couldn't move fast enough. Bryce rolled away from her, ripping the tunic tangled about his legs in his rush to get out of the den before he did something both of them would come to regret.

"I am so sorry." In truth, he was only sorry that he'd been asleep, but an apology seemed appropriate. "I meant no ill-intent, no disrespect. I—"

"Cease," Marianne replied. "Let us just be gone from here."

Without another word, he turned around and when she joined him, they backtracked toward the stream. Once their morning necessities were done, he stopped her and asked, "How is your ankle?"

Marianne lifted her foot and made a circle with her toe. "It seems fine." She touched his side. "What about you? Does the wound bother you overmuch?"

The only thing that bothered him overmuch was the getting of the wound. It still rankled that this mere slip of a woman had stabbed him. "It was not that grievous of a cut. It will be fine."

"Grievous or not, it could still fester."

"Fear not. I will not die from a flesh wound."

She frowned, before looking away for a moment. When she returned her gaze, Bryce wondered if her sorrowful expression was from guilt or concern. Before she could say anything, he turned around and headed in the direction of the main road, crunching the frost-covered grass as they walked.

To Marianne, it seemed as if they had walked for hours in an uncomfortable silence before the main road come into view. Bryce raised his hand, signaling her to stop. She waited behind the safety of a large tree while he scouted about the area.

The act reminded Marianne of her brother Rhys. How many times had he issued an order to his men with nothing more than a simple hand gesture? And how many times had he done the same to her, knowing she'd understand what he wanted?

Her chest tightened with a different kind of longing—one that beckoned her to the comforts of home. The thought of returning to the only home she'd known made her both happy and fearful. She'd be relieved to be within the familiar, strong walls of Faucon.

How would her brothers and sisters-by-marriage welcome her back? Would it be with open arms, or would they be ashamed of her?

If they discovered the actions that led to her abduction, they'd be so disappointed in her. She could live with their anger because time would ease the ire.

But how would she live with herself knowing she'd destroyed their trust in her? Rhys, and her parents before their deaths, had taught her to honor not only her family name, but to also honor herself.

On a reckless whim she'd tossed those lessons aside for a mere night of pleasure. To add to her dishonor she'd not just lusted for a man neither she nor her brothers knew, but she'd taken a great risk in tempting him to kiss her.

Marianne's breath caught in her throat, and her cheeks burned. And when he'd finally succumbed, she'd reveled in his touch so much that she'd asked for more of the same.

Bryce of Ashforde had been the one to rein in the desires that could easily have gone too far. She'd nearly begged him to take their shared kisses further, yet he'd kept her honor intact. He'd been right—whatever heights of passion they could have reached last night would have left her feeling guilty and ashamed this morning.

No matter how hard it would be to live with her brothers' disappointment, she needed to return home—as quickly as possible. Before she asked Bryce for more than just kisses.

Ah, but she shamefully hungered for more than just the feel of his mouth on hers. Yes, outside of marriage her thoughts were sinful. But perhaps marriage is what she wanted from this man. Marriage and a lifetime of sharing his days…and his nights.

And what better way to ensure Rhys's approval than for Bryce to escort her back to Faucon? Regardless of the welcome, would not her brother be grateful to Bryce for her safe return?

The sound of horses approaching jerked her out of her thoughts and sent her a few steps back into the denseness of the forest. She was tired of hiding, of seeking safety. Marianne longed for her sword, or the jewel-encrusted dagger back in her chambers. At the very least a bow and quiver of arrows. A weapon of any sort would help lessen her fear.

For now, since she intended to remain alive, she hid behind a bramble of near-dead bushes and peered out toward the road.

One of the men shouted, "Lord Ashforde!"

She recognized the deep raspy voice as Warehaven's. Instead of leaving her hiding place, she stayed where she was. For whatever reason Bryce called Warehaven friend, to her and her family the man was an enemy. She'd not give him the opportunity to play her foul.

It seemed very opportune to her that this Warehaven arrived in camp mere hours before they were attacked. Was he somehow connected to her kidnapping?

At his next shout, Bryce answered back. Yet, she still remained hidden. Something bade her be wary. Granted, the sudden illness in her stomach could be simple worry. The chill rushing through her could be from the cool air and the dampness of her gown.

Even so, she would wait until Bryce beckoned her to come into the open. For now, she was in the perfect position to watch the two men and listen to their conversation.

Dismounting, Warehaven asked, "Where have you been? We've traveled back and forth on this road at least half a dozen times since the sun rose."

"We circled around, down by the stream last night. I thought it safer to hike here through the forest than to come back through the camp."

"We?" Warehaven looked around. "I don't see your lady. Did you lose her?"

Bryce also looked around the area. His gaze stopped on her for a heartbeat before finishing his search. "I left her right here. She can't be far."

Marianne frowned. He'd seen her. So, why did he lie to the man he called friend?

The Dragon of Warehaven made an odd noise that sounded to her like a cross between a grunt and a snort. Perhaps that was the sound he thought a true dragon made. It was irritating to say the least.

Bryce turned his attention to the men with Warehaven, then he asked, "How did you fare?"

"They lost three men. You lost one, and another with minor injuries. We buried all four after the remaining intruders left."

"I see you found the horses."

"A few…mine, yours, Sir John's. The rest were theirs.

We even have two extra now, along with their cloaks, weapons and supplies." Warehaven laughed before adding, "Spoils of war, I say."

"Agreed."

"Are you certain you wish not to take refuge at my lair for a few days?"

Marianne slapped her hand over her mouth. Hopefully, she stopped the gasp from escaping. She was not going to stay at Warehaven's *lair* for any length of time. Bryce could do as he pleased, but she was going home.

Her one night of merriment had gone on far too long as it was. If they weren't already, her brothers would soon be turning both Normandy and England inside out looking for her.

Bryce started to say something, then paused. Finally, he said, "Nay. We are close enough to Ashforde to take respite there for a day or two before heading to Faucon."

Warehaven sighed. "Isabella and Beatrice will be sorely disappointed." Both men laughed. Then, he added, "But I understand."

"You are welcome to join us."

At that offer, Warehaven's laugh bounced off the trees. "No. I thank you, no." He added something that Marianne couldn't quite hear. But the tone he used was obvious—he was teasing Bryce about something.

What did Warehaven think the two of them were doing? Now, she felt the returning warmth of embarrassment heat her own face. His thoughts probably ran along the lines of what her brothers would mistakenly think. She shook her head. It had just been a kiss. Nothing more.

And this morning was simply a happenstance. When

a man and a woman slept next to each other, something untoward was bound to occur. Since she'd not make the same mistake again, it was an occurrence that could not be repeated.

Bryce's voice interrupted her musings. "The choice is yours. After I see Marianne to the safety of her brother's keep, I will join you at Warehaven. Do me the favor of seeing to my men until I arrive."

"You are not traveling to Ashforde alone."

"Nay. But I need no more than Sir John and one other. The lighter the load, the quicker the travel."

"True."

"If I might offer a suggestion." Bryce appeared to debate his next words. "Stay away from Carisbrooke."

"Since I've no wish to explain your absence, that was my plan." Warehaven mounted his horse and looked down at Bryce. "I wish you success at Faucon. God speed." Then he and all but two of the men disappeared down the road.

Warehaven's comment about success puzzled her. What type of success would Bryce seek at Faucon?

"You can come out now."

Marianne stepped out from behind the bushes. She half expected Bryce to say something about her reaction to Warehaven, but he said nothing. Instead, he held out his hand. Once she clasped it with her own he led her to a horse. After wrapping a warm woolen cloak about her shoulders, he helped her onto the saddle.

With his hand still resting on her thigh, he looked up at her. Marianne sucked in a breath at the overwhelming sadness etched on his face, dulling the ice of his eyes and turning down the corners of his mouth. "He is like a brother to me...the only one I have ever known."

There was no doubt that he spoke of Warehaven. She defended her action. "He is a traitor to King Stephen and an enemy to Faucon."

"This is a war where families fight on different sides and friends kill friends." A flash of anger sparked in his eyes, wiping away the sadness. "Your brothers are not here. Jared poses no threat to you. I will not have him treated in that manner again."

She bit the inside of her bottom lip to keep from saying anything. The oddities of this war aside, why did Bryce defend such a traitor? How had he come to consider this man a brother?

He tightened his hold on her leg. "Did you hear me?"

Marianne flinched at the sharp tone of his voice. "Yes."

"Good." He relaxed his hold and stroked a thumb across her thigh. "Come, it is time to go."

"To Ashforde?"

A crooked smile eased the hard planes of his face. The familiar mind-robbing gaze held her in place. "Yes. I have been away far too long. There are things I must see to before journeying to Faucon."

Managing a keep was no small feat and Marianne was well aware of the countless tasks required. Surely he had a capable squire who acted as seneschal seeing to the day-to-day workings of Ashforde?

Perhaps this squire was not as trustworthy or experienced as Bryce wished. Or perhaps, like her brother, he chose to maintain a close eye on his holdings.

Either way, it was none of her concern. She would be happy just to have a safe, dry place to rest her head.

Chapter Eight

Faucon Keep, Normandy
October 22, 1143

"I will wait no longer." Rhys stared down the length of the table, at the faces of his wife, brothers and sisters-by-marriage. At his statement, each face displayed varying levels of dismay, worry and fear.

Lyonesse sat to his right. She placed a hand gently on his wrist. "It has only been sennight, Rhys. Should you not wait another day or two before taking up arms?"

"No." He slammed his fist on the well-worn tabletop. "Seven nights have been seven too many." He tried to keep the edges of anger and impatience from his voice, but knew by her flinch that he'd failed miserably.

He looked to his younger brother Gareth for help. "What say you? How much longer do we keep our search close to Faucon while waiting for a ransom demand?"

"We have waited too long already." At Rhian's hiss of displeasure, Gareth looked down at his wife. "I can no longer sit here worrying. I must do something to find either Marianne, or someone who knows of her whereabouts."

"How can you be certain she did not simply run away with a lover?"

Every head turned to stare at Rhian.

Gareth sputtered before declaring, "She would do no such thing."

Darius, the youngest brother, tried to reassure everyone by saying, "We would have received some type of message from her."

"Marianne has more honor than that." Rhys's words came from behind clenched teeth.

All three brothers had spoken at once, causing Rhian to slink down in her seat. She lifted her hands up as if to ward off an imaginary blow. "I apologize. I only meant that perhaps she had found someone she cared for— someone she knew you would not find adequate."

Rhys sat straighter in his chair at the head of the table. "What do you mean by that?"

All three women, Lyonesse, Rhian and Marguerite laughed wryly.

"Oh, my dearest husband," Lyonesse shook her head before continuing, "How many men have asked your permission to take Marianne as wife?"

Darius's wife Marguerite asked, "And how many have you turned away?"

"Did you ever once ask her opinion about any of the men?" Rhian wondered.

Rhys leaned his forearms on the table. "And that is what you think this is about? That a girl took it into her head to worry her family because she fancied a man?"

"Girl?" Gareth and Darius asked at once.

"Have you looked at her of late?" Darius asked. "If you but opened your eyes, you would see that our little sister is a woman grown. She is well past the age she should be married."

Gareth added, "And if you cannot see it, she will inform you of the fact in no uncertain terms."

Rhys frowned. It was disconcerting to learn his entire family had all lost their wits at the same time. But it did not change the situation. "Be that as it may, Marianne is still missing. We have received no demand for ransom. Nor has she sent a missive telling us this was her decision."

All nodded in agreement. Perhaps they had only lost a portion of their wits.

"We need to decide now…do we waste more days waiting?" He rose from his seat. "Or do we take matters into our own hands?"

Without hesitation, Gareth and Darius stood.

The three wives only sighed.

He kept his attention on his brothers. "I will meet you in the bailey in an hour. Bring some of your men and be armed."

Before the women could think to dissuade him, Rhys headed toward the doors at the other end of the great hall. When he was halfway across the chamber, Melwyn the captain of his guard entered the keep.

"My Lord, our search of the area has proved fruitful. I have something for you."

The smug smile on Melwyn's face gave Rhys hope that this *something* would be information about Marianne.

As the others rushed to join the two men, Melwyn motioned behind him. Two guards bodily escorted a bruised and bloodied man into the keep and dropped him at Rhys's feet.

"What is this?"

Melwyn urged the man to talk with a boot to his leg.

"My lord comte, we…I did not know…I thought she was…" He buried his hands in his face.

Rhys grasped the front of the man's tunic and hauled him to his feet. "Who?"

"The girl. At the faire."

He shook the man.

"Rhys." Lyonesse stepped forward and tugged on his arm.

He glared down at her and easily shook off her hold. "Leave me be." Turning his attention back to the now crying man, he ordered, "Tell me what you know."

"A man paid us to take the girl from the faire. Since she was alone we gave it no thought that she was your sister."

"My sister or not, what did you think to do with her?"

The man began to sob in earnest. "We were to kill her, but thought we would have a little…some sport first, my lord."

Gareth cursed and stood next to Rhys. "Did you have your sport?"

"No. No. Before we could…that is…she told us who she was before anything happened."

"Where is she?" Darius had joined them.

"Why did you not bring her back to Faucon?" Rhys's heart pounded in fear of what this man and his friends might have done.

"We were too afraid."

Darius snorted. "With good reason." He repeated his question. "Where is she?"

"I do not know."

"What?" All three brothers shouted in unison.

At their shout, the man wet himself. A puddle formed beneath him. Rhys released the quivering scum, not caring that he landed in his own urine.

Melwyn drew his sword and pointed it at the man now curled in a ball on the floor. "Would you like me to finish questioning him?"

"It appears by the blood on his face that you have already done enough." Marguerite's tone of disapproval was obvious to all.

Darius looked back at her and ordered, "Close your mouth."

Lyonesse grabbed Marguerite's arm. She kept her voice to a whisper as she explained, "It is all right. Melwyn knows his job. 'Tis what he does best."

Rhys shook his head at Melwyn. "Nay." With his foot to the man's shoulder, he pushed the prisoner up into a kneeling position. "Where is she?"

The crying had stopped. Obviously, the man knew what fate awaited him. With a ragged sigh, he admitted, "We thought to make more gold. But I feared crossing the channel, so the others took her to Hampshire without me."

"And did what with her?"

"They were to use her as a prize for a game of dice."

The women gasped. Already emotional from carrying her second child, Lyonesse burst into tears. The other two women wrapped their arms about her and escorted her toward the stairs.

Rhys stared at his brothers and wondered if the horror etched on their faces was also on his own.

Melwyn smiled as he reached for the man. "My lord?"

Rhys nodded, insisting, "Make it quick." He glanced at his wife's retreating back and at the crowd beginning to gather at the far end of the chamber. "But not in the hall." He then left the keep with Gareth and Darius right behind him.

The cool air blowing against his face helped to ease his suddenly roiling stomach.

"A prize? Like a piece of horseflesh or a bag of gold?" Darius's ragged whisper floated away with the wind.

Gareth calmly strode to the nearest building and slugged a hole through the wooden wall. Then, nursing his bleeding knuckles turned and asked, "When do we leave?"

Rhys swallowed hard. "I need to see my wife first. I suggest you both do the same. But I wish to be on the road well before the sun sets."

"We will find her." Darius sounded as if his throat was thick with suppressed emotion. He then headed toward the keep.

"Of course we will," Gareth agreed before he too went in search of his wife.

Rhys stared out across the bailey and did something he rarely did anymore. He prayed.

Chapter Nine

Ashforde Keep - Devon, England
October 24, 1143

A day and a half later Bryce breathed a sigh of relief as the bend in the road leading to the small town on the outskirts of Ashforde came in sight. The ride here had been uneventful...more or less.

They'd stayed away from the larger towns and avoided keeps altogether. He'd not spent enough time in Devon to know who would fall on the side of friend, or who would be foe. With Faucon's sister at his side, he'd not wished to chance meeting up with someone who knew her, or her brothers.

He'd maintained a respectful distance from Marianne and to his relief she'd seemed to welcome his action. They'd ridden side-by-side, talked of nothing of any importance and he'd refrained from touching her as much as possible.

Yet his muscles were strung as tight as a readied bow.

The chill in the autumn air did little to cool the near feverlike heat that bedeviled him day and night.

He wasn't so young that he didn't recognize the carnal lust that set him so on edge. Nor was he so old that he could blithely ignore his attraction toward Marianne.

But now, with Ashforde almost in sight, his ragged pulse evened. He would be able to lose himself in manual labor. And drop into bed at night with nothing more on his mind but sleep.

There was one thing he wished to complete before reaching Ashforde. He called out to the small group, "Hold up."

He handed Eustace some coins, ordering, "We will stop here for a spell. Go into town and purchase something to eat."

While the two men were noncommittal about the idea, Marianne sighed. "Thank God." She dismounted, tied the horse to a nearby tree and stretched.

He too dismounted, motioning John to do the same, then joined her. "It is safe to assume you find the plan agreeable?"

"Yes. I was near to begging for a brief stop."

"Good. Wait here. I need to speak to my man."

"Sir John, come. I wish a word with you." The younger man frowned, but fell in step alongside him.

Once they were out of Marianne's hearing, Bryce leaned against a tree. "How are you faring?"

John's frown deepened. "I am well. Why do you ask?"

The direct approach seemed the best answer. "You drink much more than the others."

"Oh." A flush reddened his already ruddy complexion. "I'd not realized it caused any reason for concern."

"You wouldn't have ended up in a stream the other night if you'd had your wits about you."

John shot a glare toward Marianne, before he shrugged. "I believed her lie about a bauble. It had nothing to do with how much I'd imbibed."

"That may well be the case. But I cannot always stop to determine if your actions are due to someone's lie, or your own clouded mind."

"Shall I return to the empress?"

"No." Bryce jerked away from the tree. "Keep your voice down."

"If I may speak freely?"

"No one said you could not."

"This quest for revenge against Faucon is not going as you had said it would."

"Nor has it since the beginning." Bryce was well aware that little had fallen easily into place since he'd started this quest. That didn't explain why the man Empress Matilda assigned as captain of Ashforde's temporary guard had taken up drinking to excess. "You drink because all does not go according to plan?"

If that was the case, Sir John was in for a lifetime of drunkenness.

"No. I drink to rid my mind of the woman I love."

That statement only confused Bryce more. "Did being ordered to serve me take you away from your betrothed?"

"No. The woman I love was given to…another."

"Does this drinking change that fact?"

John shook his head. "So far, no. But I thought I would be occupied ferreting out information at Faucon, not escorting his sister coast to coast."

His tone had turned bitter. His scowl darkened. "Do you not approve of the duty, or of the woman?"

"Both. But more of the woman herself." Sir John paused a moment, then added, "She is haughty and acts as though she is better than the rest of us."

Bryce turned his attention to Marianne. He'd not noticed that about her. But even if she had given John that impression, it was true.

He brought his focus back to his man. "This war has created two types of people, John. Those who give the orders and those who follow them. We are mercenaries who spend most of our time following orders." He nodded toward Marianne. "She comes from a family who issues the orders."

"But not our orders. She comes from a family who would gladly see us dead." Suppressed rage emanated from him like a dark cloud.

Bryce didn't like Sir John's tone or attitude. Nor did he feel at all comfortable with the way the man glared at Marianne. Did John despise her because of her brothers, or herself?

The wisest course of action would be to immediately relieve Sir John of his duties and send him back to Empress Matilda. Without someone else to put in his place, Bryce knew that option was closed to him. Besides, he had no idea how the empress would react to such a move.

Until this situation could be changed he would maintain a close eye on John. He kept his thoughts to himself and said, "Marianne of Faucon is not our enemy. My plans for revenge never included harming her. Do you understand that?"

"Understand? Yes. Agree? No."

John's tone became even more sarcastic, his attitude more belligerent. Bryce squared his shoulders, straightened his spine and glared down at his captain.

His title and position might be new to him, but dealing with arrogant pups had always been the same. A strong physical presence and harshly spoken words went a long way toward putting them in their place.

"I did not ask for your agreement." When John's eyes widened for the briefest moment, Bryce knew his tactic had worked—for now. "I only require your service until I can find my own men. Then you will be free to return to the empress if you so wish. Can you do that without taking your anger out on an innocent woman?"

John hesitated as if thinking about his answer. Finally, he nodded, "She isn't exactly innocent, but I would hate to jeopardize your plans for Faucon."

"Good. And unless you know something I don't, leave the drink alone. It will do nothing to get your woman back. You need think of another way."

At that, John's mood appeared to lighten considerably. He smiled, but Bryce noted that the mirth did not reach his eyes. "Oh, fear not, my lord, I am working on another plan for that."

"I wish you luck." He ignored John's snort and waved toward the small clearing. "Let us fill our bellies, then be on our way."

Seated against a tall oak, Marianne swallowed the last bite of the bread and cheese Eustace had brought back from the nearby village. "Is the village far from here?" She rose, now eager to stretch her legs, to walk about, to do anything other than get back on the horse.

Eustace nodded. "Aye, 'tis very near." He pointed at the bend in the road. "Just beyond that curve."

"Good." She turned to Bryce. "I cannot abide the thought of getting back in the saddle just yet. I will walk into the village and await you there."

He jumped to his feet. "No."

His eyes flashed, his voice sounded choked. Marianne cocked her head at the oddness of his reaction. "Pray tell why ever not?"

He appeared to stumble for words before saying, "I know not what kind of welcome awaits us in the village."

When Eustace opened his mouth, Bryce cast him a warning glare. The older man blinked and closed his mouth.

Marianne took a step forward, crossed her arms against her chest and stared up at him expectantly. "Is there danger in the village? Do brigands control the road? Do criminals hide in the shadows?"

Bryce ran a hand through his hair, and then shook his head. "No."

She narrowed her eyes. "Then what are you hiding?"

"Nothing. There is nothing to hide." He looked everywhere but at her.

"My, my, what an awful liar you are." She uncrossed her arms, shook out the crumbs clinging to the skirt of her pitiful gown and headed toward the road.

"Stay here. I said, no."

His sharply spoken words stopped her in her tracks. Marianne turned around slowly. "Give me a reason to do as you bid."

"I don't bid you to do anything. That was an order."

She stared at the shimmering ice of his eyes, the hard set of his mouth and the lines creasing his forehead. Obviously, there was something wrong in the village. Something he did not want her to know.

And that only increased her determination to discover what it was that had him so worried.

"An order?" She took a few steps toward him. "I thought I wasn't your prisoner. Has that suddenly changed?"

Bryce took that, oh, so familiar to her man in charge stance. Head held high, shoulders squared, spine straight, hand hovering just above the scabbard hanging at his side. He glared down at her and said, "I can make it so."

Even his voice had changed—deepened to the near growl of a man on a battlefield.

She wanted to laugh. Did all men have the same mannerisms? Were they born with them, or was it something they learned? In the next heartbeat she wanted to cry. She did not know about all men, but right now Bryce looked like a blond Faucon and the homesickness hit her with a force that threatened to knock her to her knees.

Instead of laughing, or goading him into an argument, she walked back to the oak tree and sat down.

Bryce cursed before ordering his men, "Ride on ahead. I will catch up."

When the men left them alone, he stood over her. "Marianne?"

Her concentration was focused on her churning stomach. Would the food she'd eaten stay there? So, without looking at him, she replied, "What?"

He lightly tapped her outstretched leg with his foot. "What is wrong?"

Wrong? Why would anything be wrong? He ordered her about like a bully…like an overly arrogant man… like her brothers did.

Marianne sniffed. Good Lord above, now she was about to cry like some silly, weak knees lackwit. She swiped at her eyes before the tears fell.

Bryce crouched down beside her and tipped her head up with the side of his hand beneath her chin. "Oh, I see. You are feeling sorry for yourself."

She jerked her head away from his touch. "No. I am not."

"Good." He grasped her chin and turned her face toward him. While brushing the traitorous tears from her cheek with the backs of his fingers, he continued as if nothing were amiss. "I am glad to hear that, because I see no reason for a Faucon—even the youngest one—to ever feel sorry for their lot in life."

Marianne knew if she opened her mouth, a sobbing whine would issue forth. Something quite childish would come out, like—*I want to go home,* or *I miss my family.* She was seventeen, well beyond the age of whining.

But she did want to go home. And she did miss her brothers and their wives dreadfully. While her brothers had been away from Faucon for months on end, she had never been away from home by herself.

This journey had been…enlightening, much more than she had ever bargained for when she snuck out of the keep to find a few hours of freedom. Now, she simply wanted to throw herself into the arms of her brothers. She wanted them to rail at her, chain her in her chamber, smother her like the overprotective falcons they were.

She choked at the vision that thought created in her mind. Inane or not, it was true, this fledging falcon was not ready to leave the safety of the nest.

Instead of speaking she closed her eyes and took a long shuddering breath.

Bryce sighed before releasing her and rising. "You miss your home and your family. There is no shame in that."

Marianne froze. She opened her eyes and stared at his feet through a blur of tears. "How do you know this? What sort of trickery gives you the ability to read my mind, know my thoughts?"

"It is more that I guess, or sense your feelings, than know your thoughts."

She felt her brows rise in surprise. "'Tis more than simple guesswork on your part."

"It is more like an instinct." He paused. "I do not know how this happened. I cannot explain this strangeness where you are concerned. But it is there nonetheless. I am able to sense your feelings, your moods. If any trickery or bedevilment is involved, it was cast by you."

Marianne quickly looked around. "Oh, aye, you would have me stoned as a witch."

"Be still. There is no one about."

"I cast nothing on you. Nothing."

His exasperated sigh drifted into the woods. A heartbeat later, Bryce ordered, "Get up."

Unwilling to argue through the tears choking her throat and unable to think of anything but the comforts of home, Marianne rose to her feet.

"Look at me."

That was a command she could not obey. It was bad enough that he knew her feelings, sensed the sadness and longing of her heart. She could not turn her tear-streaked face directly to his. Would not permit him to witness the depth of her sadness.

"Marianne, I may not be one of your brothers, but my arms are just as strong." Something different in his tone of voice, a warmth she could not identify, wrapped around her heart. "My shoulders are just as wide. I am more than capable of taking your burdens upon myself."

When she remained frozen in place, uncertain what he wanted her to do, he whispered, "Come here."

Without further hesitation, she went willingly into the safety offered in his embrace. He wrapped his arms around her and held her close.

She knew in her mind that he offered comfort and safety. But her heart wanted nothing more than to sob against his chest.

Bryce stroked her back. "There is nothing wrong with finding release in tears."

A small laugh raced through the thickness in her throat. He'd done it again—guessed, or sensed her innermost urge. "I do not normally cry like a baby."

"It requires no special skill to know that." He laughed against her ear. "A woman who rides down a foe with a horse and uses a sword as a lance to kill another, would not be one who typically resorted to tears."

"I just…it is simply…" Marianne gave up trying to explain.

"Two days ago you said that you would be afraid later." He swayed gently back and forth, as if rocking her in his arms. "Do you think perhaps your *later* has arrived?"

She sniffed and tried to stop the undignified quivering of her chin before saying, "A man does not cry when afraid."

"I am sure you've had the opportunity to notice, but in case that is not true, you are not a man, Marianne. You are an inexperienced woman of what, seventeen, sixteen? I would find it more odd if you were not overcome with tears on occasion."

He rubbed his cheek against the top of her head. "Although, I find it quite distressing that your sadness makes me want to cry along with you."

The sudden image of the two of them crying together like little children drew laughter from her. A hard, broken laugh that before she knew what happened turned to sobs.

Bryce said nothing. No words of censure, no teasing left his lips. He only held her closer, his cheek resting against her ear and let her cry.

Finally, what seemed to her hours later, her cries turned to hiccups. He leaned away slightly, brushed her hair back from her face and asked, "Do you feel any better?"

Marianne nodded.

"So, now if I bluster at you or tease, you will not take offense?"

"You did not bluster or tease, you ordered."

"Such an odd occurrence for a man to issue orders."

"Issue them to your men, not me."

He smiled and cupped her cheek. "Ah, yes, snapping is much better."

His hand was warm against her skin. She rubbed her cheek against his calloused palm before lifting her head.

Marianne gazed into his steady look and felt her pulse come to an abrupt stop. She frowned as a sudden certainty settled into her heart.

It no longer mattered where he came from, or who he was. She cared not why he considered the traitor Warehaven his brother.

She narrowed her eyes slightly and stared harder into his. What she saw deep in his undisguised look took her breath away.

Bryce would be the man to provide her with all she'd longed for. He would be the one to hold her heart gently and give it the love she deserved.

Marianne had thought falling in love would be something that happened over time and after she'd wed whichever man Rhys finally settled on. While she'd already decided her brother's choice would be this man, she hadn't expected love to hit her like a blow from a studded mace.

She'd never thought to find it in the warmth of a compassionate embrace, or the clear unblinking stare of a pair of ice-blue eyes.

Without breaking the connection of their gazes, she lowered her arms and quickly stepped back. "Oh, my." Her hushed whisper of surprise hung between them.

By the expressions of first confusion, then horror flitting across his face, she knew Bryce had felt the stirrings of love, too.

Marianne swallowed the smile threatening to curve her lips. The thought might scare him now, but she'd see to it that he soon realized his heart would be safe in her hands.

He shook himself as if waking from a dream and waved toward the waiting horses. "Are you ready?"

She nodded. For him she kept her tone light and said, "Yes."

But inside her head and deep in her heart, her voice shouted in joy. "Oh, yes, I am ready. I am more than ready, my love."

Eustace had been correct. The small village outside Ashforde was just beyond the bend in the road.

Marianne realized that Faucon was huge compared to most villages, but she'd not known that something this small existed outside the protecting walls of a keep.

A few scattered huts lined the dirt road. Another building that appeared to be the blacksmith, had a lean-to off the side with a plank table and some benches. She deduced that this was the villagers' gathering spot.

There was no place for worship, no stalls for vendors, no stables for horses other than what existed at the smithy.

Stranger to her was that nobody hailed them as they rode through. Did people live here?

"Bryce, where are the villagers?"

He nodded ahead. "You'll see shortly."

The road twisted again and headed downhill. When they got close to the top, Bryce slowed their pace. "Do not expect to see Faucon."

She leaned toward him and touched his arm. "It does not matter if Ashforde is not as rich or strong as Faucon. It is your home and that is enough."

His mouth twisted to a grimace. "Ashforde…" He glanced toward the sky. "It is…" Finally, he shrugged. "It is nothing." He waved her forward. "See for yourself."

The woods opened to a clearing. Marianne jerked her horse to a dead stop. The field between the woods and what must have at one time been a walled keep was blackened by fire.

She lifted her perusal to the mounded hill across the way. Freshly cut timber planks formed a wooden palisade around the bottom of the hill. Wooden towers—also newly built, flanked the gates.

The burnt ruins of what once had been a good-sized keep lay in piles outside the gates. Construction on the new keep at the top of the mound had just begun.

"What happened?" She couldn't envision Faucon in such ruins. Just the thought made her sick. "Was there a siege?"

"No."

Bryce's harshly spoken answer drew her attention from Ashforde Keep to him. She leaned away from the anger etched firmly on his face, turning it into a mask of hatred. Her horse must have felt her retreat, because it sidestepped away from Bryce.

"If there was no battle, what happened here?"

He nodded toward the pile of ruins, then waved at the still scorched fields. "Obviously it was set afire."

"Were you here? Did many die?"

He shook his head. "No, I was gone and as far as I can tell none of my men died, but seven villagers perished."

"Who would do such a terrible thing?"

Chapter Ten

Bryce debated. Did he tell her the truth or not?

If she did not believe him, the sword he'd found in the ashes of the fire was stored in a clothing chest at Ashforde. Once there, it would be easy to unsheathe the weapon it contained and hand it to her. She would see the falcon etched on the blade and soon come to realize who had laid waste to his property.

But he'd witnessed the moment when she'd comprehended how deep her feelings for him could run.

The idea to tie her heart to his and then use her as revenge against her brothers was moot. The first deed was done with no intentional action on his part. And now, to his amazement and regret he had no wish to use her so badly.

In fact, his greatest urge at this moment was to protect her. He silently cursed his own softening heart before saying, "I do not know. We have yet to find those responsible."

"The rest of your men are still looking?"

He laughed. "The rest of my men?"

"There were only five at Hampshire. I'd just assumed the rest were here at Ashforde."

"Yes. In a manner of speaking." He nudged his horse forward. Marianne did the same. "Half my force disappeared with the fire."

She gasped. "You said no lives were lost."

"I know not if they are dead or alive. When I returned to Ashforde, they were…gone. There were no bodies amongst the ashes. I was searching for them when I heard about the dice game." The half lie only pricked at the edges of his honor. He had been looking for his men. He just thought to find them at Faucon. And he still might.

"So, you only have a guard of ten men?" Her horror-laced question would have been amusing if it were not so close to the truth.

"In total there would be twenty-one. I lost one during the battle at the camp and ten are still missing."

At Marianne's sudden silence Bryce glanced at her. Her concentration was directed toward Ashforde Keep. She studied the keep…rather, she studied the construction site before scanning the open field, then the woods.

He sought to reassure her, "We are so far away from any battle that it does not take many men to hold this keep."

"Oh, yes, I can see that by the thick stone walls and the imposing towers."

He stared at her. "Sarcasm does you little justice."

"I am sorry." She had the decency to blush. "It just slipped out."

He inched his beast closer until he could touch her arm. "I will let nothing happen to you. I'll deliver you safely to your brothers, or die trying."

"I thank you, but I would prefer you stayed alive."

"Well, yes, it would be my choice also."

"How long will it take to rebuild?"

"A few years from what I am told."

"It appears that it will be a good-sized keep. What was it like before?"

Bryce cursed his lack of forethought. He should have planned for her to ask questions he'd be unable to answer. Again, he chose to lie as little as possible. "To be honest, I am uncertain. Ashforde was only recently given into my care. I had been here once, for half a day, before it was destroyed."

"Oh. Then you hold Ashforde for your liege?"

How much of the day's politics did her brothers tell her? If he admitted that he was the Comte of Ashforde, would she then know which crown he served? It was a risk he was not willing to take.

"Yes. I hold it for my absent liege." Since it was not unusual for the lord of any given area to be absent, she shouldn't question his untruth. Most were attending either Stephen or Matilda.

"Is that how you know Warehaven?"

She was fishing for information. He had no way of knowing if it was an intentional tactic on her part, or just simple idle conversation.

"Jared and I fostered together. We have known each other since we were little more than boys."

"Where did the two of you foster?"

He urged his horse to a quicker pace. The sooner they were inside the keep, the sooner he could find something else to occupy her mind.

Marianne watched speechless as Bryce left her

behind, nearly racing for the keep. She could tell herself that he was anxious to oversee the work being done. Or that he was glad to be home.

But she suspected that would be a lie.

She chattered like a squirrel to pass the time. She had not expected to discover that the man who held her heart, might also be the enemy. Is that why his name had caused something in her mind to twitch? Had she overheard it while listening to her brothers discuss Stephen and Matilda? Certain that was the case, she questioned it no further.

What else had he not told her while he had held her in his arms? What other secrets did he hide while kissing her to a mindless wonder?

Another fear seeped into her. The only thing worse than suspecting him of serving the empress, would be to learn he was already wed.

Marianne wanted to kick herself for being such a complete fool. She'd not even asked if he had a wife.

Surely he would not have kissed her so passionately had he been wed? She took a deep breath, hoping to cool her newly born outrage. There was no sense getting angry or upset before she knew the truth.

Until she had the opportunity to ask him the questions needing answers, she would keep her ears and eyes open.

By the time she rode between the twin gate towers, Bryce was standing in the middle of the bailey. A young boy led his horse toward the stables.

Marianne dismounted and handed the reins of her horse to another waiting boy. She turned slowly, taking the time to inspect Ashforde Keep…or what someday would be Ashforde Keep.

Men and women quickly ducked their faces back to their tasks—a sure sign they had been caught staring at her. She didn't blame them. Not only was she a stranger, Marianne knew she looked a fright.

Bryce directed her toward a thatched hut halfway up the earthen mound. "I thought perhaps you would like to rest and bathe." He gave her gown a brief study before adding, "And I will see what I can do about finding you something to wear."

He kept his distance as he led her to the hut. Each silent step added weight to the tension knotting her shoulders. Marianne would be the first to admit that she'd never possessed any amount of patience. How long would she be able to hold her questions inside?

When they reached the hut, Bryce held the door open, letting her pass through first. To her utter relief, there was no one else inside. For some reason she'd thought there would be a servant or two bustling about.

She waited until he closed the door and started across the small one-room abode before she leaned her back against the door. "I must ask you something."

He paused. His shoulders rose and fell with the deep breath he took before turning to face her.

The worried frown creasing his brow made her wonder if she truly wanted to know.

Marianne twisted the skirt of her gown between her fingers. Yes, no matter what the answer, she had to know. She vowed not to shout, whine or cry. She was an adult and quite capable of retaining a measure of calm while querying him and waiting for the answer.

She opened her mouth and all sense of decorum flew out the small window of the hut. "Bryce, are you married?" She winced at the obvious trembling of her small, pathetic voice.

"Married?" A laugh smoothed out the creases of his frown as he stepped toward her. "You want to know if I am wed?"

"Yes." Marianne's legs trembled. She flattened her back against the door for support. "It seems a reasonable question, considering."

"Considering what? Is this not something you might have asked before urging me to kiss you?"

"I did not—" She swallowed her denial and had the insane urge to slap the overly cocky grin from his face. An urge she quelled by sticking both hands behind her.

He stopped before her. A breath of air would not fit between them. Bryce stroked a fingertip along the line of her jaw. "I would never use you, or a wife, that harshly, Marianne. Ease your mind. I am not wed."

Relief took the tension out of her body. Marianne suddenly felt as if she could easily pool to the floor of the cottage like the fine linen of an overlong gown.

"Your bath should soon be here." His lips wisped across her forehead as he spoke.

She forced herself not to look up at him. To do so would only result in another kiss. As much as she longed for his lips on her own, they were not alone in the woods.

They were in a keep with people about and unfortunately it was now time to remember who she was.

A kick from the outside of the door bounced the wood against her back, sending her sailing into Bryce's strong embrace, knocking the breath out of her.

He grasped her arms, then maneuvered them away from the door. He quickly brushed his lips against her cheek before releasing her and moving a discreet distance away.

Two men carried in a large, banded wooden tub, which they set down before a small metal brazier in the corner of the cottage. While three other men emptied buckets of steaming water into the tub, the first two attached a pole to the side and draped a length of cloth tent-like over it.

Behind them an older woman carried a basket containing supplies for Marianne's bath and a small three-legged stool.

The older woman shooed the men from the cottage, including Bryce, before setting her basket down on a bench that she then dragged to the side of the tub and placed the stool into the tub.

"Can I get you anything else, my lady?"

Spellbound to the steam escaping from the makeshift tent's opening, Marianne waved the woman away and slowly moved toward the heaven before her.

A bath. A wonderful, hot, private bath. Just the thought of sinking into the clear sparkling water sent goose flesh racing up and down her arms.

"Well then, I leave you to your bath." The woman paused at the door. "You might wish to lock this behind me."

Without taking her eyes from the tub, Marianne felt for the locking bar and dropped it in place. She headed for the bath, literally peeling off what remained of her ragged clothing and dropping the remnants on the floor in her wake. Naked, except for her leather boots and stockings, she sat on the bench to remove those.

Marianne rooted through the basket. She picked the

wax plug off a vial of oil and poured the thick, yellowish liquid into the water. The steam rolling off the water soon filled the cottage with the scents of rosemary and lavender.

She plopped the stiff boar-bristle brush into the water, wondering if it'd be strong enough to scrub the filth from her skin.

After taking the leather cover off a small jar of soap, she sniffed, then held it away from her nose. If the brush did not do the job of removing the dirt, the strongly-scented rosemary soap would. No matter. At the very least she'd be clean, disinfected and would have that nice outdoor woodsy smell—which was far more preferable than the stench clinging to her now.

Marianne forced herself to climb sedately into the tub instead of jumping into the water. She sat down on the small stool inside and immediately rose to discard the seat. It prevented her from soaking all the way to her chin in the luscious water.

The fact that she could not stretch out her legs and lounge like she was wont to do in Lyonesse's specially made tub at Faucon was of little concern. She drew the curtain fully closed, planted her feet on the bottom of the tub, rested the back of her head on the wooden side and closed her eyes.

This sinful luxury was a slice of heaven and she'd not ruin it by thinking of what she could not have at this moment.

She didn't want to think of anything. Not about her foolishness, or of what would happen once she returned home to Faucon. There would be enough time to worry about all of that later.

She sighed and let her arms float on the top of the water. Right now, she simply wanted to soak, relax and let the warmth of the water seep into her tired, sore muscles.

Marianne inhaled a nose full of cold water and came awake with a choking gasp. She jerked upright in the tub, splashing water over the sides.

"Are you all right?"

Bryce's question startled her further and she knocked over the pole holding up the curtain.

She swatted at the fabric now trailing in her bath. "How did you get in here?"

His footsteps came closer. "Through the roof."

So much for locking the door. "Stay back."

"No need to panic. I am just going to right your tent."

"I am not panicked."

His hand jutted through the opening of the fabric. He waved it around looking for the pole and found the top of her head.

Marianne smacked his hand away, then grabbed his wrist and guided him to the wooden pole.

Once he reattached it to the tub, he fluffed the fabric back into place around it.

"You have to be freezing in there."

She curled her arms around her bent knees. "I am. Go away."

"I have more hot water."

Marianne stuck a hand through the tent's opening. "I thank you."

"No."

He was clearly laughing at her. She could hear it in his voice. Leaning over, she poked her head out the opening.

Aye, laughing just as she'd expected. But he wasn't lying. He did have two more pails of steaming water. She hoped begging would work in this instance. "Please, my lord, may I have the water?"

Bryce looked up at the ceiling and rocked back and forth on his heels. "What do I get?"

"That depends. What do you want?"

"That depends. What are you offering?"

Marianne wondered if it was possible to break one's teeth by grinding them together. She relaxed her jaw and had a most excellent offer for him. In what she hoped was her most sultry voice, began, "How about…"

He came a step closer. "Yes. Go on."

"When I am all clean and sweet-smelling…"

Another step closer. "Mmmm…so far it sounds good."

"And finished with my nice warm bath…"

The last step brought him next to the tub. He knelt down so they were eye to eye. "Yes…" His warm breath grazed her chin.

"I promise not to kill you in your sleep."

He laughed. "That sounds fair. If you move aside, I will dump the water in."

"No, thank you. Just set the pails by the tub and leave. I can manage them on my own once you are gone."

He did as she asked with the pails, but instead of leaving he stretched out on the narrow bed.

"What are you doing now?"

"Resting."

"Not on my bed."

"Our bed."

Perhaps she offered him too much. Maybe she would kill him in his sleep. "What do you mean *our* bed?"

"It seems Sir John told everyone we were married."

"What?" Marianne flinched at her own shout.

"He thought it would be an easier explanation than the truth and would keep everyone from asking too many questions."

Marianne hauled one pail up and over the edge of the tub. She needed to get this bath finished so she could set things right.

Bryce continued his explanation. "I was angry at first. But he has a point."

A pointed head perhaps. She dumped the other bucket of water into the tub. "And what would that be?"

"It saves me from explaining how I won you in a game of dice."

Marianne dropped the empty bucket. It rolled across the floor. "And you agreed that lying was the better of two evils?"

"How would you rather the people of Ashforde regard you? As my wife, or as—"

"Your whore."

The leather straps of the bed creaked. "I did not say that." His voice was a little louder, so she assumed he'd sat up.

"There was no need to say it. Nonetheless, it was implied." She globbed some soap onto the brush and began scrubbing her feet and legs.

"Why would anyone think that?"

"I know not how you were raised, but at Faucon, an unmarried woman does not go about with a man unless there is someone else in attendance."

"A chaperon."

She scrubbed her arms, wincing as the stiff bristles

found cuts and scrapes she'd not known existed. "Yes. A chaperon. A maid. A brother. A sister. Someone."

"Is that what you want? A chaperon?"

Marianne bent over and dunked her head into the bath. While soaping her hair, she cursed, then answered, "No. What I want is another bucket of water to rinse my hair."

The leather straps creaked again. His footsteps rang out as he stomped to the door. The locking bar hit the floor and the door squeaked on its hinges. Marianne paused and smiled to herself. He actually went to get her more water.

Bryce returned before she was done scrubbing her head. Ice-cold air blew across her wet body. She rubbed the soap from her eyes and saw that he had removed the curtain.

"Bend over."

"What?"

Before she had the chance to cover herself with her hands, a bucket of water sluiced over her head. Clean water. Yes. Warm water. No.

"What the hell—" She all but leapt from the tub.

Another bucket of cold water cut off her curse. He picked up both empty buckets and headed for the door. "I'll get some more."

The instant the door slammed behind him, Marianne jumped up and grabbed a drying cloth from the bench. Her bath was over. She wrapped the oversized cloth around her, tucked the end in and raced toward the door.

The locking bar was not heavy, but it was on the floor. She nearly lost the cloth when she bent to retrieve the bar. She got the bar in place just in time, too. Because the moment she stepped back, Bryce slammed into the door. She heard an expletive on the other side.

"Open this door," he demanded.

"No. Thank you. I do not need any more water. I'm done."

"Marianne."

"Bryce." She tried to match his deadly tone.

When he didn't respond, she went back by the brazier and took a seat on the bench. There was another cloth in the basket and a wide-toothed comb.

The sun was setting. She had nothing else to do the rest of this day except try to untangle the nest she called hair. She dragged the still dripping mess over one shoulder and toweled off as much water as she could before painstakingly working the comb through to the very ends.

The calming activity set her mind to whirling. Even if her suspicions were correct and Bryce did serve the empress, what did it matter? Stephen and Matilda would not live forever. Had not her own brother Darius married the widow of the enemy?

And had not every member of her family welcomed Marguerite and her son with open arms? Marianne had never heard one word of censure.

Aye, there were a few small…minor differences. Darius and Marguerite had been in love as children. And Darius didn't require Rhys's approval for his marriage.

Surely there was a way to gain his approval? Marianne's eyes widened. Her hand stopped midair. She could think of one sure way to gain his blessing on a marriage to Bryce.

Her heart raced at the thought and she dragged the comb rather sharply through another snarl, breaking a tooth off the comb.

Her brothers would be livid, she thought, as she tossed the broken comb tooth into the fire. Their wives would be horrified. But she could talk to her sisters-by-marriage. She could explain how much she wanted to become the Lady of Ashforde. They would eventually understand and would be able to bring their husbands around.

The only person she had to convince was Bryce himself. Would honor keep him from letting her seduce him? Would it make him feel tricked into marrying her? And if it did, would he soon get over it?

Marianne heaved a sigh. One step at a time. First the seduction. How did one go about seducing a man completely? Heat fired her cheeks. She'd have to do so in a manner that led him to believe he'd done the seducing.

Easier said than done considering she had no idea where to start.

A small scratching sound caught her attention. Marianne frowned and scanned the darkened cottage. Nothing. Although, she did see a brace of candles which she lit before resuming her combing.

There. Again, a small scratching, scuffing sound. It seemed to come from the ceiling. Before she could pinpoint the noise, or the source, Bryce lowered himself through a hole he'd made in the thatch work.

He landed on his feet, reached up with his sword and moved the roofing back in place before turning to smile at her.

"Did you miss me?"

Marianne could not help but notice that Bryce had bathed. His hair was damp around his face. She said nothing, but turned back to the brazier. "Were you gone?"

He came up behind her and took the comb from her hand. "Allow me."

In less than a dozen tugs, Bryce stopped. He nudged her up from the bench and pulled the stool over. "You sit there." He took the seat on the bench.

His legs stretched out on either side of her made the perfect resting place for her arms. He said nothing when she took advantage of the position. He methodically worked the snarls out of her hair.

She drew lazy circles on his knees. "This is quite sinful."

"It is."

"My family would be horrified."

"They would."

"But I do appreciate your help."

"I know."

"And your hands in my hair feel so…so…" She searched for the right word. "So delightful."

"Delightful?"

She ignored the choked sound of his voice and softly moaned before leaning her head back to rest against him. Marianne froze at finding the hard length beneath her shoulder blades. Now his short answers and choked tone made perfect sense.

She quickly sat up and pulled the cloth tighter around her. Now what? She was certain this would be the perfect time to try her seduction tactic but suddenly found herself at a loss.

Bryce rested a hand on her bare shoulders. His touch nearly burned her skin. "Marianne, I do not deny that I want you. But I am not a brute to take what I want by force."

She rose and walked toward the brazier. Her legs

trembled. The fire from her shoulder had worked its way down her body. Just the thought of being naked and alone with him, made her head spin. If his kisses stole the breath from her body, she couldn't begin to image what his touch could do.

He cleared his throat, tossed the comb into the basket and rose. After drawing a hand through his hair, he nodded toward the bed. "You sleep there. I will place a blanket on the floor."

He turned to grab a blanket from the bed and Marianne knew it was a chance she could not pass up.

With all the longing and need she could muster, she turned around and whispered, "Bryce."

As he turned back to face her, she released the cloth and let it ripple down the length of her body to pool on the floor.

Chapter Eleven

Bryce's mouth went dry. Candlelight flickered off her pale skin, highlighting the luscious curves in the fire's warm glow and shadowing the graceful valleys.

For the first time in years his hands shook. Her need, the longing he heard in her voice humbled him, making him feel as green and inexperienced as a virgin.

Afraid his mind played tricks, he took slow steps forward, unwilling to break the carnal dream if that's all it turned out to be.

He stopped mere inches from her, wanting to reach out and stroke the pale flesh of her breasts. To trace the gentle curves of her hips.

But when he met her overly bright, trusting gaze, he knew that no matter how much he wanted her, he could not lie to her any longer.

"Marianne." He tucked a long ebony wave behind her ear. "I do not serve King Stephen."

"I suspected as much." She looked away for a moment and he held his breath. Would she reconsider this last brash act now that she faced the truth?

Marianne hiked her chin a notch before turning back to him. "Who do you serve at this moment, Bryce of Ashforde?"

He swallowed past the lump forming in his throat. She knew his loyalty rested with Empress Matilda. Yet Marianne was ready to give herself to him.

Bryce's chest swelled at the knowledge that she would choose him over her family. He dropped to one knee, took her hands in his and rested his forehead against them. "I serve you, Marianne of Faucon."

The rest. He had to tell her the rest. "We need to talk. We need to…"

She urged him to his feet, pulled her hands free and ran her fingers through his hair. "I care not about talking. You can say whatever you wish on the morrow."

"But…"

She molded the length of her body against his. The feel of her soft breasts pressing against his chest, her thighs leaning against his own and her lips brushing against his neck nearly did him in. "Marianne."

"No." Her fingers covered his mouth. "I will not feel ashamed in the light of day. I want you." Her other hand trailed down his chest and across his belt. "I need you to quench the fire you alone started."

Before she could move her hand any lower, he swept her up in his arms and laid her on the bed.

Still fully clothed he stretched out alongside of her. Oh, aye, he wanted her like a dying man wants salvation.

But even more he wanted to give her the satisfaction she craved. He longed to answer the unasked questions torturing her mind and to ease the fear of the unknown.

There would be time for his fulfillment later—when

she knew what to expect and the odds of her bolting in confusion were lessened.

She plucked at his tunic. "Bryce?"

He grasped her wrist and held her arm down at her side. Before she could say another word, he covered her mouth with his.

Marianne's fevered longing wanted more than this gentle caress of his lips. She wanted to be swept away by the passion he'd ignited that night in the cave.

This care and gentleness hinted of the contentment her sisters-by-marriage wished for her. And she wanted none of it. She would rather be singed by the hot flames of mind-stealing desire she knew Bryce could create.

Unbidden, a moan of need and unanswered longing raced up her throat. It was a keening sound that he obviously understood more than she.

Accepting the invitation she unknowingly issued, he deepened his kiss, each stroke of his tongue more demanding than the last. Marianne followed his lead, reveling in the certainty that he would banish her worries of being only content.

He released her wrist and stroked the flames she'd been seeking to life. The roughness of his calloused hand brushing over her breast pebbled her nipple and reawakened the fiery ice she'd come to expect at his touch.

Yet, this touch was different somehow. It was not a gentle caress meant to soothe, or a hesitant exploration. No, his movements were steady and sure as he traced a path of desire from her breasts to belly to thigh to knee and back again.

Tension hummed the length of her body and settled as a needy throb between her legs. Marianne arched toward him seeking release from the growing frustration.

Bryce broke their kiss with a ragged laugh before sliding his lips along her neck. The breath-taking tension she thought could not possibly grow any stronger only increased when his lips found her breast.

Before the gasp of surprise could fully escape, he slid his hand between her slightly parted legs, turning her gasp to a moan. Marianne curled her fingers in the damp waves of his hair.

Bryce fought his own building tension. What had been meant as a way to satisfy her curiosity and frustration had quickly become his own battle for control. One he wished not to lose.

The mound beneath his kneading palm throbbed with each beat of her heart. He dipped a finger between the soft folds and found the pulsing ridge.

Marianne jumped at the unfamiliar touch, but in the next instant arched against his hand. He circled his tongue around one swollen nipple and glanced up at her face.

A fine sheen of perspiration shimmered on her flesh. Her eyes were tightly closed, the expression letting him know that she was at the point of near painful pleasure.

Soon she would leave the pain and fall into the deep well of complete pleasure. It would be so easy to strip off his clothes, push his erection past the thin barrier to her womb and take his satisfaction with her.

She would not fight him. At this moment, she would most likely welcome him into her arms and body.

But he couldn't do that to her. He would gladly show her pleasure, but he would not take her maidenhead. That would be her husband's task. As much as he longed to be that man, Bryce doubted if her brothers would let it happen.

He increased the pressure of his fingers. Almost instantly Marianne's hips rose off the pallet.

"Bryce!"

His name rang out from her lips in a breathless gasp of surprise. He recaptured her mouth, swallowing her cry of wonderment.

Bryce gathered her into his arms, burying his face in her hair. Spent, Marianne's breathing eased and the pounding of her heart eventually slowed.

However, the heavy rapid drumming of his own heart threatened to beat through his chest. No full-fledged battle had made breathing this difficult. Nor had any made his hands shake the way they did now.

"Oh, my." Having found her voice, Marianne breathlessly admitted, "Perhaps delightful wasn't the right word." She kissed the spot beneath his ear and drew her fingernails up his back.

Unable to stop his ragged groan, he pushed himself up on his elbows and dropped a kiss on her damp forehead. "Climb beneath the covers and I will return shortly."

"You are leaving?"

"Yes."

She toyed with the hair at the nape of his neck sending a chill down his spine. "But you did not...I thought perhaps we could..."

By the sultry tone of her voice and the heavy-lidded gaze, he knew she was more than ready for more love play. If he stayed in this cottage any longer he would oblige her—and satisfy his own raging needs.

"No." He pushed himself up. "I have to go." He rose and jerked down the covers beneath her, then pulled them up and tucked the edges in around her. "Go to sleep. I will return soon."

"Where are you going?"

Bryce grabbed her still-damp drying cloth from the floor. "To find a cold stream."

"I thought you had already bathed."

"At this moment, I require a bath of another kind."

Marianne watched his hasty exit although her smile was tempered by the memory of her own recent frustrations.

He had given her such pleasure while taking none of his own. She stretched like a well-fed cat and ran her hands down the length of her body. Her skin was alive, her touch recalling the sensation of his hands upon her.

Marianne curled onto her side with a sigh. Now that she'd had her first hint of what made her brothers and sisters-by-marriage giggle and moan, she wanted more. Much more. Bryce had woven a net of magic while fully clothed. What would she discover if he were as naked as she?

If he had taken her into the clouds with nothing but his hands and lips, how far could she go if he...if they...? Without finishing the thought, all of her pulses kicked to life. Marianne pressed her legs together tightly.

Suddenly overwarm, she threw back the covers and sat up. The night's cold air brushed over her heated skin, sending a true chill up and down her spine. Effectively dousing the fire in her veins. She smiled. That explained his need for a cold stream.

Maybe when he returned she could convince him that a cold bath had not been necessary.

Until then, she needed something to do. Sleep was out of the question. If she burrowed back under the covers, her mind would only badger her with recent memories of Bryce's touch.

Padding quickly across the cold floor, she tossed a few more coals onto the dying fire in the brazier, grabbed the comb from the bench and raced back to the bed. Since she had no clothing to wear, she pulled the top cover up over her shoulders and tucked it around her crossed legs.

She worked the comb through her hair. Thankfully, it was no longer matted together in nests mice would fear. But the wavy mass easily snarled and it took more than a few moments to work out all the tangles.

While she plaited the detangled length into braids, Bryce returned. He stood in the doorway wearing only his shirt and braies. "You were supposed to be sleeping."

"Not until you returned." Marianne patted the bed. "Come, join me."

He closed the door, dropped his boots, then tossed his other clothing, belt and sword atop the small table. When he turned toward her, he ran his hand through his still-wet hair. "I'm not certain that would be a good idea."

"I am." She tied off her braids with strips of fabric torn from her old clothing, then flipped the lengths behind her. "Come." Marianne held out her hand. "I promise not to tempt you beyond reason."

He laughed. "Too late."

"I am not letting you sleep on the cold floor." She climbed beneath the three layers of covers. "I'll sleep here." And then lifted the top layer. "And you sleep here."

"The floor would be safer."

"Fine, then we will both share the floor." She moved to rise.

"Nay." He sat down on the edge of the bed. "You never give up, do you?"

"How would I ever get my way if I gave up so easily?"

Bryce shook his head and pushed at her shoulder. "Roll over."

She turned to face him.

"No. Face the other way, Marianne."

"Coward."

Once her back was to him, he climbed beneath the top cover. "At least I know when to retreat."

"Retreat?" She giggled. "What is that? 'Tis not a word I know." Her childish laughter ceased when he wrapped his arm around her and pulled her back against the hardness of his chest.

"Retreat is what keeps you alive in the face of death when all else has failed."

"Is that what you fear at this moment, Bryce? Death in my arms?"

He pulled her even closer and covered her breast through the covers. At her gasp, he placed his lips against her neck.

Marianne's heart leapt to her throat. Every spot in her body that could throb, sprang to life and did just that— throb and burn with reawakened need.

When her breathing turned ragged, he answered her question with one of his own. "Tell me, Marianne, do you think you could die from wanting?"

She sucked in a chest full of air, then cried, "Retreat."

He relaxed his hold, slid his hand to her stomach and moved a hair's breadth away. "Go to sleep. We have a long ride ahead of us tomorrow."

"To where?"

"Faucon."

She was not ready to go home yet. "I thought we were staying here a couple days."

"I have changed my mind."

It would be easier to complete her ruination here, in the close quarters of this small cottage, than it would be on the road. Marianne's mind spun faster and faster, seeking any excuse that would keep them in Ashforde at least another night.

Finally, she asked, "Did I do something wrong?"

"What?" He sounded tired, but added, "No. No, you did nothing wrong."

If all she had was this one night, what would it require to seduce him into finishing the deed? She curled against him, pressing her buttocks into his groin.

"Oh, for the love of—" He smacked her rump. "Behave and go to sleep."

Even without the layers of thick covers she'd not have felt pain from his halfhearted swat. She stretched out. "Please, Bryce, I wish not to go home just yet."

"And I wish not to take you home." His sigh was exaggerated probably for her benefit. "Marianne, if it were possible I would keep you here, in this cottage, unclothed, in my bed for a decade or more. But you have brothers who are responsible for you."

"I am responsible for myself."

"You may like to think so, but you know full well the truth is that until Comte Faucon gives your hand to some man in marriage, he is responsible for you."

Her heart skipped a beat. "I thought…" She frowned. "I mean…" Had she misread him that badly? "But you…"

He tugged her closer and rested his chin atop her head. "You thought I would offer for you?"

Marianne nodded.

"What do you I have to offer, Marianne? I have no keep and little gold." One day the little lies would pile up and choke him. "I do not even serve the same crown. I have most likely killed men your family considered friend. If I am very, very careful and have even more luck, I may be permitted to leave Faucon alive. I would never be permitted to leave with you at my side."

"You have much to offer. Ashforde will be a fine keep when it is finished. As for gold, my bride portion will be enough for the both of us. You are neither too young, nor too old. You are brave and strong. And my brothers would never kill the man who rescued their sister. Why would you think such a thing?"

He rubbed his cheek against her hair. "You will not get your way in this, Marianne."

Why was he being so stubborn? "You are wrong. My family will come to love you as I do."

His snort of disbelief prompted her to add, "And I do love you."

"What do you base this love on, Marianne? You desire me. You like kissing me, arguing with me, being with me. Just as I enjoy doing those things with you. But you have not known me long enough to love me."

"My heart does not know the span of time. It only knows that it beats for you. I do love you."

Bryce closed his eyes against her fervent admission. She wasn't going to give up. He'd known that, in the same instant that he'd realized a marriage between them would never be permitted.

A realization that had hit him with the force of a boulder being launched from a swinging trebuchet the moment he stepped into the icy stream. The Faucons were not going to let their sister marry a man who not only served the empress, but who had nothing in the way of worldly possessions.

How would he keep her safe? He had nothing but a cottage to live in. A thatched cottage surrounded by a flimsy wooden palisade that would probably not keep out the wild dogs let alone an attacking force.

Even if he could keep her safe, how would he keep her alive this coming winter? The food stores had gone down in flames with the keep. What had remained of the fields had been burned.

A fact he could not hide because the Faucons, or one of them, were responsible.

She tried turning over and he held her tighter, effectively keeping her in place.

"Bryce, please."

He winced at her plea and knew he had to call an end to this conversation before they ended the night hating each other.

"Marianne, men do things during war that they would never consider at any other time." He had to believe that the Faucons would never have taken all from him in such a manner if it were not for the fight over the crown. "Unforgivable things that cannot be righted without bloodshed."

"What does that have to do with us?" She paused, and he had a sick feeling he knew which way her thoughts were headed. "Have you done something that would cause my family to seek your death?"

She might have been willing to choose him over her brothers in matters of sex, but he knew where her loyalties lie on all else. She'd known her family her entire life, but she'd only known him a few short days. No night of love play could erase the ties that held her to her family.

"No. I've done nothing. But nobody knows how long this war between Stephen and Matilda will last. No mage can tell where it might lead each of us."

"But—"

"Cease." He squeezed his arm about her. "Stop looking for arguments that will not sway my decision. You are wasting your time and mine." He relaxed his hold. "Go to sleep, Marianne."

Many slow heartbeats thumped by and she remained quiet. Bryce silently thanked God she was not a woman given to tears.

The candles sputtered out and he stared into the settling darkness of the cottage. The glow from the embers in the brazier cast flickering light and shadow to dance across the far wall.

Finally, after what seemed hours, the embers burned to near nothing and darkness overtook the small one-room cottage.

Bryce gently pulled the sleeping woman in his arms closer. Certain she would not hear him, he whispered, "Marianne, you will always hold my heart."

Chapter Twelve

Marianne jerked awake at the sound of Bryce's curses. She wiped the sleep from her eyes and found him standing in a puddle of water staring up at the ceiling.

"What is wrong?"

"It rained last night."

She sat up, dragging the covers along with her. "I hate to say anything, but is that not where you came through the roof?"

He turned to her with a look that said he did not require the reminder. She bit the inside of her mouth to keep from saying anything else, or worse…laughing.

Bryce pointed at an overflowing basket near the door. "The old woman brought you some clothing and food."

Marianne bounded from the bed and eagerly dragged the basket over to the bench.

"I wouldn't be too excited. It is doubtful there will be anything of quality."

Puzzled, she looked at him. "I have no idea where you gained your mistaken perception, but I have not had a new bliaut or gown in almost a year and those were remade ones Gareth bought at a faire."

"I am simply saying that the fabrics might be woven a little less fine."

"Oh, aye. It is commonplace for me to run about the fields and the cliffs in silk and samite." At his reddening face, she relented. "Since I have never been to court, I do not own such finery. Anything in this basket will be a gift I treasure." She waved him out of the cottage. "Go find a thatcher to fix your roof."

"I apologize. I am not at my best this morning."

Marianne batted her eyelashes at him. "I did not notice. Go."

When he finally left, she dug through the basket and came up with a pair of men's braies, which would be a welcome addition beneath a gown. Especially if she was going to be on the back of a horse for the next few days.

There were three bliauts and two undergowns to choose from. Marianne took the worst of the lot. It made no sense to her to ruin good clothing. Not when the people here at Ashforde obviously had so little.

Between her own hose and boots, the braies, dyed bliaut and patched gown would suffice. Once she'd fixed her hair, washed up and dressed, Marianne sat down at the small table.

Her nose told her that she'd find food beneath the cloth-covered dishes. Her stomach growled its agreement.

The first dish contained a meat pie. She sniffed… sage, thyme and dark wine…then smiled in anticipation. Someone at Ashforde knew how to cook. The next, a bowl, held cheese and bread. Not just any bread, but a round loaf of dark, fresh, warm bread.

She whipped the cover off the next dish to find pear tarts baked to perfection and drizzled with a spiced honey sauce. Again, she put her nose to work. Cinnamon, nutmeg perhaps, but definitely cloves. There was also a pitcher of cider and one of water.

If she were the polite, patient sort of guest, she would wait until Bryce was finished and could join her. Marianne picked up a small eating knife. Thankfully, no one ever accused her of being polite or patient.

A sudden stomping from the roof sent dirt drifting down toward the table. Marianne gasped, jumped up and dragged the table out of the way. It did not prevent all of the dirt from landing on her feast, but she had managed to save most of it by replacing the cloths over the dishes.

She sat back down and shouted, "Having fun up there?"

"Oh, aye. Care to join us?"

"Thank you, no." She took a bite of the pie and closed her eyes. With her mouth half full she shouted, "If you do not employ this person as your cook, you are crazed."

"What?"

"The food. It is wonderful. Hire the cook."

Bryce descended the ladder and stuck his head in the window opening that she had uncovered to let in the morning light. "Are you planning to save me any?"

"No." She took another bite and made a grand show of how good it tasted. She rolled her eyes, shuddered with pleasure and licked her lips once she'd swallowed.

"I'd best hurry then."

"Aye, you'd best."

Once she had eaten her fill, she assured herself that the food was safe under their cloths then went to lean against the door frame. She watched Bryce assist the thatcher. It was interesting to see the lord of the keep running up and down the ladder chasing for tools and bundles of reed material. She was especially amused by the way the older man kept shooing Bryce off the roof.

But what really held her attention was the fine display of flesh. Now that the men were finished, Bryce had removed his shirt while running the tools back down the ladder.

Seeing him in nothing but the flicker of candlelight had not done him justice. She realized that he had a strong chest and muscular arms. What she had not seen in the dim light were the well-defined ridges of his torso.

Since he was fair-haired, he didn't have the thick dark hair covering his chest like her darker-haired brothers. She decided that she rather liked being able to see the play of muscles contracting and relaxing.

On his final trip past her, he stopped. "What are you doing?"

"Oh." She stared at his chest and ran her tongue across her lips. "Just watching you...work."

He flexed his muscles, curled his arm and flexed the bulge there, too. "Happy?"

She should have been embarrassed at her forwardness, but embarrassment was the last thing on her mind. Marianne shivered visibly. "No. But I could be."

Her action and statement brought a flush to his cheeks. He stepped closer. "You are a wanton miss."

"And who is to blame for that?"

"Not me."

She laughed softly and put her hands behind her back to keep from touching him. "Are we still leaving today?"

"Yes." He pulled his shirt over his head. "I need to check on the supplies and food stores for the time I will be gone, talk to Edwin the man I am leaving in charge of the keep, dress, eat and then we will be on our way."

"Is there anything you would like me to do?"

Bryce laughed, a low, passion-laden sound that made her knees weak. "I can think of a few things."

Marianne backed into the cottage, crooking her finger at him as she did so. "Perhaps you would care to, I don't know…eat…dress…or…something, before seeing to the keep?"

He reached out and grasped her wiggling finger. "Eating and dressing would be fine. But that *something* would not be wise. Come with me. I will show you what there is to see of Ashforde."

"Gladly." They'd be on horseback for the next few days. A walk now was more than welcome.

Bryce pulled her next to his side, keeping a hold of her hand. She glanced down at their interlaced fingers and said nothing. A strange way to act for a man who insisted a match between them would not work. Perhaps he wasn't as certain as he thought.

They slogged through the mud toward the planked path that led up to activity taking place near the top of the mound. He pulled his foot from another boggy spot with a loud sucking noise. Holding up the edges of her bliaut and gown, Marianne couldn't resist commenting, "You grow nice mud here at Ashforde."

"I know. They assure me that it is much more pleasant the two or three days a year when it doesn't rain."

She knew that he exaggerated. But when she looked around the grounds, she understood the need. It had rained all night, flooding every inch of ground. Between the workmen going to and fro, the horses and the others, it looked as if a storm brewed on a sea of mud, creating wave after wave of muck.

The ooze threatened to overtake the planks laid for ease of walking and pushing carts or wheelbarrows. The sight brought back childhood memories.

As they walked side by side on the planks, Marianne said, "This reminds me of the last time my sire enlarged Faucon."

"How so?"

"According to my mother's rants, he intentionally chose the wettest year to begin construction. They argued about it endlessly. She harangued him about everything being covered in mud and he would tromp it all in on purpose."

"How old were you?"

"Maybe six or seven."

"It must have been boring to spend that year inside."

"Inside?" She frowned. "Ahh, you mean because I was such a fragile, dainty flower of a girl?"

"I take it you were not."

"My mother had already dealt with three boys. To her chagrin, I was determined to be her fourth. It amused my father to have something else to argue with her about."

"He liked to argue?"

"No. What he truly liked was to soothe her after he'd tormented her into a near blind rage."

"Ahhh. That explains your penchant for mockery."

"Yes. It is a habit all Faucons share."

"All?"

"Sad, but true." She touched his shoulder with her free hand and looked up at him. "Beware of Rhys. He can be harsh and sarcastic to a fault in his attempt to goad you into starting a fight."

"I will keep that in mind." He surveyed the area, then brought his attention back to her. "When did your parents die?"

"About eight years ago."

"Who took care of you after that?"

"Rhys when he was at Faucon." Marianne shrugged. "Or Gareth when he was about."

"And when they were both gone?"

"Serfs and freemen—the villagers. The guards. I do have a nursemaid who has stayed with me."

"It would have made more sense to send you to another keep with a woman about."

"Why? So I could learn to be a lady?"

Bryce hitched an eyebrow in her direction. "Would that not have improved your chances for a good match?"

"Perhaps." As far as she was concerned, she'd already found her match. And he currently held her hand in his. "But I think I learned more about running a keep and taking care of soldiers and servants by staying at Faucon. There, I had many people to teach me what was necessary. At another keep I would have had one woman to teach me her way. Who was to say her way would have been the best?"

When he fell silent, Marianne added, "And this past year, I've had Lyonesse to teach me all about being a lady." She laughed at the thought.

"The lessons have been amusing?"

"Considering they come from a woman who possesses, and has been known to use, her own armor. Yes. It has been amusing."

"Good Lord."

They reached the top of the mound and Marianne released Bryce's hand so she could take in the scene laid out before them. "Oh, Bryce, this is a perfect spot for your keep."

From ground level, looking west, she could catch glimpses of the sea through the trees. In the other directions the trees had been cleared, providing an unobstructed view of any who would approach.

Beyond the clearing to the north, lay fallow fields. Blackened now from the fire, but maybe by next summer they could be filled with growing crops. What would his people do for food this winter though?

The thought of them starving to death during a harsh winter made her ill. "Bryce?"

"Hmm?"

"The fields are gone. What about the crops?"

"They were destroyed."

"What about food? The meal I had this morning, where did it all come from?"

He pulled her against him briefly. "Fear not. No one here will starve. I've ordered what I hope will be enough supplies to last through the winter and into the spring. Provided we are not attacked again."

"Supplies?" She glanced around Ashforde. "I see nowhere to store grains or a mill or anything."

He pointed toward the row of buildings going up between the mound and the palisade wall. "For this winter, those will be the storage sheds. One of my men has made a deal with the mill in the next town to process the grain."

"This all must be costing you a fortune."

"And then some. Thankfully, I have a generous liege and eight years' worth of gold won on the tourney circuit."

What he needed was a sinfully wealthy wife. Marianne tucked that tidbit away for later. It could perhaps be useful bait.

She turned her attention back to the keep. To the south, she saw that a practice field had been set up. Right now it was empty except for the quintains and jousting list. There were no targets standing, no lances or bows or arrows stacked up for use.

The depth of what one could lose in a fire had only teased at the edges of her mind until now. When Bryce had said he'd lost everything, he had literally meant every item he owned.

Her heart ached for him. She hoped those responsible suffered as great a loss.

Marianne pointed toward the forest. "What are those posts about a third of the way to the trees?"

"They are where the outer wall will be built...when the keep is finished."

"You'll leave the palisade in place?"

"In a manner of speaking. It will be rebuilt as a stone curtain wall."

"Ah, so you will have two baileys."

"Yes. I was hoping to someday have the villagers relocate inside the wall. It would be easier to protect them if they were closer."

"After losing nearly everything in the fire, I am certain they will be more than willing. Have you approached them with the idea?"

"Not yet. I will on my return."

She turned and studied the foundation for the keep.

Naturally, the larger area would be the main building. To the left was a smaller foundation that she assumed would eventually be the kitchens. "What's the narrow passageway between the two foundations?"

"It'll connect the kitchens to the main keep."

"At ground level? Won't the great hall be on a higher story?"

Bryce nodded. His face lit with excitement. "I saw this contraption recently that I wanted to try here." His words came faster with his enthusiasm. "There will be a vertical tunnel of sorts that extends from the hall to the lower level. Instead of having to run the food and service ware up and down steps, we will install a sort of dry well with a series of pulleys and chains."

"And a basket for carting the items?" As the vision took form in her mind, Marianne shared his enthusiasm. "So the food will be pulled up to the hall and the dirty dishes and empty ones can be lowered back down?"

"Yes. Exactly."

She was skeptical, but curious. If it worked properly, it could save much time and energy. On the other hand, if it did not work, someone could get seriously injured. Another passageway caught her eye. "And that one?"

He looked at the clearing sky. "Can you build a keep without secret tunnels?"

Marianne laughed. "You must speak to Marguerite, my sister-by-marriage, or Darius about hidden tunnels inside a keep. From what I understand, her first husband excelled at building them."

"Thornson?"

She didn't try to hide her surprise. "Yes. How did you know?"

"It is almost impossible to find a master builder who does not bring up Henry of Thornson and his tunnels."

Bryce took her hand. "We should go."

She wished not to leave so soon, but knew he would see through any tactic meant to stall their departure. Halfway across the inner yard, she saw the older woman. Marianne nodded toward her. "What is her name?"

"Bertha. Why?"

"Bryce, you really should consider having that woman move into your kitchens."

"The food is that good?"

"Better than good."

He called Bertha over. When she joined them on the planks, Marianne gushed, "I just wanted to thank you ever so much for the clothes and the superb meal."

"I am gladdened you enjoyed the food." The woman blushed a deep red. "But it was truly nothing, my lady. My daughter and I made a great many pies last night for the men to eat today. And the pears were left over from yesterday's meal. I simply warmed up the sauce."

Marianne looked up at Bryce. "Did you hear that? The most delicious sauce I have encountered and she claims to have simply warmed it up, like it was nothing."

Bryce took the gentle hint. "Bertha. As you know, Edwin is going to oversee things here while I am away." He added for Marianne's benefit, "Edwin is her husband."

"Oh. What could be more perfect?" She noticed that Bertha's back had straightened with pride at the responsibility bestowed upon her mate.

"I agree. What I'd like to know, Bertha, is if you would be interested in overseeing Ashforde's kitchens?"

The poor woman took a faltering step backward. Bryce caught her arm to prevent her from falling into the mud.

"My lord? You are but teasing me!"

"I would never do such a thing. Truly, Bertha, I would be honored if you would accept the position."

"But a kitchen that size requires someone with experience I do not possess."

Marianne interrupted the discussion. "How many children do you have?"

"Eight, my lady. And I care for my dead sister's four."

"My, my, twelve children. And they are all hale and hearty?"

"They are, yes." The woman sighed. "But I am a bit weary chasing them about. Thanks be to God, they are almost all grown now."

Bryce laughed before picking up Marianne's train of thought. "If you can raise twelve children, you can assuredly oversee a kitchen." He paused before adding, "You might even find it easier."

Now Bertha laughed. "Perhaps you are right. Running a kitchen might be less exhausting. I could even put some of the older ones to work." She nodded. A smile lit her entire face. "I would be honored to accept your offer, my lord."

"Good. I will discuss the particulars with you upon my return. Until then, you and Edwin can perhaps start thinking of the items you will need."

Once the woman left them, Bryce tipped his head to Marianne. "Thank you."

"My pleasure. We handled that quite nicely, did we not?"

He was slow to respond and she wondered what

thoughts circled around in his mind. After a time, he answered, "Yes, Marianne, we did."

Bryce walked her to the door of the cottage. "I have a few things left to do, then I will return and we can be on our way."

"Take your time."

Left alone, Marianne started picking up their discarded clothing and bathing cloths. Someone else would have to carry out the tub, but she gathered the bathing supplies, putting them back into the basket.

She started making the bed and sat down. Performing these mundane chores seemed natural to her. She couldn't seem to keep her own bedchamber tidy, but she would gladly do so for Bryce for the rest of their days.

They had handled Bertha successfully—together. He'd picked up on her hints as if they'd been husband and wife for many years.

She rose and looked out the still-open door toward the mound. Ashforde would be a sight to behold once it was done. It would take years to get it running to perfection. Years of hard work, trial and error before it ran as smoothly as Faucon.

In her heart she knew it was a task she and Bryce could do together. Having someone to share the work with, made the load lighter. She would be happy to share the work of Ashforde with him.

If only he would listen.

Somehow, between here and Faucon, she would find a way to convince him that she was right.

Marianne turned back to the task at hand. She would finish making the bed, then find him some clean garments to change into.

Bryce's clothing chest was in the corner of the room and she opened the lid. She lifted out a shirt and braies. Beneath them was a long wrapped package that looked like it concealed a sword or scabbard.

There appeared to be hose beneath the package, so she pushed it out of the way and rummaged for the hose. Her search rolled the package to the rear of the chest, unwinding the wrapping as it moved.

Not wanting him to think she'd been digging around out of curiosity, she grabbed the sword and unwound cloth and set them on the bed so she could rewrap the weapon and return it to the chest.

Marianne reached out to straighten the sword on the cloth and froze.

She bent closer to the bed. "No." Her hushed whisper roared in her ears. It was not possible.

She picked the weapon up and carried it to the light streaming in through the door.

Countless questions ran through her mind. She kept coming back to the first one—how had he got her sword?

Chapter Thirteen

Marianne fought hard against the imaginings taking form in her mind. This weapon could not be hers. She was certain that her sword was in her chamber at Faucon.

She drew an unsteady fingertip down the falcon engraved on the flat of the blade. She then studied the cross guard. While it was a close replica, it wasn't quite right. Neither were the wrappings around the grip.

She closed her fingers over the grip, and raised the weapon, checking the balance. She then thrust the weapon out and felt the blade jiggle inside the hilt. Whether from poor workmanship or hard use, the tang had loosened. No, this definitely was not her sword. But at first glance it was a remarkable copy.

Her hand shook. Who had gone to so much trouble replicating her sword? And why?

Each question only created another. Where had Bryce found this? Why did he have it? Why was it hidden in his chest? And why had he not shown it to her?

Marianne sat down so hard on the bed the leather

supports creaked in protest. Someone loyal to Empress Matilda had a copy of a weapon that belonged to a supporter of King Stephen.

For what purpose? Something foul was afoot, involving her brothers and Bryce. She needed to know what and why.

Did he even realize it was her standard engraved on the blade? Or did he think it was one of her brothers?

His business with Edwin complete, Bryce walked through the open door to the cottage. He half expected to see Marianne stretched out naked on the bed. She had made it quite obvious last night that she had no great desire to return to Faucon so quickly. He wouldn't put it past her to use such a tactic to stay at Ashforde another day.

She was on the bed. However, she wasn't naked. And in her hands she held a sword. He glanced to his open chest and dragged in a deep breath of air before turning his attention back to her.

He kicked the door to the cottage closed and asked, "What were you doing in my chest?"

"Where did you get this?"

He stepped away from the hard coldness of her voice. It was as if the last day had not taken place and they were now bitter enemies. "I told you last night there were things we needed to talk about."

"Talk."

"Put the sword down and we will talk."

She ignored him and rose. Planting her feet, she gripped the weapon with both hands. "If you want me to put the weapon down, you will have to take it from me."

Bryce shrugged. If that's the way she wanted it. He had already seen her fight. Her weak side was to the left, so he feinted to her left.

He sidestepped and turned away from the blade that was too long and heavy for her to handle. Before she could bring the tip of the weapon up, he grabbed her left wrist and squeezed. "Drop it."

She shook her head. "Why do you have a Faucon blade?"

He would answer all the questions she had after she was unarmed. He squeezed harder. Marianne gasped and flinched, but she opened her fingers and the weapon clattered to the floor.

Bryce pushed her down onto the bed. "Sit." He put the sword back in the chest and let the lid slam closed.

While his back was turned, she stood and paced the cottage.

"Sit down!" To his amazement, she did, but not on the bed. Instead, she took a seat on the bench. He stood in front of her and put one foot up on the bench next to her. After resting one forearm on his thigh, he leaned toward her. "You ask. I will answer."

Marianne tried to move away. Which was the reason he had taken such a stance to begin with. It put him close enough to keep her in place. He easily reached out and grasped her shoulder.

"Where did you get that sword?"

"I found it in the smoldering ashes of what once was my keep."

By the expressions that quickly crossed her face—confusion, surprise, anger and sadness—he knew she was battling what her mind was telling her.

"Why would you have found it there? How did it get there?"

He shrugged. "I know not. Perhaps during the fray, the owner dropped it and left the weapon behind."

"You think a Faucon burned down Ashforde?"

"Had it been you, what would you have thought?"

Obviously unwilling to believe in that possibility, she shook her head. "When did the fire happen?"

"This last summer."

"Rhys was home. Darius was at Falcongate."

"There is still one more brother."

"No. Gareth is rebuilding Browan. He would not have had the time, nor the inclination."

"It would not have taken much time to speak of. Browan is not that far from here. No more than a day's ride up the coast."

"No. It was not Gareth." She vehemently defended her brother. "Besides, that sword does not belong to any of my brothers."

Bryce choked. "Who would be foolish enough to carry a sword with falcons engraved on the blade?"

Marianne stared up at him. "Me."

"I beg your pardon?"

"Me." She waved toward the chest. "That poorly made weapon is a copy of my sword. Not my brothers', but mine."

He'd never considered that Marianne would possess her own weapon. Although, after knowing her, he should have given it some thought. "How can you tell?"

"Easy. We have our standards etched on the blade. Rhys's is a golden eagle. Gareth's is a falcon ready to attack. Darius's is a falcon at rest."

"And what is that one if not a falcon ready to attack?" Yet another sign pointing to Gareth of Faucon as the culprit.

"The raptor on that blade is a nesting falcon. It is perched on a ledge, looking down at its nest. What looks like scratches in the etching, are actually grass." She lifted her eyebrows and cocked her head. "Now which one of us do you think might best be considered a nesting falcon?"

He bit back his groan. Of course the nesting falcon would be her. "How do you know one of your brothers did not use your weapon to draw the trail off them?"

At that she laughed. "They would not act so cowardly. And that weapon is only a copy."

"You sound certain."

"I am. The grip is too long. The pommel is not counter-weighted correctly. I should have easily been able to handle that sword. But without a good balance between the blade and the hilt, I was unable to defend myself."

He knew these things, but her knowledge rendered him speechless.

Marianne continued. "The cross guard is wrong. Mine is trilayered. It has a fine layer of bone between the layers of wood and is cross wrapped in leather. And the tang on that sword is loose. I would never use my weapon so poorly to loosen the tang from the grip."

Bryce knew how that might have happened from experience. Someone had used the side of the weapon in a hacking motion against another blade or something equally hard. Either way, it had knocked the blunt end, the top end, of the blade loose from the hilt.

He'd made the mistake once of slamming the edge of his sword against a rock in anger. During his next battle, the blade had flown out of the hilt. A good way to court death.

If one of her brothers had not burned Ashforde to the ground, who did? And why had they led him to believe that the deed had been committed by a Faucon?

He wasn't positive that it was not a Faucon. This was a turn of fate he had not expected. And it was something he would have to figure out soon.

"What are you thinking?"

Bryce sat down beside her and made no comment about her inching away. He was too concerned about the matter at hand. And her putting a distance between them might not be such a bad thing. "I am not saying I believe your brothers are innocent. But if it wasn't one of them, who could it have been?"

"Obviously, someone wanting you to believe it was a Faucon."

"Yes, that's quite apparent."

"Do you have enemies in common?"

He leaned back and stared at her. "Marianne, think. My enemies would be Faucon's allies. Their enemies, my allies."

"I'd forgotten that."

"It wouldn't necessarily have to be a common enemy."

"Perhaps someone wanted you to believe it was my brothers, knowing you'd retaliate?"

"I suppose that is possible, but I find it hard to believe. Up until this summer I was but a mercenary with no men at my command."

"What happened this summer to change your circumstance?"

"I saved my liege's life and ended up with Ashforde."

"What a shame, although Ashforde is a worthy prize."

"The comment about the empress was uncalled for."

Marianne cocked one shoulder. "Do not wait for an apology."

Her mockery could be amusing, when the situation called for humor. This moment, however, was not one of those situations. Her mocking sarcasm only served to anger him.

Bryce rose and walked away from the bench. "I would not expect you to apologize."

"I hear your words, but your tone implies something else. What did you truly mean?"

"You are a Faucon are you not? 'Tis my understanding they apologize for nothing."

Marianne leaned away from the anger wafting across the small cottage toward her. It was hot enough to burn her flesh. "I see you have a high opinion of the Faucons. How do you warrant such notions when you do not know them?"

"Rumors abound. And even if only half of them are true, I can easily assume arrogance runs in your family."

"Arrogance?"

"Yes. An overzealous belief that they alone rule their world and those they consider beneath them."

Marianne had the sudden wish to be a mouse, a small rodent sitting in the corner of Empress Matilda's court, just so she could listen to the falsehoods told about her brothers.

"Hmm. Interesting opinion. Then I would imagine there are those who believe the Faucons are due their just reward."

"Perhaps."

"And perhaps you would be one of those people? Is that why you feel so justified in your quest for retaliation?"

Bryce cleared the distance to the door in three long strides. He threw it open and pointed up at the mound. "No. I do not base my need for revenge on rumors or opinions. I justify it solely on that. On the complete and total devastation of Ashforde."

"Cease!" She rose and faced him. "How can I make you understand that they did not destroy Ashforde?"

He slammed the door closed. "You cannot know that."

"Oh, I can and I do. Bryce, they are not monsters. I care not what you have heard."

"How many men have died at the end of their swords?"

"In battle. Only in battle. None of them, not Rhys, nor Gareth or Darius would ever seek another's death without provocation."

"Oh, and they tell you everything do they? I find that hard to believe."

"What's to tell? I live at Faucon. I reside in the keep. Eat my meals in the hall with the men. There is little I do not hear."

"And you go on campaign with them and sit at the war tables, too?"

"No. Stop it." Marianne paused to catch her breath. She was going about this the wrong way. "Each of them is well respected by their people. Their villages and fields are well tended. Those living in the villages and working in the fields are well cared for. For all their blustering, my brothers would go out of their way to help anyone in their employ, or in their care."

"You paint such a lovely picture with words." His lips curled briefly into a sneer. "Words are meaningless. I have only actions on which to base my opinions."

She winced at his heavy sarcasm. The urge to tell him

that he was every bit as arrogant, mocking, and self-assured as her brothers were was strong. But she knew that would get her nowhere. It would most likely only make matters worse.

"Tell me, Marianne, if they care so much, so greatly for those in their care, why are you here?"

She frowned. "Pardon me?"

Bryce shrugged. "Was it their great care that watched over you the night at the faire when the four varlets grabbed you?"

"The four varlets?"

"Yes, the four ragged-appearing men who snatched you out of the crowd."

Marianne took a step back on leaded feet. "How do you know that?"

"You told me."

"No." She shook her head. "No, I did not tell you that."

"Yes, you did. You said your first mistake had been going to the faire alone."

"That was all I said."

When Bryce's eyes widened for the space of one heartbeat, before narrowing again, Marianne felt ill. Sick to her stomach and sick at heart. "You were at Faucon."

"Aye."

"For what reason?"

"Revenge. Why else would I be there?"

Before her knees gave out beneath her, she sat back down on the bench and wrapped her arms tightly about her stomach.

Bryce silently cursed his anger—and stupidity. He'd not meant for her to discover the chain of events that had led them to this point. At least not just yet.

"Marianne, at the time I was certain in my belief that one of your brothers had destroyed all I owned."

"And now?" Her voice was so small, so forlorn that he wanted to run and hide from the hurt he'd caused her.

He stood by the bench and looked down at her. When she turned away, he knew he was in more trouble than he would be able to handle.

"I truly do not know. The proof I have claims it was them. But it all makes little sense."

"Why did you rescue me?"

Sadness had edged out the anger in her tone. He wanted to lie—to protect the heart he'd only begun to touch. But a sick sense of honor forced him to say, "To take you back to Faucon."

"You said last night that sometimes men did things that caused blood to be shed." She stared up at him. "Did you intend to use me to get to my family?"

He held her gaze and admitted. "Yes, I had every intention of doing just that."

Marianne's lower lip trembled. But she drew it between her teeth for a moment to stop the motion. "And last night, was what? An easy way to tie my feelings to you? Or a way to get even with the Faucons for what you mistakenly think they did to you?"

He ached from the pain he'd caused her. The urge to gather her into his arms and ease her fears nearly overwhelmed him. But he feared such a display would only make her trust him less.

So, instead of holding her to his chest, he grasped her chin and lifted her face to his. "You are free to think anything of me that you wish. But know this, Marianne, had I wanted to use you so harshly, I would have used you thoroughly and completely. You would have been returned to Faucon ruined. Do you understand that?"

She closed her eyes. "I understand only one thing this moment." When she opened her eyes and returned his gaze, Bryce's chest squeezed at the loss of trust he saw there. "I only know that I want to go home."

He had not the words to take away her pain. Nor did he know what to do. He released her and then headed toward the door. "Then let us be gone from here."

They started out of Ashforde in what felt like hours to Marianne, although she knew it had been only a matter of moments.

She hurt. Not just in her heart and mind, but in every limb and every muscle. It was if someone had physically beaten her.

No matter how much his deception hurt her, she'd not cry. Marianne stared at the spot between her horse's ears. Sir John and Eustace again accompanied them. She'd not give Ashforde, nor his men, the satisfaction of seeing her tears.

Yet, for all she tried, she could not summon up the rage, or the anger that would give her the strength to get through the next few days of this journey.

Worse, she could not even control the urges of her own body. Every time Ashforde looked back at her a tingle ran down her spine. Just then, he rode back to her. He rode beside her for a moment, as if waiting for her to say something to him. When she did not, he leaned over and adjusted the cloak about her shoulders. Her heart raced at his closeness.

A moment later, he returned to his men and her heart squeezed with pain.

It mattered not. She could have lived without Rhys's approval of a marriage to this man. Her brother would have gotten over his objection sooner or later.

But she could not live with a man she could not trust. Every day she would wonder and worry if this was the day he would seek revenge against her family.

Her chest constricted and she swallowed down the ever-threatening tears. No, she would not cry. Perhaps if she repeated that often enough, it would be true.

Chapter Fourteen

Faucon, Normandy
October 28, 1143

By the time they reached Faucon's lands things between them had only worsened. For three days she had ignored him. It wasn't so much her silence that bothered him, as it was her complete lack of emotion or recognition. Bryce wished she would yell, scream or lash out at him in some way. At this moment he would welcome even her tears. But to treat him as if he no longer existed unsettled him beyond explanation.

These last few days of seeing to her needs—food, drink, warmth and shelter—ensuring her safety had fast become a habit he wished not to give up. He would gladly spend the rest of his days seeing to her safety, needs and desires. But he was not foolish enough to dwell on dreams that would never come true.

He was equipped to deal with men in battle, not

women. And especially not one whose feelings he'd so thoroughly crushed.

He fully understood her fear for her brothers' welfare. What about him? Was he not owed a measure of vengeance for what he'd lost?

The more he thought about it, the angrier he became. Just three days past, she'd not only been ready to defy her brothers by giving herself to him, but she'd professed to love him. And now he was relegated to a position not only beneath her brothers, but to some level lower than a slug.

Certain there would be no welcome at Faucon he'd ordered Sir John and Eustace to remain behind at Hampshire. They'd wait a fortnight for his return before making their way to Jared at Warehaven.

For some reason, he'd mistakenly thought if the men were not about, Marianne would feel free to voice her anger…or her fear. And now that they'd crossed onto Faucon's demesne lands the opportunity to end this silent torture fast slipped away.

Ahead lay the fork in the road. The path to the right would lead them directly to Faucon Keep. The path left went deeper into the woods.

When they reached the fork Bryce muttered a curse before he brought his horse to a halt. Without turning around, he asked, "What do you wish me to do, Marianne?"

She came to a stop beside him, shooting him a dark look that spoke volumes. He had the urge to jump back from the heat of the flames. Instead, he shook his head, "Besides dying in some slow, exceedingly painful method, what do you wish me to do?"

"About what?"

Thankfully, he'd known she'd choose to be difficult, so he wasn't surprised. "Ashforde. Your brothers."

"Ashforde has nothing to do with me."

He wished that fact were not so true. "Your brothers then."

Marianne said nothing. Which did surprise him, so he offered, "Do you wish me to swallow my quest for revenge?"

"Would you?"

What better way to completely unman himself than to permit those responsible for the destruction of Ashforde to walk away unscathed? Ignoring the sudden twitch in his groin, he answered, "Yes. For you, I would geld myself."

Marianne winced at not only the literal vision that admission created, but at what it would mean to Bryce. She twisted the reins between her fingers, staring first at the path that would lead toward the hunting lodges and the lake, then down the path that would take her home.

Would any one of her brothers be willing to walk away from what they considered a matter of honor?

That answer required no thought whatsoever. No, they would not.

And that's what it was to Bryce—a matter of honor. She understood that. And if he sought vengeance against someone not in her family, she would urge him to satisfy the thirst eating at him. To do otherwise would be to, as he put it, geld him.

She could not permit him to shame himself in that manner. To unman him in this matter would change who and what he was. Marianne closed her eyes, wishing she could hide from whatever the future held. "I cannot ask you to do that, Bryce."

His sigh was audible. "Then what do you wish me to do?"

Take me in your arms, kiss me, love me and make this heaviness in my chest go away. Shocked by the sudden turn of her mind, she kept that wish to herself. Even if he could soothe the hurt she suffered, it would be nothing more than a temporary respite from what lay ahead.

"I know not. It is not right for me to make such a decision."

"Not right?" His words broke on a strangled choke. "None of this is right. It is not right that we could not meet under different circumstances. Nor is it right that I hurt you. It is not right that you hold my heart in your hands and I can do nothing about it. Nothing is right."

Speechless, she fought to ignore the sudden stuttering of her heart.

Before she could find her voice, he continued, "I only ask what your wishes are in this matter. That is all. You need make no decision for me. Just tell me what you wish could happen."

Half to herself, she said, "I wish you could discover who truly destroyed Ashforde before doing anything else."

"What is to stop us from doing just that?"

"Us?" Her breath caught as he placed his hand over hers. Her heart squeezed and his touch sent warmth oozing through her marrow. She felt her anger begin to melt.

"Yes, Marianne. Us. Would it be so unusual for two people to work together toward a common goal? Are you not curious about the sword? Do you not wish to discover who would be so bold as to copy your weapon?"

Yes, she would like an answer to that mystery. This

entire happening was not some simple misunderstanding like she'd witnessed countless times between Rhys and Lyonesse. This matter was more than an appraising stare from a stranger, or a wink and a nod toward a comely woman.

Lives were at stake. Lives of those she held dear. She stared at the hand covering hers. Was not Bryce's life also dear to her? No matter how she'd treated him on this journey, he'd seen to her needs and kept her safe without complaint.

She wanted so badly to trust him, to know that she could count on his words being true. Had he not admitted to rescuing her only to use her in his quest for vengeance?

Her mind drifted back to his first declaration four nights past. Thinking she'd been asleep, he'd whispered that she'd always hold his heart. And now he'd just as much confessed the exact same thing.

Marianne closed her eyes against all the confusion buffeting her. Had she not cried out to Gareth that her heart was deserving of love?

Bryce insisted that a match between them would not be allowed. But he also insisted her brothers had destroyed his keep.

Could he be wrong on both counts? If she ignored what she saw and refused to hear the words brushing her ear, she could feel the spark of hope flare deep inside. It was a tiny pulsing ember that would not be extinguished.

She was home. She was safe. And anything was possible.

Marianne lifted his hand and rubbed her cheek against his knuckles. "Who do you serve, Bryce of Ashforde?"

He moved his horse a step closer, turned his hand over and cradled her cheek. "You. I serve you, Marianne of Faucon."

Her palfrey fidgeted at his closeness. She reined in the beast and turned it toward the left, away from Faucon Keep. "Then follow me."

Darius of Faucon walked back to where he'd secured his horse. It seemed the youngest Faucon had finally found her mate. Unfortunately, the man did not serve King Stephen—a fact Marianne obviously knew by her last question.

She didn't appear to be a prisoner. The way she looked at Ashforde, the way she touched him, made it apparent that whatever circumstances had brought the two together, she had freely given this man her heart.

He swung himself into his saddle, thankful that he'd followed the two without being seen. At least now he knew Marianne was in no danger. He also knew where she was headed and had a pretty good idea of what would happen at the hunting lodge.

A part of him wanted to ride ahead, stop her and drag her to the keep. But had he not once done the same? And he'd been younger when he and Marguerite had clumsily consummated their love.

He had no wish to shame Marianne in the manner their sire had shamed and disowned him on that long-ago night. So, he'd give her this night. Once Rhys discovered what was afoot, this night might well be all she'd have.

Darius backtracked to where his captain Osbert waited with their bound and gagged prisoner.

"Did they continue on to the keep?" Osbert asked.

"Nay, they go to the hunting lodges."

The captain's soft whistle frightened a quail from the underbrush. "The comte will be livid."

"Yes, he will. Fortunately, the man she is with is also a comte." Darius frowned. "I wonder if this new Comte of Ashforde possesses the fortitude to stand up to Rhys." For Marianne's sake, he hoped so.

"Perhaps a flea in his ear would not be out of place?"

"I was thinking the same thing." He glanced briefly at the prisoner they'd captured in Hampshire. "'Tis a shame our prisoner cannot tell us anything more."

So far, the only thing they had learned was that Ashforde had kidnapped Marianne in retribution for the destruction the Faucons had wrought on the comte's keep. But something about the man's furtive glances, his fast way with words, kept Darius from believing what he said.

While parts of his story might well be true, the rest was highly suspect.

Osbert offered, "I can try again."

Darius shook his head. "No. Give him time to think about his future. He will come around…if he is a smart man."

He had better come around. Else Rhys's captain Melwyn would ensure the man had no future—except the kind found at the bottom of a grave. This Sir John would rue the day he ignored Osbert's comparatively easy questioning.

"I will go to the main lodge and see if I can catch Ashforde alone for a moment or two." He nodded toward the prisoner. "You take our…guest…to the far lodge. I'll catch up with you there. We'll head into Faucon after everyone is abed."

It would be easier, and perhaps wiser, to avoid the family for a time than it would be to lie to them. If any discovered that Marianne was near, in the company of a man, they would rush to her side. He preferred that she return to the keep on her own.

As the three men made their way out of the forest the rumbling of carts and pounding of horses urged Darius ahead to the path. He waved Osbert to hold back a ways.

Once the procession passed, Osbert joined him, leading the prisoner along. "Now who arrives?"

Darius had to laugh. Ever since the faire goers finally left, peace had settled once more around Faucon. Only the family knew of Marianne's disappearance, and they were anything but at peace. Now the Comte of Glynnson had arrived. His timing could not have been any worse.

"It appears that Glynnson has once again changed sides."

The Comte of Glynnson ran back and forth between King Stephen and Empress Matilda more often than Rhys bathed. Which was a good jest because ever since Lyonesse had commissioned her two-person tub, she and Rhys had taken to bathing together daily. He laughed. They could call it bathing if they wished, but everyone else knew better.

"So he brings his entourage to Faucon? Why not go directly to King Stephen?"

When Darius turned around to answer his captain, the wideness of the prisoner's eyes caught his attention. Did he fear Glynnson? Or just the man's presence at Faucon?

"I don't know the answer to that, Osbert." But he did

know that the next few days at Faucon should prove interesting and perhaps dangerous for all.

"There is a lean-to around back for the horses." Marianne dismounted outside the lodge. The largest of the lot, it was situated the farthest from Faucon.

"If you'll see to the horses, I'll see what provisions are inside."

Bryce led both palfreys away, while Marianne opened the door and stuck her head inside. The shelters were seldom used by humans, but oft inhabited by numerous animals. She'd learned long ago to check for wild beasts before entering.

On one of her trips here, she'd stumbled across a family of stoats that had made their nest with the mattress stuffing. Thanks to an unsecured window shutter, she'd discovered how vicious a mother stoat could become while protecting her kits.

The creatures might look amusing while bouncing about a field, or toying with their prey. But to her young eyes, the sharp pointy teeth had appeared a foot long.

The setting sun angled in through the door providing light to the back of the lodge. Certain no birds, bats or other animals sheltered within, she went inside and rummaged through the single chest anchored against the far wall.

Obviously, Darius no longer made regular use of this lodge. The only items in the chest were bedcovers, a pot for cooking, flint for making a fire, a net and a dagger. She tossed the flint and dagger on the small bed.

"The horses are settled in for the night." Bryce walked in and after a quick glance around the room, said, "All the comforts of my home."

He was seeking to ease the tension that had followed him in the door. Marianne shrugged. "'Tis a simple shelter for the hunters. Darius used to keep it stocked, but it seems he no longer does so."

Bryce peered out the door. "Will any of Faucon's men be about looking for poachers?"

"No. It may sound unusual, but this time of year Rhys leaves his forest open for huntsmen. He claims it keeps unlawful activity to a minimum to do so."

"He simply permits strangers to come and go as they please?"

"He patrols these forests regularly himself. Would you risk angering the Comte of Faucon on his own land?"

"Under normal circumstances?" Bryce shook his head. "But it seems to me that I am going to do just that on the morrow."

"The difference is that you will not be alone." Marianne glanced toward the sun. "My stomach is calling for food."

"Then I best be practicing my hunting skills before the sun sets." Bryce eyed the flint. "Can you get a fire going?"

"Of course I can." She waved toward the chest. "There is a net in there if that will help."

"Yes, my lady, it will." He scooped up the net, tossed it over his shoulder and headed outside. Halfway through the door, he turned around and came back to her.

Baffled, Marianne asked, "What…"

He cut off her question with one of his own. "Will you be here on my return?"

She looked up at him. A frown creased his forehead.

She could easily torment him and make him wonder. Or she could soothe away his worry.

Marianne decided she'd tormented him enough these last three days. "Yes, I will be here when you return. I promise."

Seemingly satisfied with her answer, Bryce left.

Once he was gone and the fire burned in the pit outside the dwelling, Marianne pulled her cloak tightly about her and took a seat before the fire. The warmth of the blaze chased away the pronounced nip in the air. It would prove to be a cold night.

Thankfully, she had more than covers to keep her warm this night. A flush added heat to her cheeks. It was unfortunate that she'd chosen the hunters' shelter the farthest distance from the keep. She would welcome a chance to speak to Lyonesse, or any of her sisters-by-marriage before Bryce returned.

She desperately needed someone to tell her the difference between love and lust. What made her think of him constantly? He was on her mind whether she was happy, or so upset she could barely think.

Love or lust? Which one caused her heart to pound so and her palms to dampen? Would this overwhelming emotion grow stronger over time, or would it fade away?

Did anyone know the answers to her questions, or was the answer found only by risking all?

She stared into the leaping fire and wondered what had become of her ability to think rationally.

Bryce grabbed the pheasant and broke its neck before it too could escape. He had tried three times to catch a fowl with the net. Twice he'd captured only fallen twigs and leaves. He swore he could hear the birds laughing at him from a distance.

After rolling the pheasant up in the net and slinging it over his shoulder, he started back down the path toward the lodge and Marianne.

A knife against his throat stopped him cold. Without thinking, he reached for his sword. Added pressure on the knife and the hot trickle of his own blood running down his neck stayed his hand.

"Comte Ashforde, are you aware that falcons mate for life?"

By God, which brother was this? The blade slid across his throat nicking him beneath the chin before a hand grabbed his shoulder and spun him around.

The man standing before him was his height, lean and about his age. From what he'd heard the Comte of Faucon was older by a few years and had a scar running the length of his face. The second brother was rumored to be a giant of a man. This could only be the youngest brother, Darius.

Bryce drew a hand across his throat. Certain the cuts were not fatal, he finally answered the man's question. "No. I was not aware of that."

Darius had drawn his sword and held the tip against Bryce's chest. "You are now."

"I gather you are Darius of Faucon?"

"I am. Hand me your sword and sit down. We are going to talk."

Bryce had the distinct impression that Darius was going to talk and he was going to listen. Curiosity prompted him to do as ordered.

Once he took a seat on the cold ground, Darius leaned

against a tree. His easy posture didn't fool Bryce for an instant. He knew that if he made any sudden or unexpected move, Faucon's sword would pin him to the ground in the space of a single heartbeat.

"You are a poor hunter."

Bryce could not argue with that. "I am out of practice is all."

"If you are as bad at everything else as you are at hunting, will you be a poor provider for my sister?"

This was not quite the conversation Bryce had expected. "I beg your pardon?"

Darius leisurely wiped the blood off his dagger. "Let us not play the simpleton. I told you that falcons mate forever. If my sister truly holds your heart in her hand, then I can only assume you will do the right thing by taking her as your wife."

Heaven above, the man had heard them talking back at the fork in the road. "What if she does not agree?"

Faucon roared with laughter. The sound sent a flurry of birds scattering from beneath bushes and the tops of the trees. The same birds that had been unwilling to be captured in Bryce's net mere moments ago. "I saw the look on her face. I heard the tone of her voice. She has already made up her mind on the matter."

Bryce swallowed hard. Darius had been hidden behind him. He had unwittingly left his back unprotected. The man could have killed him at any time, and the realization of that now sickened him. Almost as much as this discussion.

"Perhaps. What does it matter though? 'Tis doubtful the comte would agree to such a match."

"True."

Then why were they even discussing the possibility? Was Marianne's brother crazed?

Darius sighed. "Let me start over. I captured your man just outside Hampshire. He's already admitted that you kidnapped Marianne with the intent of using her as bait to gain revenge against our family."

Bryce swallowed hard. "That isn't quite correct."

"I gathered as much. But I also gather that it is close enough to the real events to get you tossed in Faucon's tower for the rest of your natural life."

"How did you capture my man? Which one do you have?"

"I have been tracking you since you left Devon. The older man apparently remained in Hampshire, but the younger one seemed intent on following you across the channel. I simply offered him the use of my ship."

Sir John was following him? Bryce frowned. The men Empress Matilda chose for his use were not well known to him. Why would John have so openly disobeyed a direct order?

Darius continued, "I would say either your judgment of the men you employ is lacking, or you do not pay them enough. Either way, this one talks far too easily and seems to enjoy embellishing the truth so that it does not fall in your favor."

Still contemplating Sir John's motives, Bryce answered, "I did not employ them."

"Ah, a boon from the empress to go with your new title and property?"

That caught Bryce's full attention. "You have me at a disadvantage. It seems you know everything, while I remain at a loss."

"Let me share with you what I do know."

"Oh, please do." Bryce winced at the heavy sarcasm evident in his tone.

Faucon ignored it and began to tick off what he knew. "You are the new Comte of Ashforde. Your keep, fields and most of the village were destroyed by a fire that none of the Faucons started."

"Why should I believe that you are innocent?"

"What would any of us want with Ashforde?" Darius sounded genuinely confused. "Our family's lordship of these lands are hereditary. The properties of Faucon are vast enough to satisfy all of us for generations to come."

Bryce had the sinking suspicion that Darius was not lying to cover up any nefarious activity of either brother. Meaning that Marianne had been right all along.

"I also know that you are loyal to Empress Matilda," Darius paused to smile before adding, "But you serve only Marianne of Faucon."

Why did he have the feeling that her brother was laughing at him?

"I know that you won my sister in a dice game. I can only assume you meant to bring her home right away, but had urgent matters to see to at Ashforde first. And that accounts for your delay."

"I—"

Faucon raised his sword, stopping Bryce's explanation. "You meant to bring her home right away, but had urgent matters to see to at Ashforde first."

If this was some kind of hint, Bryce thought it was in his best interest to accept it. "Yes. That is it precisely."

"Good. I also know that my sister would never hold

the heart of a man who was unable to stand up to Comte Faucon."

Bryce's eyes widened. What was this Faucon trying to tell him now?

Darius must have recognized his confusion, because he cursed, and then asked, "Do you love Marianne, or do you seek to only play with her heart?"

"I would not do that to her. Yes, I love her, but it is a hopeless sort of emotion."

"Do not make me beat you."

At that statement, Bryce's temper flared. "If you think you could, feel free to try."

Darius nodded. "Yes. That is the attitude you will need to hold on to your love."

"What? Do not speak in riddles." He was growing weary of this game. It was getting dark; if he did not head back to the lodge soon he would never find it.

"My wife does not support King Stephen. It has made no difference, I still hold her love dearly. This war for the crown will not last forever. From what I can tell, Marianne loves you and will for the rest of her life. If you return even a portion of that love, you will fight for her."

"I would fight Satan for her, but I will not fight a member of her family."

Darius slapped the side of his sword against Bryce's arm. "Yes, you will. Rhys will be after your head. I can only do so much, the rest will be up to you. You will have no choice but to stand up to him, to fight him if need be."

"And how will I deal with Marianne's anger if I do so?"

Darius laughed again and sheathed his sword. "I am giving you this night." He turned and walked away, adding over his shoulder. "If you are unable to figure out the answer to that question by morning, then you do not deserve the heart she has freely given you."

Chapter Fifteen

Utter disbelief still swirled about Bryce's thoughts as he strode into the clearing around the small lodge. If he understood Darius of Faucon correctly, the man was giving him permission to bed Marianne.

Why on earth would Faucon do such a thing? He had not given Bryce the impression that he disliked his sister. In fact, it seemed quite the opposite was true. So what would he gain if Bryce followed through on his suggestion?

He found it impossible to believe that Darius was acting in what he considered Marianne's best interest. Then again, he found a great many things impossible to believe at this moment.

If the Faucons did not destroy Ashforde, who did?

How had Sir John permitted himself to be captured and what had he said? Why would Empress Matilda put such an untrustworthy man under his command?

His mind elsewhere, Bryce tripped over a bag left near the burning fire. Inside were cheese, bread, salted pork and a full wineskin. He studied the line of trees surrounding the clearing and saw nothing.

Since the food hadn't been left here by wood sprites, he assumed it came from Darius. Had Marianne seen, or talked to her brother?

Bryce's heart hitched. Was she still here? He picked up his pace and nearly ran through the door of the lodge.

A fat tallow candle burned on top of an upturned bucket near the head of the bed. The flickering light was more than enough to illuminate the small room, assuring him that Marianne had indeed remained here.

The sight of her sleeping on the narrow bed eased his fear, but did nothing to slow the heavy pounding of his heart. He set the netted pheasant down on the chest.

"What did you catch?"

Startled by her question, Bryce held up the bag. "Pheasant."

Marianne sat up on the bed. "And what did you trap in the net?"

He looked at his raised hand and groaned. "I caught a pheasant in the net. But someone left this in the clearing."

"Who? I saw no one while you were gone."

"I am fairly certain it was your brother Darius."

"What happened to your neck?" Marianne's voice raised an octave, drowning out his answer. She nearly leapt off the bed and raced across the floor.

"I am fine." He placed the bag of food on top of the chest and grasped her hands as she reached toward his neck.

"Fine?" She shook off his hold. "You are bleeding."

"'Tis nothing but a scratch." He tried stepping away from her ministrations and backed into a wall.

She leaned against him. "Now hold still."

"Marianne," Bryce said. "Truly, it is nothing to fret over."

"I'll make that determination, since you can't even see it." She shook her head and tsked. "It needs to be cleaned. Go sit down on the bed."

"I said it is fine." The last thing he wanted to do was get anywhere near the bed.

She ran her fingers across his neck and held up her hand. Bryce's throat convulsed at the blood coating her fingers.

He'd not realized how close Faucon had come to severing his head from his neck. "I thought it was just a scratch."

"From what? And do not attempt to tell me it was the pheasant."

"I told you already. Your brother Darius."

Marianne stopped her fussing. "Darius? You did not mention seeing him."

"I most certainly did. Your scream drowned out my words."

She shot her nose up in the air and put her hands on her hips. "I never scream."

"If you say so."

After digging some rags out of the chest, she pulled the wineskin from the bag. "Go, sit down and let me at least get rid of the blood."

Bryce glanced from her, to the bed, then back to her. "I do not think it wise to use the bed."

Marianne's startled expression begged for an explanation. Before he could offer one up, she pushed him toward the bed. "Fear not, Bryce of Ashforde, I will not attack you…" She smiled up at him before continuing, "…just yet."

"'Tis not you I fear."

"Then who? It cannot be my brother, since he obviously let you live."

"For this night he did, yes."

She tipped her head and frowned. "Does he know I am here?"

"Yes."

"And he permitted you to return without a fight?"

"Yes."

"Hmm." Her frown deepened. "I wonder what he is up to this time."

"I have been wondering the same thing."

Marianne untied his belt and placed it and his sheathed sword on the floor next to the bed. "What did he say?"

"Are you seeking to distract me?"

She raised the hem of his tunic. "Bend over." Then she pulled it off over his head and tossed the garment on the bed.

"You are seeking just that."

"I am seeking to get you out of your chain mail so I can clean off your neck."

Bryce gently moved her aside. "Is there a stream nearby?"

"Yes, about a hundred paces behind the lodge. But it is frigid. You will freeze to death."

"That is doubtful." With the heat racing through his veins it would be impossible for him to freeze. He headed for the door. "I will be back anon."

Marianne waited until he was some distance from the

door before falling onto the bed with laughter. Once again he was going to use an ice-cold bath to cool his ardor. Little did he realize that would last only for a short time.

She'd already decided to make full use of their time alone this night. Bryce of Ashforde was the only man she would have for a husband. If Rhys decided to forbid such a match, she would run away.

And if for whatever reason, Bryce himself decided he did not want her as his wife, then she'd have no man and this night would have to last her a lifetime.

Marianne gathered up his sword, belt and tunic along with her cloak and boots, and piled everything atop the chest. She pulled a stool next to the bed to use as a small table. Then she took the food from the bag and placed it on the makeshift furniture. She left Bryce no choice but to sit on the bed.

She undid her braids and finger combed her hair. Marianne let the riotous waves fall freely about her shoulders and back. She had overheard women working in the keep say that a woman's unbound hair was the devil's work. It tempted men to run their fingers through the forbidden locks. And that would lead to other lustful acts.

It was time to see if those overheard tales were true or not.

Certain Bryce would return soon, Marianne tugged at the lacing on the back of her bliaut and let the gown slide from her shoulders, down her body and to the floor. She stepped out of it and added that to the growing pile on the chest.

The night air had turned cold, so she quickly removed her hose and after tossing them toward the chest, she raced to the bed. Not yet bold enough to remove her thin chemise, as she would normally do before getting into bed, Marianne dived under the covers and tugged the hem of the long undergown down to cover her legs.

Once settled in bed, her mind began to swirl from one question and thought to the next. Darius knew she was here alone with Bryce and yet he had not come to the lodge to order her home to Faucon. Did that mean he condoned this fledgling relationship?

If so, had he conveyed that message to Bryce? She could not imagine any one of her brothers giving any man permission to spend a night alone with her. They saw her not as a woman, but as a child.

It made no sense. But she was not about to question the boon she'd been granted.

What would it take to convince Bryce this night might well be all they had? Would he set aside his honor for passion? Would he set it aside for love?

The door to the lodge creaked open, setting butterflies loose in her stomach.

Bryce peered around the door. "Are you awake?" His words seemed to shake.

Marianne took one look at him and ordered, "Your lips are nearly blue from the cold. Get in bed."

He dumped his chain mail to the floor and shook his head. "I thought I would go sit by the fire for a spell."

"Bryce, it is cold out there. With the night air and your wet skin and hair we'll not have to worry about Rhys killing you."

"The fire is warm. Go to sleep." She heard his teeth chattering from across the lodge. It reminded her of the intense cold of the shelter they had found that night by the stream and knew he must be suffering as much, if not more, than she had.

She rolled onto her side and stared at him. "What are you afraid of?"

"Afraid?" His eyebrows disappeared beneath his hair. "I am afraid of nothing."

He sounded oddly like a child. Marianne pointed at the food. "Then come over here. Sit down and wrap the blanket around you. You can tell me what my brother had to say while you eat." And to her ears she sounded oddly like a scolding mother.

These were not the images she'd intended to have this evening. No, the images she wanted were much more… carnal…adult…and definitely not motherly or childlike. She shivered.

"Are you cold?" Bryce sat down on the edge of the bed, careful to leave some space between them.

"No…" She'd started to say she wasn't cold at all, only repulsed by the strange twist of her thoughts. But she quickly changed her mind. "I am freezing." She shivered again.

He unfastened his boots and kicked them off before swinging his legs up on the bed. Bryce pulled her against his chest, muttering, "I have a sneaking suspicion that you may not be as cold as I am."

Marianne sighed. This was so much better. The damp chill of his body sent a real shiver down her spine. She snuggled in closer and slid her arm across his waist. Bryce's heart thudded a steady, soothing rhythm against her ear.

"So, what did my brother have to say?"

"He has been trailing us since Hampshire."

"Alone?"

"I do not believe so. I am fairly certain he said his man was with him. Although I only saw Darius."

That was unusual. "I wonder where Osbert was." Osbert was normally Darius's shadow, following her brother everywhere he went.

"Guarding their prisoner, no doubt."

She placed a hand on his chest and rose up enough to stare down at him. "Prisoner? What prisoner?"

"Sir John."

"*Your* Sir John?"

"He is not precisely *my* Sir John, but yes, he is the man they have captured."

"I fail to understand how that could have happened."

"That makes two of us. It seems John did not heed my order to remain in Hampshire. Instead, he took it upon himself to follow us."

Marianne lay back down on his chest, asking, "To protect you perhaps?"

Bryce snorted. "'Tis doubtful. But there's more. Once captured, John saw fit to confess all my misdeeds."

"Misdeeds?"

He stretched, trying to get comfortable on the narrow bed. "Oh, yes, my abduction of you. And my quest for revenge over Ashforde."

"What did Darius have to say about Ashforde?"

"That the Faucons would have no reason to destroy the keep."

"I had already told you that." She kept most of the smugness from her comment.

"Yes, but not quite in the same manner."

"Is that when he cut your throat?"

"No, he did that when he first came up behind me. It was an effective way to get me to drop my sword."

"So, do you believe me now? Have you come to realize that none of my brothers destroyed your property?"

"A small part of me still wants to believe it was them. Only because my bruised honor demands satisfaction. But, yes, I do believe you."

Marianne sighed. She could not begin to imagine how all of this information would translate when it was told to Rhys. "Apparently, my brother now knows as much as we do?"

Bryce brushed his cheek across the top of her head. "I fear he knows more than we do."

She couldn't contain her laugh. "Now that is not possible."

"I would not be so sure of that, Marianne. Not only has he watched us for over a day, but he overheard us at the fork in the road." At her sudden intake of breath, he agreed, "Yes, it is an embarrassing thought, is it not?"

"Surely he was but teasing you."

"No, he repeated our words back to me without fault."

Oh Lord, above. Marianne could just imagine Darius's smug, laughter-choked voice. "And he let you come back here, knowing full well we would be alone tonight?"

"Yes. But there is still more to it than that." Bryce reached over to the makeshift table and plucked a hunk of bread from the offerings. "Are you hungry?"

The rough, near raspy tone of his question made her wonder what Darius said. Certain she'd find out in due time, she answered, "Yes. A little."

He sat up on the bed, dragging her along. Once she

was sitting with her back against the wall, he picked up the stool and let her choose what she wished, before returning it to the floor.

Between bites, Marianne drew him back into the discussion. "What more did he have to say?"

"Well, just that the comte will do his best to intimidate me."

"That much is true. Rhys always uses intimidation first. Many times it saves him from having to use force." She took a swallow of the wine to wash down the cheese. "Do not let him get away with it though. Stand up to him."

"That is what Darius suggested." He reached toward the stool, asking, "Do you want any more?"

"No. I've had enough, thank you." With no water or cloth handy, she licked the crumbs from her fingers. Before going to work on her other hand, she paused to ask, "Was there anything else he suggested?"

At Bryce's silence, she looked at him. His stare seemed to burn through her. An expression of combined need and want set her heart to racing.

"Bryce?" Marianne turned around, coming up on her knees to face him. She rested the palms of her hands against his chest. His heart pounded with the same furious rhythm hers did.

She slid her hands beneath his shirt. His flesh was now hot beneath her touch. It did not take him long to warm up. Nor her. Leaning closer, she asked in a whisper, "Did he say anything about us?"

With a groan, Bryce pulled off his shirt and reached for the hem of her chemise. Marianne used the rocklike plane of his chest for leverage and rose enough for him to pull the fabric from beneath her.

Before she could settle back onto her knees, he whipped the garment over her head, tossed it to the floor and pulled her against his chest, whispering hoarsely, "He said that falcons mate for life."

The feel of his strong arms around her sent a shiver trembling the length of her body that had nothing to do with the chill of the night air. Even her fingers shook as she stroked the line of his stubble covered jaw. "Aye, that they do."

He buried his face in her hair. "Since I know not what the future may bring, I have not the right to ask you to share all of your tomorrows with me."

Marianne pushed herself up, straddling his waist. The heat of his taut stomach burned the soft flesh between her legs. She gasped at the contact, but looked down at him. "None of us are guaranteed a tomorrow. We have nothing more than this moment and hope for the days to come. I will share this night with you. Each and every day I will pray for one more night."

He reached up and stroked a breast. She leaned into his touch, gasping as he brushed a thumb across the stiff peak of her nipple before sliding his hand up behind her neck.

Bryce pulled her down to him and placed a line of kisses across her forehead, down her cheek toward her mouth. With his lips barely touching her own, he said, "Then let me love you this night and we'll both pray for tomorrow night."

His ragged words thrilled as no other. She stretched her legs out, resting fully atop him. The hard bulge pressing into her thighs let her know that Bryce's passion was as enflamed as her own. "Yes, please, love me."

With a low rumbling groan he rolled her onto her back, coming to rest with his legs straddling hers and the bulk of his weight on his elbows. She wrapped her arms about his neck, running her fingers through the ends of his still-damp overlong hair.

His mouth came down on hers. This was no brief, light kiss like the ones from moments ago. No, this was a fiery caress that stole the breath from her body and all thought from her mind. A fierce caress that promised more passion than she could imagine and demanded she respond in kind.

Every inch of her flesh burned with desire and pulsed with a desperate clawing need. She clasped her arms tighter about his neck, and arched her back seeking to get closer.

Bryce tore his lips from hers and raggedly asked, "Do you trust me, Marianne?" Twin flames from the candle flickered in his eyes.

"Yes."

He reached up and pulled her arms from around his neck. When she moved to place them on his back, he slid out of her embrace.

Before she could fully miss the warmth of his body covering hers, Bryce followed the line of her jaw with the tips of his fingers, before trailing his touch down her neck.

"What are you…" Marianne's breath hitched when his stroking fingertips circled her breast.

"I intend to savor every moment of this night." The next circle was smaller, spiraling up the curve.

"I want to memorize every soft inch of you."

His hot breath grazed her ear. She gasped when he

caressed her swollen nipple. The gasp turned to a moan when the warmth of his mouth replaced his fingers.

He trailed his touch lower. Taking time to stroke lush bedevilment across her belly and down the tops of her legs. His touch danced around her knees, finding a ticklish spot that made her giggle and squirm. At the same time it provided him the opportunity to slide one of his long, muscular legs between hers.

The sweeping strokes up the inside of her thighs turned the giggles to gasps of pleasure.

And when his torment focused on the most sensitive spot between her thighs, her breath stopped. He dipped a finger between the throbbing folds of flesh. Frantic with a burning need, Marianne blindly grasped at his shoulder, "Bryce, please."

He moved away from her only long enough to strip off his braies before kneeling between her parted legs.

Marianne reached for him, but he answered not by coming into her arms, but with a smile worthy of the devil himself. He parted her thighs and bent forward to caress her hot sensitive core with his lips and tongue.

Marianne thought she would burst into flames. Gripping the bedcovers, she fought for breath to ease the rapid pounding of her heart and the mindless throbbing of her body.

It was like falling off the edge of a cliff, twirling and spinning into a bottomless chasm of nothing but pure mindless pleasure.

Her legs stiffened, and without conscious thought her spine jerked off the bed.

Bryce's deep groan brushed against her ear as he came over her. "I will try not to hurt you."

She could barely make sense of his words through the fog of desire. Hurt her? How? Before she could find the answer he entered her in one fluid thrust.

Marianne experienced no more than a sudden flash of pain that faded before she fully noticed it. She must have flinched, because Bryce had gone still. "No. Don't stop." She arched against him, trying to find the perfect rhythm for their bodies. Hesitantly he matched her rhythm.

Soon a wild abandonment carried them away. Marianne swirled faster into the chasm until a cry of satisfaction tore from her lips.

Bryce echoed her cry with a heavy shudder and a deep groan as he followed her into the chasm.

Damp with perspiration, panting for breath, he collapsed on top of her. Marianne wound her arms around his back, kissed his neck and shoulders until she could no longer draw in air.

He moved onto his side, curling an arm around her, he pulled her close. They both drifted off to sleep, her back tight against his chest and one hand cupping her breast.

Chapter Sixteen

The first thing that broke through Bryce's sleep-laden mind was that a cool breeze brushed over his naked body. From the coldness of his legs, he had been uncovered for some time. Without opening his eyes, he reached for the bedcovers.

Unable to locate them, he stretched and begrudgingly opened one eye. He easily found the missing covers. They were wrapped around Marianne.

She sat on the stool, cloaked in the covers for warmth, munching on cheese while quite boldly staring at him.

"What are you doing?"

"Mmm. Eating and watching you sleep." She had the audacity to wiggle her eyebrows at him.

"And are you enjoying yourself?"

"Immensely."

He had learned long ago that fair-haired people blushed quite easily. It mattered not if they were male or female, the telltale mark of embarrassment would rear its ugly head with the least provocation.

This was one of those times. He could feel the heat slide over his cheeks. It was no use seeking to hide it, in the end the redness would become more pronounced. So, he propped up his leg closest to her, trying to conceal his erection.

"It is no use. I have already studied it quite closely." At least she had the decency to blush along with him. "Its nudging woke me earlier."

That was enough for him. She would have him babbling like a tongue-tied lad if he did not stop her. Bryce swung his legs over the other side of the bed and pulled on his braies. "Egad, Marianne. Cease."

She burst out laughing. "I am sorry. But I find your body fascinating. It is so different from my own."

"Thank the Good Lord for that." Bryce hauled her up from the stool and silenced her with a kiss. Once she melted in his arms, he kissed her a little deeper before sitting her down on the bed.

She stretched out and patted the empty spot he'd just vacated. "There is no rush to return to Faucon. We could stay here for a day, a week…a lifetime."

"As inviting as that offer sounds. I promised Darius I would take you to the keep this morning."

"But I am not ready to face them and the chastisement sure to come."

"*You* are not ready?" Bryce shook his head. "It is not your life being risked with this visit."

"I will not let them harm you."

"I do not require your protection."

"But—"

"Enough!"

Her eyes widened at his shout, but she remained silent.

He ran a hand through his hair. "I wish not to argue with you this morning. I just want this meeting finished so we know where you and I stand."

"I thought we stood together." All traces of amusement gone, she asked, "Was I wrong?"

"No." He sat on the edge of the bed and pulled her and her covers onto his lap. "No, you are not wrong."

She leaned against his chest. "I think perhaps you worry overmuch about my family."

"I don't know, Marianne. They may treat you well because they love you. I believe I have much to fear."

"If anything befalls you at their hands, I will die."

He wrapped his arms around her, holding her close. Her words and the intensity he heard in her voice frightened him more than facing an army of Faucons. "Hush. Do not say that. Do not even think those thoughts."

"But what would I do? Where would I go? I could not live with them if they brought you harm."

Bryce rested his cheek atop her head. He'd not thought of this happening. He offered the only solution he knew. "If anything would happen to me, take my sword and go to Jared at Warehaven."

"You would send me to The Dragon?"

His chuckle felt out of place as it left his lips. "Yes. I would. Marianne, he is not a bad man. Jared is no more a dragon than your brother is a falcon."

"There are so many tales about him."

"Who? Jared? Or Rhys?" When she didn't answer, he said, "That is all they are—tales told by men who do not know any better. And like any sane man, Jared does not waste his time trying to correct the overblown stories. He uses what he can to his advantage and ignores the rest."

"What could he do for me?"

"He will keep you safe and make certain you want for nothing."

"I don't want his gold."

"His gold?" Bryce leaned away and looked down at her. "No. I have been a mercenary since I was big enough to mount a horse and hold a sword. My needs were little, so my money chest grew. The amount grew more when I started taking part in tourneys."

"Oh."

"You seem surprised. How else could I afford to rebuild Ashforde if I did not have the coin to do so?"

"I thought you oversaw Ashforde for your liege?"

Bryce glanced briefly toward the ceiling. "That was not exactly what I said."

"It is what you led me to believe."

"I am sorry for that, but it seemed reasonable to do so at the time. I am the Comte of Ashforde."

"Oh! That is truly good news."

"Why?" He doubted if Marianne was excited about him having a title or wealth for any reasons related to greed. So, he wondered what caused her sudden burst of glee.

"Because, you will be facing Rhys on an even level. He cannot simply have you put to death. Nor can he just lock you away in a cell without demanding a ransom."

No. But with his liege lord's or the king's sanction, he could demand satisfaction in a trial by combat. Bryce could think of no worse sentence than that. It was not that he feared dying. He feared Marianne's heart breaking at either outcome.

He didn't voice those thoughts. Instead, he agreed with her. "Aye, it is possible that this title may help somewhat." He pushed her off his lap. "But if we do not get on our way, Faucon's army may come looking for us."

Marianne stared across the empty field toward Faucon Keep. For the first time in her life the imposing structure did not bring her a burst of joy.

Pride, yes. But it did not appear to welcome her home.

Bryce touched her cheek. The warmth of his palm did much to soothe the sudden pounding of dread in her temples.

"They will welcome you with open arms."

She turned toward him, slipped her hand behind his neck and pulled him closer. "Chase away the cold snaking around my heart. Kiss me."

He whispered against her lips, "Gladly," before covering her mouth with his own.

"If the two of you are finished, perhaps we can continue on?"

Marianne leaned away from Bryce. "Darius, where did you come from?"

"I was out for my morning ride and thought I saw a raven-haired wench who looked like my little lost sister." He rode alongside her and dropped a kiss on her forehead. "It is good to have you home."

"That remains to be seen." She lifted one eyebrow as she looked at him. "I would introduce you to my companion here, but I understand you have already met."

Darius leaned forward and looked around her to Bryce. "Ah, yes, Comte Ashforde. How are you this fine day?"

Bryce rubbed his throat. "Fine, so far."

"Good. Since the saints have chosen to smile on you, the rest of this day should be just as fine."

When Marianne and Bryce both stared at him, Darius explained, "I am the only brother in residence today. We do not expect Rhys and Gareth until tomorrow."

The stiffness went out of Marianne's spine. She relaxed, letting her shoulders fall with a deep, heartfelt sigh. "Thank the Lord for this favor."

"Before you thank Him overmuch, remember, the wives are at Faucon."

The prospect of facing her sisters-by-marriage failed to renew her worry. While she cared deeply for them, their disapproval would not cut as sharply as her brothers'.

Darius reined in his impatient horse. "Ready?"

At her nod, the party raced across the field toward Faucon.

Marianne laughed as the wind tore through her braids, undoing the hastily made plaits. The breakneck speed was exhilarating. The carefree abandonment was a most welcome relief from the slower pace of the journey from Ashforde.

Without slowing, she and Bryce followed Darius through the gates of the outer wall. They raced across the bailey and between the twin towers of the curtain wall. They stopped only when they reached the inner courtyard.

"Ho! What is this recklessness?" A guard ran toward them, half a dozen others on his heels.

Darius swung from his saddle, waving toward Marianne and Bryce, declaring, "These misbegotten spawns of Satan chased me from the woods. Toss them in the tower, for their intent was to do me harm. We shall feast on their bones this night."

"Aye, my lord." An older, gruff-looking man pulled Marianne from her horse, engulfing her in his mail-clad arms. "'Tis good to see you safe, my lady."

Had someone told her the moon would never shine again, she would not have been more shocked. She patted his shoulder, "And it is good to be home, Sir Melwyn." When he released her, she asked, "Who is with Rhys?"

"With all of your brothers out searching for you, the comte thought it best for me to remain behind." Melwyn, her brother's captain, looked none too happy with that decision.

"He could not have left a better man in charge. I am certain the ladies and all at Faucon appreciate his wise decision."

Melwyn looked at her as if she'd grown horns before he snorted. "What a pretty speech. Thank you." He nodded toward Bryce. "And who is this pup?"

With a laugh, Marianne turned to Bryce. She extended her hand beckoning him to join her.

When he clasped her hand and stepped to her side, she said, "This is Bryce, Comte of Ashforde. He rescued me and kept me safe."

Melwyn glanced at their still joined hands before he nodded to Bryce. "Comte of Ashforde?"

"Yes. And I gather that you are Comte Faucon's man?"

"I am sorry." Marianne shook her head at her lack of manners. "Yes, this is Sir Melwyn, Rhys's captain."

Melwyn's bushy eyebrows came together over his searching eyes. He studied the newcomer to Faucon a moment, before extending his hand. "I will take your sword."

"Melwyn!"

"Cease." Bryce's sharp order drew raised eyebrows from the other men. He released Marianne's hand. "'Tis his duty to Faucon. I am a stranger here. My motives are suspect and rightly so." He softened his tone. "And if I am unarmed no one has a reason to seek my life."

Marianne glared at Darius. "I hold you personally responsible for his safety."

Her brother graced her with a look she could not decipher. Finally he said, "You make too much of this, little sister. Nothing is out of the ordinary here unless you make it so."

She hated it when he talked in riddles. Why could he simply not say what he was thinking?

Bryce unsheathed the weapon at his side. He grasped the blade and extended the hilt toward Melwyn. Once the captain relieved him of the sword, he said, "There is another one tied to the back of my saddle. I would appreciate it if that sword was placed in Marianne's care."

Melwyn freed the wrapped bundle from the back of Bryce's saddle and handed Bryce's sword to one guard, who promptly headed toward the armory. The captain handed the package to another. "See that this finds its way to Lady Marianne's chamber."

Before the uncomfortable silence could fully descend, a small group of women rushed toward them.

Marianne left the men and nearly flew across the distance separating her from her brothers' wives. When she entered the circle of their arms, everyone talked at once.

"Thank God, you are home."

"Where have you been?"

"What happened?"

"Oh, Marianne, we have been worried sick."

"Your brothers are beside themselves with fear."

Each question and statement blended in with the next. Until Rhys's wife Lyonesse sucked in a loud breath. "And who is that?"

Marianne, and the others, followed her line of vision. Marianne sighed. "That is the man I am going to marry." A soft smile curved her lips. His returned smile lit her heart.

Silence rippled through the small gathering. Lyonesse grasped Marianne's shoulders and turned her around to face the wives. All three narrowed their eyes and intently searched Marianne's suddenly hot face. Finally, a soft whistle escaped Lyonesse's mouth. "Oh, so that is the way of it?"

Darius's wife Marguerite stared across the short distance toward her husband. "Is he aware of this?"

Marianne glanced over her shoulder in time to see Darius nod, then shrug in answer to his wife's questioning stare. Knowing it was useless to lie, she admitted, "Yes."

Gareth's wife Rhian asked, "Is this why you have been gone? You ran away with this man?"

"Oh, no." Marianne shook her head with a passion. "I did not leave Faucon of my own free will. Bryce truly rescued me."

It was imperative that they believe her. She grasped Rhian's slender fingers, but swept her gaze across all three faces. "I would do no such thing without seeking your counsel, surely you know that."

Marguerite's sigh briefly lifted her shoulders. "It appears a discussion is in order."

Lyonesse broke away from the others. "More than one." She arched her reddish brows at Marguerite and Rhian. "You see to Marianne. I will quiz Lord Ashforde."

Marianne gritted her teeth. "We do not need to be quizzed or lectured."

"Oh? Is that so?" Lyonesse stepped closer. "I gather you are not yet married?"

Marianne lifted her chin a notch. "Not yet."

Lyonesse narrowed her eyes. "But you have taken advantage of your freedom to act as though you were?"

She couldn't have stopped the flush racing up her neck and face if she'd tried. Marianne felt the heat of her blush burn her cheeks. She glanced at the ground before returning Lyonesse's stare. "You cannot be certain of that."

All three wives laughed at her. Rhian spoke first, "We were not, until now."

Marguerite cleared the confusion. "Your reddened cheeks and rebellious attitude speak louder than your words, Marianne."

Lyonesse came even closer. She stood toe to toe with Marianne. "You have committed these acts, made this decision without your brothers' approval. You had no right to shame your family in such a way. If you were too blind to see to your duty, your man should have seen to it for you. Aye, little sister, a discussion is highly in order."

The anger welling up in Marianne's chest threatened to burst. "And which one of you went to your marriage bed with your maidenhead still intact?"

Marguerite cleared her throat. "Keep your voice down."

"No." Marianne backed away from Lyonesse's glare.

"No, I will not keep my voice down. You thought to find me a husband who would make me content. I have no wish to be content. I want what each one of you has. I want to be cherished. I want to be loved. I need to feel—"

"Marianne, hush." Bryce grasped her arm and swung her around to face him. He palmed her cheek. "Not here. Not like this."

At first she thought Darius had grabbed her and she tried to pull away. But the thumb stroking across her lower lip and the warm fingers sliding around the back of her neck keeping her in place did not belong to her brother. They were too familiar, too welcome to belong to anyone but Bryce.

She relaxed and hung her head. "I am sorry. I was not thinking."

Lyonesse's mouth fell open.

Rhian placed a hand over her heart, whispering, "Oh, Lord."

Marguerite choked back a gasp before leaning against her husband.

Darius broke the shocked silence by placing a hand on Bryce's shoulder. "Well, I think it is safe to say that we are all in agreement here. We need to get to know you better. And quickly."

"Before tomorrow might be the wisest course of action." Lyonesse rested her hands on her protruding belly. "Shall we go inside? I need to sit a spell."

Before Darius drew Bryce along with him, he leaned down and whispered in Marianne's ear. "Even though it is none of your affair, yes, Marguerite was a maiden still on her first wedding night."

She closed her eyes briefly, and then touched his arm. "Please, accept my apology. I am sorry."

"As well you should be. You need to learn to stop and think before opening your mouth, Marianne."

She knew the truth in his light chastisement. However, he was the only one who followed that advice and he'd not been present to pass the lesson on to her.

Bryce stroked her lip one more time. "Are you at ease now?"

She leaned into his palm and met his concerned gaze. "Aye."

He drew his hands away slowly. "When you feel the need to shout or argue, come to me. Do not take your anger out on your family."

"But…" Her words trailed off at his pleading look. She nodded her agreement.

Darius waved toward the keep. "Shall we?"

He led the way into Faucon Keep with the wives following. Bryce and Marianne brought up the rear of the small party.

Each lost in their own thoughts, it was a silent procession.

Once inside the great hall, Lyonesse tsked. "I nearly forgot." She looked askance at Marianne and Bryce. "We have company that I need to see to." With a wave toward Rhian and Marguerite, she suggested, "Marianne, why do you not seek your chamber and perhaps a bath. Lord Ashforde, my sisters will show you to a chamber and see to your needs. We can all gather in my solar afterward."

Bryce nodded in agreement. "I thank you, my lady."

Before the group could go their separate ways, the

sound of people approaching caught their attention. Marianne had barely glanced toward the strangers when Bryce's strangled groan drew her attention.

He froze, as if suddenly rooted to the floor. His sun-darkened face appeared to pale.

Marianne took a step toward him. "Bryce, what is wrong?"

The question no sooner left her mouth than a petite blonde threw herself at his chest, nearly knocking Marianne to the floor in her haste.

The woman's hands were all over his face and shoulders and she declared, "Bryce, my love. You have come for me."

Chapter Seventeen

Even through the voices raised in shock and outrage, Bryce could hear the shattering of Marianne's heart. He could feel the pain ripping through her chest and taste the salt of the unshed tears shimmering in her accusing glare.

Before he could set aside the woman clinging to him like an unwelcome vine, Marianne ran from the hall.

Unable to extricate himself without tossing Cecily bodily across the chamber, Bryce turned a pleading glance toward Darius.

His rescue was forthcoming in the form of a sword's hiss as it was pulled from the encasing scabbard.

Darius called out to Lord Glynnson, "Could you remove your daughter from my prisoner?"

"Prisoner?" Cecily nearly shrieked. "This is the Comte of Ashforde. What right do you have to take my betrothed prisoner?"

"I am not your betrothed." Bryce's denial of her claim was lost beneath the shouts and cries of the others present.

How had this happened? Why were Glynnson and his family at Faucon? Empress Matilda had repeatedly assured Bryce that Glynnson fully supported her and would not switch his allegiance back to King Stephen.

Otherwise he never would have taken this offered betrothal under consideration. The final document was stored in his saddlebag—unsigned and undelivered.

That had been only one of his recent mistakes. The moment he knew Marianne held his heart in the palm of her hand, he should have sent the unsigned document to the empress along with a missive stating he would not be exchanging any promises with Cecily of Glynnson.

He never should have waited. His only defense was that he'd been distracted by other matters.

Cecily's plaintive wails grated on his ears. Where was the cold, collected lady he'd met before? He stared down at her. While her manners and voice bespoke of a distraught lover, her eyes were emotionless…as cold as ice.

Stunned, he realized that her outrageous display was staged. Why? For whose benefit did she act in such a manner?

It started as a small twitch deep in his body. A twitch that quickly grew to a burning churn eating away at him. He suddenly felt as if he were no more than a pawn in a game where he did not know the rules. A game he did not understand.

At this moment, being held as Faucon's prisoner would be welcome respite. It would give him the solitude needed to clear his befuddled head and think.

Lord Glynnson pushed his way through the still gathering throng. "Here, here, Cecily." He pried at her clutching fingers. "Stop this caterwauling and leave the man be."

"But, Father—"

"No. Listen to me, daughter. Either release him this instant or we will leave here immediately."

With a great show of reluctance, Cecily sheathed the claws she'd dug into Bryce's shoulder and slowly lowered her arms.

Darius slid his weapon between Bryce and Cecily; using it as a wedge he forced Bryce to step back. "Enough of this most entertaining welcome." He pushed the tip of his sword against Bryce's chest, ordering, "Go."

For a heartbeat Bryce wondered if he'd made a mistake by issuing his silent plea for Darius's help. At this moment it appeared the man would be honored to run the blade through his chest.

Darius directed him toward the stairs leading to the upper chambers. The wives followed, leaving the Glynnson family behind.

Once they were out of sight, Darius lowered his sword. Bryce was unable to contain his sigh of relief.

One of the wives walked by him muttering, "Do not get too comfortable, my lord."

Another brushed by him and without pausing for an answer, she asked, "How could you?"

"This is for Marianne." He winced as the third one slapped his cheek before spinning away to follow her incensed sisters.

Darius waited until the heavy door to a chamber slammed closed behind the women before he waved Bryce toward the next flight of stairs. "Go. Up one more."

"I am heartened that you saw fit to assist me."

"As well you should be."

Bryce paused at that statement. But a sharp prick in his back got him moving up the steep stairwell once again.

"Do not mistake my help in rescuing you from Glynnson as a sign that I might defend you in any future confrontations."

"Such as those involving the comte?"

"That and any other member of my family."

When they arrived at the landing, Bryce turned to ask, "What is the possibility that I might be permitted to explain this to Marianne?"

"Are you a wagering man?"

Obviously, since he had diced for Marianne and won. "Yes."

"Then it would be safe for you to assume the odds are not in your favor." Darius opened the door to what Bryce recognized as a cell.

"I am your prisoner then?"

"For the guaranteed protection of my sister's heart and the continuation of your own life, consider this your best option."

His feet felt like lead as he stepped over the threshold into his cell. Bryce turned to Darius and asked, "Could you at least give her a message?"

"Certainly."

"Tell her I am not betrothed to that woman. No one else but Marianne can lay claim to my heart."

Marianne bodily pushed Darius aside and stood in the threshold. "That was made obvious by the way she threw herself into your arms, Lord Ashforde."

She moved away from Darius's grasping fingers and walked into the cell. "Close the door."

Darius hesitated a moment too long. Marianne kicked the door closed in his face. "You can leave now."

"Marianne, this is not wise."

"I have no intention of being wise, brother. Leave me alone." She glared at him through the small window cut into the thick iron-strapped door. When she was certain he was gone, she turned to Bryce.

"Well?"

She had already hinted at her rage by calling him Lord Ashforde. He looked at her, searching her face in an attempt to judge the level of her ire. The red eyes and deeply creased frown quickly conveyed that she had gone from being angry, to being outright livid with him.

"I am not betrothed to her." He held out his hand, hoping she'd clasp it in her own.

"So you say." She sidestepped him and crossed the small cell to stand in the corner.

"Why would I lie?"

"Why would you not?"

"Because you hold my heart in your hand."

Marianne held out her hand, palm up. She closed her fingers as if holding an imaginary object. While staring him straight in the eyes, she tightly closed her fingers about the object that he guessed represented a heart.

Once her fingers turned red from the exertion of clenching them, she opened her hand and acted as if she flung the now crushed object to the floor. To add to her theatrics, she stomped on the imaginary heart while wiping her palm against the skirt of her gown.

"That is what you did to my heart. So, why would you assume I would keep yours safe?"

Oh, she was livid all right. But Bryce was relieved to

see she was still so angry that she had yet to recognize her own heartache. That meant he still had time to explain. If he could keep her good and outraged long enough.

He knew that once she accepted her hurt, she would not listen to him. That is what she had done before and he would not take the chance of it happening again.

He crossed his arms against his chest. "Are you finished?"

"Yes." She stepped away from the wall. "Yes, I am." Marianne lifted her chin and headed for the door.

He waited until she walked by him and then lunged. Wrapping his arm around her waist, he pulled her against him.

"Let me go!"

Bryce laughed—more to fortify himself for what he was about to do than anything else. "Not until you hear what I have to say."

"Never."

He lowered his lips to her neck and when she swatted at him, he easily pinned her flailing arms to her sides.

Once she was secured by his embrace he resumed his teasing. Bryce trailed his tongue down the length of her neck, pausing to nip at the soft flesh beneath her ear and again where her shoulder started.

"Stop it this instant."

He ignored her order and shifted her body so he could restrain her with one arm. He nudged her still-unbound hair away from her neck with his chin, exposing more of her soft flesh to his touch.

Her heart pounded beneath his forearm. A slight twist brushed his arm up the curve of her breast.

She choked off her soft gasp. "Ashforde, release me."

Lord Ashforde was now simply Ashforde. Bryce smiled against the nape of her neck. She was getting closer.

He twisted his arm again, this time brushing a little higher. While trailing his lips against her neck, he slowly slid his free hand up the length of her thigh, pausing ever so briefly at the top. His touch slid higher up her belly and over his arm until he could tease and caress the swollen nipple pushing against the fabric of her gown.

Bryce felt her near surrender and slid the arm restraining her lower, so he could stroke between the hollow of her thighs.

"Damn you to hell, Bryce." She cursed breathlessly and turned around in his embrace to beat her fists against his chest. "What? What do you have to say to me?"

With his arms still around her, Bryce lowered his mouth to hers. "Kiss me, Marianne." She parted her lips, sliding her hands up over his shoulders.

He wasn't certain how, but he tried to convey the depth of his love for her in the sensual caress of their tongues. He pulled her closer, deepening their kiss, silently praying that she understood what he was trying to tell her.

When his own knees weakened, he groaned and slid his lips toward her ear. "I am not betrothed to Cecily of Glynnson." He threaded his fingers through her hair, forcing her head back before sliding the tip of his tongue up her throat.

"The unsigned document is in my saddlebag, Marianne." He scraped his teeth along the line of her jaw, pausing to kiss each spot.

"No promises were exchanged." He gently brushed her lips. "Do you believe me?"

"Yes." She answered without hesitation.

His chest tightened. For the first time in his life, Bryce had the sudden urge to cry with relief. He swallowed hard, forcing back the unmanly emotion.

"Even though you so cruelly tricked me into listening to you, I believe you." Marianne laced her fingers behind his neck. "Do not stop now."

With a groan, he gave her the kiss she wanted. A long, slow, give-and-take mating that had him ready to lower them both to the floor.

She squirmed against him, and then pushed away with a ragged gasp. "This is not going to be enough."

Bryce threaded a shaking hand through his hair and glanced around the empty room. "I do not think we have a choice."

Marianne followed his perusal. "There is not even a pallet in here. What are they thinking?"

"It is a cell, Marianne, not a private chamber."

"There is no call for such treatment." She turned toward the door. Bryce caught her wrist and tugged her back to him.

"No. Let it go. In all honesty, I would do the same thing." Certain she would not go running to Darius, he released his hold and stroked her arm. "Besides, I need to think and this will provide the perfect opportunity."

She came against him, resting her cheek on his chest. "What needs such intense consideration?"

"Much." He stepped back and lowered himself to the floor. With his back propped against the wall, he extended his hand. "Join me?"

Marianne sat down beside him and drew his head to her shoulder. She gently ran her fingers through his hair. "What do we need to consider?"

Bryce ducked away, turned and rested his head on her lap. "That is better. Now I can see you."

"And I you." She stroked a longish wave of hair from his face. Her fingers were cool against his still over-heated skin.

"Something is most definitely afoot."

"With?"

"Everything. Which I believe includes the destruction of Ashforde."

Marianne rested her arm across his chest. A frown lined her forehead. "What makes you think that?"

"There is the small matter of the sword that is not yours. Then Sir John disobeys my order and ends up Faucon's prisoner." He stopped for a moment. "I wonder where he is being held."

She readily supplied the answer. "In a cell in one of the guard towers."

"Now Glynnson is at Faucon."

"And that is suspect?"

"Aye, considering the empress swore the man would remain loyal to her alone."

"Glynnson?" Marianne laughed softly. "Please. The man has changed his allegiance how many times now?"

"Four or five that I can recall."

"And you believed he would not do so again?"

"Obviously. Otherwise I never would have considered a betrothal to his daughter."

Marianne placed a kiss on his forehead. "I mean no disrespect to your taste in women, but she seems a bit...overly emotional for you."

"Just a bit?" He tapped her chin with a fingertip. "And what, my lady, is wrong with my taste in women?"

"When it comes to me, you have perfect taste and judgment. But she is…I am not certain that she'd make such an excellent chatelaine for Ashforde."

"I did not know that at the time. She gave the appearance of a well-bred, well-mannered, unemotional, cold sort of woman."

"Oh, aye, cold and unemotional would suit you well." Marianne laughed.

"You share Jared's opinion of her then."

She rolled her eyes upward. "Wonderful. Now I am in agreement with a nasty dragon."

"You might be surprised to know that he suggested you would be a better match."

Marianne stared down at him with wide eyes. "Surprised does not begin to describe my thoughts." She grew serious again. "What do you think accounts for her change in manners?"

"I do not know. The only thing I am certain of is that somehow these oddities are tied together."

"What makes you think that?"

"There are too many all at one time. It is as if I am being used as a pawn for something."

"Ashforde perhaps?"

"No. Ashforde was nothing worth arranging such an elaborate plot to get me killed. The only reason Matilda gave me the charter for Ashforde is because I had the coin to improve the fortifications."

"Perhaps that's it. Maybe she's in Glynnson's debt and promised him a rich son-by-marriage. You came along and saved her life at a time when she had a keep needing someone wealthy enough to hold it."

"I'm sure that much is true."

Marianne added, "But it does not explain why it appears that someone wants you dead at the hands of my brother."

"Nor does it explain Cecily and Sir John's participation in this game."

The moment the words were out of his mouth, he and Marianne stared at each other. Bryce sat up cursing. "That is it!"

"She is the love who was stolen from him."

"And as a guard for the empress, he has nothing more than the clothing on his back."

"So," Marianne leaned forward, "once Cecily found out she was to be given to you in marriage, they hatched a plot between them."

Bryce picked up on her train of thought. "They had Ashforde destroyed knowing full well the charter left me no choice but to rebuild."

"Once the fortifications were underway, you would no longer be needed."

He raised his hand. "Wait. Go back a step. Cecily and I would have had to marry first before she could inherit the property upon my death."

Marianne rose and paced the small cell. "Could their timing have been off? They had no way of knowing that you would take it into your head to rescue me from kidnappers."

"Maybe not in the beginning, but eventually, yes, they knew." He rose and paced alongside of her.

"How?"

"Sir John knew my plans. He knew I intended to have my men take you hostage so I could rescue you. The plan was to gain access to Faucon so I could ferret out information to pass on to the empress."

Marianne stopped pacing. She put her hands on her hips and shot him a glare. "I beg your pardon?"

"Well…" Bryce shrugged and returned her glare with a sheepish grin. "How was I supposed to know I'd fall in love with you? The idea was to gain Faucon's gratitude, pass on the information and let someone else do the killing."

"How utterly noble of you."

He stopped in front of her and slipped his arms about her. "Now, now, love, that was in the past."

"And it had better stay there, or else."

"Or else what?"

Marianne's eyebrows winged above her eyes. She reached down and rubbed the palm of her hand against the bulge in his groin. "Or else there will be no more of that, my lord."

"That would truly be a fate worse than death."

She nodded. "Just keep that thought in the back of your mind."

"I will." As good as the woman in his arms felt, he could not get his mind off Cecily and John. "No matter what we think may or may not have happened, we have no proof."

"So, we must find a way to get it. I can make friends with Cecily. And I can have Darius, or even Sir Melwyn have a talk with your man."

"If anyone does speak to Sir John, see if they can discover where the missing men are."

"I will." She leaned against him. "Now, where were we?"

"Sitting on the floor talking."

"Before that."

Bryce slowly shook his head. "I can't seem to remember."

She rubbed her breasts against his chest, snaked her arms about his neck and drew his head down. "Let me see if I can remind you."

He followed her lead, letting her initiate the rhythm and strength of their kiss. Her slow and gentle exploration quickly turned passionate—demanding his complete attention.

The door to the cell banged against the wall. Before Bryce could lift his lips away from Marianne's, the sharp end of a sword pierced the first layer of flesh just above his shoulder.

"Step away or die where you stand."

"Rhys!" Marianne pushed Bryce away from her brother's weapon. "We did not expect you until tomorrow."

"Obviously."

Bryce rubbed the new wound and shook his head at the blood on his fingers. "That's the third and last time one of you draws my blood." Why did they always aim at his neck?

"The next time will be my blade through your heart. So you've no need to worry about a little nick."

"Stop it." Marianne stood in front of Bryce. "Stop this nonsense. Is this how you treat the man who rescued me? He kept me safe and returned me to Faucon. He deserves better than this."

"Marianne." Bryce tried to nudge her out of the way, but she refused to move.

"Rescued you? Kept you safe?"

From the rage-filled look on Faucon's face, Bryce was certain he'd already talked to his wife and family.

Comte Faucon grabbed Marianne's arm and nearly flung her aside. The wall stopped her from going too far.

Bryce doubled his fist and landed a blow on Faucon's jaw. "Never…ever lay a hand on her again."

The two men stood toe to toe. Not even a woman's cursing from the doorway took Bryce's focus from the man before him.

Marianne tugged at his arm. "Bryce, please."

Without taking his stare from Faucon, he ordered, "Go. Leave us be, Marianne."

Another woman grabbed the comte's arm. "Rhys, stop this right now."

Faucon shrugged off her hold. "Lyonesse, take my sister and go." He handed her his weapon. "Take this with you." A smirk crossed his mouth. "I will not need it."

Faucon's wife cursed again, "For the love of God." But she did her husband's bidding. "Come, Marianne. Leave these children to their play."

Marianne hung back. "Please, Rhys, Bryce, do not do this."

"Get her out of here!" Faucon's shout lifted the hair around Bryce's face.

If this was his method of intimidation, Bryce was not impressed. The devil comte's fierce expression and loud voice amused him more than frightened him.

He waited until the women left the cell. Then he smiled in the comte's face before asking, "Are you ready to meet your match, Faucon?"

Chapter Eighteen

Marianne followed Lyonesse down to her chamber. She walked through the doorway and paused to look about the room. While it was true that she'd only been away for a matter of days, it felt as if she had been gone from Faucon for years.

The small, but comfortable chamber held all of her cherished possessions, but they appeared childish to her now.

Instead of going into the small alcove to the right of the door, Lyonesse sat on Marianne's bed and patted the spot beside her. "Come, sit down."

It was all Marianne could do not to run from the room and back up to the tower cell. Instead, she ran to Lyonesse and dropped to her knees before her sister.

She'd only known this woman a little more than a year, but they shared so much in common. Each of them had been raised more as a boy than a girl. They each had a temper that could flare up over the slightest transgression—real or imagined. They both loved and cherished their family.

And now, they both worried about the men they loved.

Marianne's breath stuck in her throat. "What will happen?"

Lyonesse brushed her hand down Marianne's hair and shook her head. "I can only imagine that they will beat each other to a bloody pulp."

"And we will stand by and let them?" Marianne despised the quivering of her bottom lip. But not even biting it made the motion cease.

"Yes, that is exactly what we will do…for a time."

Marianne ignored the moisture gathering in her eyes. She would not cry. If Bryce and Rhys were childish enough to engage in a fistfight, they deserved whatever happened.

She stared up at Lyonesse, searching for answers. "How can you bear it?"

"Marianne, why is this upsetting you so?"

"I do not wish to see either man get hurt."

Lyonesse patted her shoulder. "That sort of fear will lead only to your own madness. You need learn to face it, Marianne. Stare it in the eye and then swallow it, until it is nothing more than another chore to lengthen your day."

"How can you dare tell me that you do not fear for Rhys's safety? I have seen it on your face."

"Perhaps. But have you heard it leave my lips?"

Marianne's mind raced over all the recent times Rhys had left to join King Stephen. Her sister-by-marriage was correct. Not once had Lyonesse voiced her fear. "No. No, I have not."

"To do so would only give it power over me. I would spend every heartbeat of each day terrified he would return slung across the back of his horse."

"I am not certain your way can be mine."

"You have no other choice." The fingers on her shoulders tightened. "We love warriors, you and I. It could be no other way for either of us. Unfortunately, it is the nature of warriors to love nothing better than fighting." Lyonesse paused, stroking Marianne's face she continued, "And now, you claim to have given your heart to a man of the same ilk as your brother."

"I have."

"Is it love or lust, Marianne?" Rhian's voice carried across the chamber over the closing of the chamber door. She and Marguerite entered the room.

"I have wondered the same thing myself." Marianne lowered her face toward the floor. "To my chagrin, I have not been able to decide."

At the sound of a heavy thud reverberating through the ceiling from the cell above, all four women stared up. Marguerite sighed before she said, "You had best make up your mind quickly, because your brothers will want an answer before they make any final decision on your Comte Ashforde."

"They will kill each other."

Rhian laughed at Marianne's hushed comment. "Nay. At least not in this manner." All three women looked at her in question. "You do not truly think this bullying of each other is going to be the end of this matter, do you?"

Marianne groaned; then she rested her forehead on Lyonesse's bent knees. "Dear Lord, what have I done? This is my fault."

Marguerite patted Marianne's back. "No, child, it is not your fault."

"How can you be blamed for growing from a child into a woman?" Rhian took a seat next on the bed.

"It is our fault. It is your brothers' fault." Lyonesse's voice seemed to trail off. When Marianne looked up at her, she shook her head. "It is mostly Rhys's fault for not listening to all of us. And for not seeing the proof before his own eyes. He would not accept the simple fact that you had indeed grown up."

Rhian added, "We should have forced him to accept an offer for you. Any offer. You would have learned to care for the man eventually."

"No." Marianne pulled away and rose. "No. Had you done so I would never have met Bryce."

Marguerite laughed. "That is the idea."

"Hush." Lyonesse waved a hand at the other wives. "Let her talk."

"I never would have known the height my anger could soar, or the sweetness in a simple touch against my cheek, or softly whispered word. Never would I have experienced such fear of a man, or such a longing in even his briefest absence."

The three other women groaned in unison.

"A look from a man *chosen* to keep me content," she glanced toward the women, "would never have made my stomach flutter, or my heart race. I would not have cared what he thought. Nor would I have tried to find a way to ease whatever bedeviled him."

She crossed to the window, stared out and paused. Had she just answered her only question? Marianne thought perhaps she had.

Rhian asked, "If he could never again take you to his bed, would you still treasure a simple touch? Would you still long for him to return from battle?"

Marguerite added another question. "Would you care about what bedeviled his mind, or his day?"

"Would contentment be enough then, or would you soon look to another for fulfillment?" asked Lyonesse.

"I would never treat him so." Marianne spun away from the window and glared at Lyonesse.

At the echo of another thud, followed immediately by yet another one, Rhian rose from the bed. "We need to stop this. Now."

Marguerite nodded. "Yes. Obviously, Marianne has answered her own and our question." She looked to Lyonesse. "It is time Rhys and the others be made aware of this."

Lyonesse rose, too. "You see to your husbands. I will get Melwyn to see to mine."

Marianne moved toward the door. The three women barred her exit. "No." Lyonesse shook her head. "You need stay out of this. Rhys will not listen to you and you could make it worse. I will order you a bath."

"But—"

Rhian said, "She is right, Marianne. Take your bath. Dress. And do what you can to gird yourself for what is to come. Your comte is not going to get out of this easily. He may need you to be strong."

"Meet my match? Ashforde, you are but an arrogant pup who still needs his arse wiped."

Bryce fully expected Faucon to laugh at his challenge. So, this baiting answer did not anger him in the least. While they were the same height and roughly the same build, Faucon was older. His chest was fuller, stomach wider, whether that was from age, or fighting remained to be seen.

Instead of waiting for Faucon to make the first move, Bryce lowered his shoulder and plowed into the older man's chest. The comte swayed on his feet, but remained standing.

Obviously, the added fullness was not from age. This wouldn't be the first, nor last, beating he took, but Bryce was determined to give as good as he got.

Faucon drew back his shoulders and slammed a fisted hand against his own chest. "Want to try again?"

By the saints, no. Instead, Bryce cocked his arm and threw a punch toward his opponent's jaw. Faucon grabbed his fist halfway to its target. "You will have to do better than that."

Both men strained against each other. Bryce was unable to force his fist forward, but Faucon was also unable to force it back.

Bryce realized the comte was accurately judging his next move by the barest flicker of Bryce's eyes. It was a good way to stay alive in battle and Faucon had perfected his skill.

So, he glanced at a spot just below Faucon's neck, and then swept the man's legs out from beneath him with one solid kick to a kneecap.

The comte staggered back, before dropping to the floor on his rear with a heavy thud. Still agile, he quickly sprang back to his feet.

But then he kept moving, lowering his head and barreling into Bryce with a force that slammed his back hard against the wall.

The room momentarily went black while Bryce

fought for breath. It gave Faucon enough time to land two blows to Bryce's face.

Blows that cleared his head, enabling him to swing back. His fist made contact with Faucon's already crooked nose. When the comte swung away, Bryce threw a punch at his lower back.

Faucon grunted and spun around. Blood ran from his nose and Bryce hoped he'd broken it.

"Ashforde, do you have any last words before I break your traitorous neck?"

"Traitor? Who is the real traitor here? Did not every baron swear allegiance to King Henry's daughter? Are they not honor bound to support Matilda's right to wear the crown?"

"No man willingly follows a woman of her ilk."

"Her ilk?" Bryce laughed at the common excuse. "Her father was a king, her first husband an emperor, how could she not be a strong woman?"

"Is that what you call her? A *strong* woman?"

"If you do not take her life into account it is easy to name her a viper who acts more like a man than a woman."

Faucon shrugged off the comment. "She is still a woman. One who is neither Norman nor English."

"You cannot hold Matilda to blame for being given to a German Emperor at such a young age. Her ways may not be familiar to us, but she has men—both English and Norman—as advisors. Advisors she respects." To himself, Bryce added, *and sometimes listens to.*

"Discussing politics is useless, Ashforde. I'll not turn my back on King Stephen."

"Nay, perhaps not. But someday the tide of this anarchy may change. What will you do then?"

"That will never happen."

"You cannot be certain of that." Bryce silently hoped his next suggestion might be worth Faucon's consideration. "Would it not be in your best interest to have ties with someone loyal to the empress?"

"What are you asking?"

"I am asking nothing, Faucon. I am going to marry your sister."

The comte roared, "Over my dead body!" before walking toward him with steady, calculating steps. "It will never happen. You have been found a traitor and will die by my sword."

Bryce shrugged. "You may want to wait a few months before killing me. Just to ensure she does not carry the heir to Ashforde."

He hoped that smugly offered information would send Faucon close to the edge of pure rage. If the man lost control, perhaps Bryce could then defeat him.

What he didn't count on was Faucon's laugh. "Marianne would not dishonor herself in such a manner."

"And if you are wrong?"

"If I am wrong, it will not matter. She still would not be permitted to marry you."

"You cannot watch her every day for the rest of her life."

The two men circled each other like snapping wolves. Bryce waited for Faucon to make another move. And he knew the comte was doing the same.

"What will you do, Ashforde? Plan to have her kidnapped again?"

Obviously, Sir John's tongue wagged with the slightest breeze. He only hoped the man wasn't dead—he wanted to be the one who meted out the man's demise. "If need be, yes."

"And will you then rescue her again? Only a spineless coward would use a woman to gain revenge."

"Your barbs are useless, Faucon. I care not what you think."

"You claim to have defiled my sister—you would be wise to care very much about what I think."

"Defiled? I did not rape your sister. No force was involved. She is a woman, Faucon, a woman who knows what she wants."

"And you think she wanted you? The first man she'd been alone with? You were nothing but a snake that she was not equipped to handle."

"She loves me."

"Of course she does—because she does not know any better."

"She is not a brainless child." Bryce suddenly found his own temper rising. How could Faucon disparage Marianne?

And what would the comte do if he discovered that his own brother had more or less arranged for Marianne to be, in Faucon's words, defiled? Bryce owed Darius much for giving him that one night. But he'd not divulge that information—not even under the promise of death.

"No? Her judgment is so lacking that she slept with the enemy. If she did so of her own free will, that also makes her a traitor."

"You would never name her such. To do so would put her life in jeopardy."

"You have no idea what I would or would not do with her."

Bryce knew Faucon was doing this on purpose. That knowledge did nothing to stop the red haze of anger from clouding his mind. "Touch her and you will die."

"Since you will be gone from here, you will never know."

Bryce lunged, tackling Faucon around the waist and knocking him to the floor. He jumped to his feet first, only to have the comte grab his ankle and jerk him back down to the floor.

Both men tussled on the floor, each fighting to get away from the other one first. Finally, Bryce slammed his fist against Faucon's ear, giving him the chance to get away.

The comte shook his head. While the blow might have stunned him, it didn't keep him down. Faucon stood up and glared at Bryce for a long heartbeat before saying, "You can stop me from declaring her a traitor."

The door to the cell swung open. Melwyn barged in with his sword drawn and pointed it at Bryce's chest. To Faucon, he said, "My lord, your wife needs you."

The comte headed toward the door. "How?" Bryce called out, stopping him, "How can I stop you?"

Faucon turned to face him. A smile that boded only ill will creased his mouth into a sneer. "Trial by combat. Tomorrow morning."

"To the death?"

Without hesitation, Faucon answered, "Aye."

Her bath done, Marianne finished dressing and sat down on the padded bench in her alcove. The thuds from the cell above had ceased while she'd bathed. Hopefully, the women were able to talk sense into her brothers.

She worried more about Rhys than the other two. Darius would need little convincing. Had he not believed that Bryce truly cared for her, he never would have let them spend the night together in the hunter's croft.

Gareth might be a little harder to convince. But not much. If Rhian could rationally explain this relationship, he would mull it over and most likely agree that the match would suit.

Rhys on the other hand was far too angry right now to listen to anyone…including his wife. Marianne was sorry she'd put Lyonesse in this position. It would take much screaming and yelling on her part to get her pig-headed husband to the point where he would even listen. There was no telling if he would ever agree to a match.

The door to her chamber opened. Marianne leaned forward and peered around the curtain that separated the alcove from her chamber.

"Are you decent?" Her brother Gareth stood at the threshold.

She rose, ran toward him and threw herself into his open arms. "I am never decent."

He lifted her off the floor in his embrace. "I know, little sister, I know." After planting a loud smacking kiss on her cheek, Gareth lowered her to the floor. "What have you done now, Marianne?"

She caught a glimpse of a hand reaching in to pull the door to her chamber closed. "Who was that?"

"Your guards." Gareth moved her farther into the chamber—away from the door.

"I beg your pardon?" When she tried to move around him, he grasped her arm, easily keeping her from opening the door to confront the men.

"Guards. Surely you remember what they are."

"Of course I do." Marianne narrowed her eyes. "They keep prisoners locked in their cells."

He tugged her over to the alcove and pushed her down on the stone bench. "They also keep wayward children from doing themselves harm."

"I am home now, what harm can I do to myself?"

Gareth knelt on the floor before her. He placed his hands on her shoulders. Marianne gasped at the sudden seriousness in his overly bright, leaf-green eyes.

"What is wrong?" Her voice shook, but not as much as the hand she placed on his chest.

"Do you truly love him, Marianne?"

"Yes." She answered him with as much conviction as possible in a single word.

"Did this man kidnap you? Did he at any time force you to do anything?"

Where had he gotten such an idea? "No, Gareth, I swear, never once did Bryce force me to do anything." She felt her face warm. "In all honesty, I would say it was the other way around."

His smile was as soft as his chuckle. "I have good reason to believe you."

Marianne could only imagine what lengths Rhian had gone to in getting this duty-bound man to love her enough to set honor and duty aside.

"Gareth, what has happened?"

"Your Ashforde is a traitor to the crown, but you know this already, do you not?"

"Aye. It matters not to me which crown he serves." A crooked grin teased her lips. "Because in the end, he serves me, Gareth."

Her brother cleared his throat and clasped her shoulders. "Marianne, he will not leave Faucon alive."

"No." She struggled against his unyielding hold, trying to break free.

Gareth easily held her in place. "You can scream, or wail, or fight all you wish. It will change nothing."

"He has done nothing. Nothing! Not to any one of you, nor to Faucon. How can you permit this?"

"Permit it? The Comte of Faucon has ordered a trial by combat. I cannot challenge his order."

Marianne's heart tripped. "Then there is a chance Bryce will not die."

Gareth's eyes widened. "Do not be foolish. If he manages to kill Rhys, I will not let him walk out the gates. Neither will Darius."

"But—"

"Dear God above, Marianne. Even if you no longer love your brother, you owe Rhys some measure of respect and gratitude."

Gareth's harsh tone made her ashamed of herself. "I do." Marianne swallowed the lump choking her. "I do still love Rhys. I always will. He is owed more than just my respect and gratitude."

She knew how much she owed all of her brothers. Rhys the most. Who had cared for her immediately after their parents died? In whose arms had she cried? Who had chased away the nightmares and fear?

Darius had not been present—having been disowned and tossed from Faucon by their sire when she was little more than a small child. While Gareth had made her laugh again, it had been Rhys who'd borne the brunt of her grief. And he'd done so without complaint.

Was there the slightest chance that Rhys still cared for her? Even if he no longer wished to see her, it was a chance she had to take.

"Can I talk to him?"

"Who?"

"Rhys."

"No." Gareth shook his head. "Marianne, everyone has already tried. There is no argument you can offer that has not already been used."

"I cannot let the men I love kill each other. I have to try."

"It does not matter. Rhys is not here."

"Not here?"

Gareth sighed before he explained, "Do you not think he knows how easily you and Lyonesse can wrap him around your fingers? To avoid the possibility, he and Melwyn have left Faucon and will return in the morn."

"In time to see to Bryce's death."

"Yes."

The lump in her throat returned. But swallowing hard no longer forced it down. Marianne bit her lip, hoping the pain would keep her from embarrassing not only herself, but Gareth, too.

He pulled her head to his shoulder. "There is no shame in crying for someone you love. It is something you will be doing for days to come, Marianne."

She felt the tears well in her eyes and shoved her hands against Gareth's chest. "No. I cannot give up that easily."

"Have you heard a word I've said? There is nothing you can do to stop this. Come the morn, you and the other women will be confined to this chamber. Guards will be placed at the door and you will remain here until all is finished."

"Why this chamber?" She knew the answer the moment she'd asked the question.

"You cannot see the practice grounds from this side of the keep."

"Am I not confined to this chamber now?"

"Not precisely. Rhys ordered the guards to keep an eye over you, that is all." Gareth warily eyed her. "Why?"

Marianne notched her chin higher. "I want to see Bryce."

"Do you think that wise? It will only make his death harder for you."

She would burn in hell before letting this happen. But she needed to talk to Bryce. He could help her figure out what to do. "No. It will be harder if I cannot bid him farewell."

Gareth shrugged. "Can you promise me that you and he will not…" He paused and Marianne saw the flush cover his face. "That you…"

She wanted to laugh, but the heavy fear and sadness in her chest overshadowed any tidbit of humor. She and Bryce had more important matters to attend to than the urgings of their desire. "Yes, Gareth. I vow that Bryce and I will not spend the night coupling in the cell."

He breathed a loud sigh of relief and then rose to his feet. "Then I will take you to him…but not for the entire night I fear."

"I care not. I will gladly welcome whatever time you can spare us." She crossed to the bed and grabbed a pillow and a cover, explaining, "His cell is cold and bare. I refuse to spend the time shivering so hard I cannot speak."

Gareth opened the door to her chamber and said something to the guards before beckoning her to follow him up the stairs to the cell.

Once they reached the cell, Gareth dismissed those guards. Marianne looked at him, speechless.

"Oh, fear not, there will be no chance for you to help Ashforde escape. I will guard the cell myself."

With that brief hope dashed, Marianne nodded. "As you wish."

Gareth opened the door to the cell, letting her enter before he closed and dropped the locking bar on the outside back in place.

Chapter Nineteen

The cell door swung open with a groan. Bryce paused over his task of inspecting his chain mail armor for obvious weak links. With only the pale light from the moon, a cursory inspection was the best he could do to ensure his death on the morn would not be caused by inferior equipment.

For some reason that was important to him. And he had no clue why. It seemed rather odd, vain even, to want his armor to be presentable. Should his mind not be on things like Marianne, or Ashforde, or all the things he would never complete, never do?

"Bryce?"

His heart slammed against his chest at the sound of Marianne's voice. He'd not expected to see her this night—or ever again. A part of him was gladdened by her presence. He could think of no greater gift for his last night in this world. Neither could he think of anything worse for her. "Go away, Marianne."

She raced toward him, throwing the items in her arms

to the floor. He barely had time to push his armor from his lap before she landed against his chest.

"No. I will not go away."

Her hands were cool and soothing against his bruised face. Her breath was warm against his ear.

Unable to stop himself, Bryce wound his arms tightly about her and buried his face in her still damp hair. She had recently bathed. He smelled the lingering traces of an all-too-familiar soap.

She was home at Faucon, with every luxury at her disposal. Yet, she bathed with his crudely made, rosemary-scented soap. The notion nearly unmanned him.

"How did you get in here?"

"My brother Gareth. He guards the door."

"Has he lost the ability to reason?"

"No." She rested her cheek on his shoulder. "Why would you think such a thing?"

"Because it was wrong for him to let you come here."

"I had to see you again." She traced the line of his jaw. "To touch you again."

"Marianne, this will only make my passing harder for you."

"You will not die, Bryce."

Did she know what she was saying? "If I do not, that means that Rhys will. Surely, you cannot be naive enough to think Darius and Gareth would permit me to live after I killed the comte?"

"Then we best get busy."

"Doing what?"

"Finding a solution to this dilemma."

He should have known she'd not give up hope.

Somehow, he needed to force her to accept the inevitable. "You think I have not tried?"

"Obviously, not hard enough."

A sharp rap on the door stopped their conversation. The door swung open again and Gareth reached in far enough to drop a sack on the floor.

This time when the door closed, Bryce heard the scrape of the locking bar as it slid into place.

Marianne rose and gathered the items she had arrived with, then she grabbed the sack. She took them to the opposite corner of the cell—the same side as the door.

"What are you doing?"

She set everything down and made a bed in the corner with the covers and pillow. She then dumped what appeared to be food and a wineskin on the bed before carrying something else to the door.

"Gareth." Marianne tapped on the small peekhole in the door. When the panel slid open she held up a candle. "This is useless without fire."

Her brother took the candle from her, handed it back lit and then slid the panel closed once again.

Marianne put the candle in a holder and set it an arm's length from the bed before coming back to him. "Come, have something to eat while we plan what to do."

When she reached down to him, Bryce hesitated. He should order her away. Say, or do anything to make her so angry that she'd not care what happened on the morrow.

He looked up at her and opened his mouth.

"Do not even try."

He blinked. "Try what?"

"To send me away with lies I will never believe." She shook her hand. "Bryce, please."

He took her hand, rose and let her lead him the four steps to the bed. "How did you know?" he asked, taking a seat on the covers.

She sat next to him and rummaged in the sack. "I guessed. It seemed something you would try in order to protect me."

"It would be easier if you despised me."

"If I hated you, we would not be in this position."

She pulled out a hunk of bread and handed it to him, dropping the sack when she looked up at him. "What happened to your face?"

Bryce moved his head away from her fingers. "I am fine. However, I do believe I broke Rhys's nose."

"Good." Marianne laughed. "Although with his luck, I bet you simply put it back in place from the last break."

The bread tasted and felt like sawdust in his mouth. He was not the least bit hungry, but he did need something to wash down the bread. "Is there anything in there to drink?"

"Yes." She handed him a wineskin. "But I have no idea what."

He didn't care if it was nothing but water. A sniff of the opened skin proved it to be wine. The last thing he needed to do this night was to drink his fill of wine. Bryce took a sip and handed it back to her.

When she offered him some cheese, he waved it off. "No. I am not hungry, Marianne."

"You have to eat. You cannot let yourself be weak from lack of a meal."

Bryce laughed wryly. "I never eat before a battle. It only makes me vomit."

"Ah." She put the food back into the sack and set it aside. "So, what are we going to do?"

He leaned back against the wall, turned her around and pulled her head down onto his lap. "*We* are going to do nothing."

When she tried to sit up, he held her down with an arm across her chest.

"Marianne, be still." He brushed the fine hairs at her temples away from her face. "Just let me look at you. Let me hold you."

"You cannot simply give up."

"That is exactly what I intend to do."

"Bryce, no. What will become of me?"

"You will grieve. For a time you will hate your brother. Then, something inside you will find a reason to live and love again."

"I will never—"

"Hush." He traced her cheekbones, trying to memorize her features. "You were never meant to be alone, Marianne. You were born to love and be loved. You may not believe me now, but someday you will find someone who will hold your heart close and keep it safe."

"You are that person."

Bryce shook his head. "Nay. Listen to it. Does your heart feel safe this moment? Does it believe there is a future for us? Or, does it ache because it knows the truth?"

"I thought you were a warrior. I thought you would fight until the end."

"It is the end." He paused, trying to find a way to explain. "When I first came to Faucon, seeking to have you kidnapped, I knew the risks. I knew there was a possibility that I could die before gaining the revenge I sought."

"That was before."

"Yes, it was. But the risks never changed. I cannot kill your brother, Marianne. I love you far too much to dishonor myself in such a manner."

"Dishonor? Honor?" Her voice rose. "What good is honor if you are dead?"

"It is honor that will permit me to die at peace, instead of begging for my life like a spineless coward."

"I would rather you be a spineless coward."

"No, you would not." He smiled at the glare she gave him. "You would not have given me a second look had you thought me spineless."

"So it will be honorable to stand there and let Rhys plant his sword in your chest?"

"Stand there? I never said I would not make him earn the right to take my life."

"No. You will fight and all the while wait for the right moment to make yourself a target."

"Yes."

"Bryce of Ashforde, I hate you." She turned her face into his stomach and slid both arms around him.

"I can tell, love."

"I cannot live without you."

Her choked statement made his blood run cold. He pulled her arms from his waist and jerked her up onto his lap. When she looked away, he grabbed her chin and turned her face toward him. "Listen to me and listen well, little girl."

"I am not a little girl."

"Then cease talking like one. You are not to entertain such a foolish notion. Not even for one heartbeat. Do you hear me?"

"You will not be here to stop me."

Rage turned the ice in his veins to fire. "How do you know you do not carry my child? You would risk its life because you could not have what you wanted?"

"Wanted? I do not *want* you. I *need* you. Like I need the very air I breathe."

"Fine. Then I will promise you this—before I die, I will warn your brother."

"You would not."

"Like hell I wouldn't."

"Go ahead. Tell him. They cannot watch me for the rest of my life. Besides there is no way of knowing if I carry a child or not."

Before she knew what he was doing, Bryce had her flat on her back. He loomed over her, his legs between hers, his hands on either side of her head.

Marianne gasped at the look on his face. It was not the look of a lover ready to gently take her to that chasm of pleasure. It was an angry, determined look of a man seeking to frighten her.

"Bryce." She touched his cheek.

He jerked his face away from her touch. "Before this night is over, rest assured, you will be carrying a child."

Dear Lord, not like this. She had only to call out and Gareth would stop this from happening. She opened her mouth…then pursed her lips tightly.

If she could not have Bryce, perhaps she could have his child to love. She need only quickly find a way to soothe his anger.

He fumbled with his braies, then pushed up the skirts of her bliaut and chemise. Without flinching Marianne stared into the ice-blue rage glittering in his eyes and wrapped her legs around his hips.

When the tip of his erection pressed against the soft folds of her flesh, she clamped her legs tighter and pushed up. Taking him into her, she whispered, "Aye, give me our child, Bryce."

He gasped, the rage turned to horror at what he'd done. When he thought to pull away from her, Marianne tipped her hips higher. "No. Stay."

She wrapped her arms around his neck. "Love me. Give me a memory to hold onto in the days to come."

Bryce gathered her into his arms. His heart pounded against her chest. His breath was ragged against her ear. "I am sorry. Dear Lord, I am sorry."

Marianne ground her hips against him. She moaned softly, before biting his shoulder. "Be sorry later."

He kissed her neck and fell into a gentle rhythm against her, as if taking her for the first time.

She wanted none of his gentleness. She burned for him. "Bryce, please." Marianne raked her nails down his back. "Take me like we will never get another chance."

He pulled up and away from her, kneeling between her legs. "Roll over."

"What?" She knew not what he wanted, and just stared up at him.

Bryce grabbed her legs and flipped her onto her stomach before hauling her up to her knees. She looked at him over her shoulder and he smiled back. "Do you trust me?"

"Yes." In all honesty, at this moment she cared not what he did, as long as he eased the throbbing of her body.

He guided himself to her, grasped her hips and pushed forward. Marianne gasped with pleasure at the sudden fullness.

And when he slid one hand around the front and teased the throbbing nub hiding beneath damp curls, she dropped her shoulders and rocked back to meet his thrust.

It was all she could do to swallow her scream. Gareth would mistake it for something other than passion.

This is what she wanted. The sudden falling into the bottomless chasm. The rapid pounding of her heart. The heat coursing through her veins. His hands on her body, filling her, completing her. Making her feel whole.

The pleasure grew until she was certain she could bear it no longer. Rising up from her elbows, Marianne pressed her back against his chest, raised her arms and clasped her hands behind his neck.

He did not break the rhythm of his thrusts, nor of his teasing hand. Instead, he added to the dizzying fall by sharply biting her neck and sliding his other hand over her breast to caress the swollen peak through her clothing.

Marianne threw back her head and bit her lip to keep from crying out her completion. Bryce stiffened against her, sinking his teeth into her shoulder to hold back his own cry.

They both fell limp onto the covers and Marianne's shudder of pleasure turned to sobs.

Bryce rolled off of her and gathered her into his arms, pulling her tight against his chest. "Oh, love, do not."

"I cannot bear it."

"I know. Neither can I, but we must find a way."

His words broke suspiciously and Marianne lifted her head to stare at him. The moisture shimmering in his eyes only made the tightness in her chest more painful.

Yes, she feared what lay ahead. But it was not fair to foist her terror onto his shoulders. He had enough to carry.

Marianne swallowed her tears. She would have many empty endless days to cry. But very little time to share with the man she loved.

She stroked his face, seeking to memorize every line, every scar. "What can I do for you?"

He grasped her hand and kissed her fingers. "When you are able, make certain Jared knows what happened. Tell him not to seek revenge, but to see to Ashforde."

"Do you have any family I should contact?" Marianne felt as if she were watching this conversation take place, instead of participating. It did not feel real.

"Nay. I am but a bastard with no family."

A sudden anger throbbed in her temples. "You are not a bastard. You are Comte Bryce of Ashforde and the man I love."

"Thank you."

"For what?"

"For these last few days. For loving me. For trusting me. Marianne, I vow I will rest easy knowing how much I was loved."

She could not trust herself to speak, so she buried her face against his chest.

"There is one other thing you could do for me."

"What?"

"Ask your brother if I can be buried at Ashforde."

Marianne drew in a long shuddering breath. "I will see to it myself."

He stroked her hair, threading it in and out of his fingers. "I do not want you present tomorrow."

"I do not have a choice. Rhys has ordered all the women be confined to my chamber. It has no view of the field."

"Good."

Her throat was raw from holding back her tears. Even her ears burned from the effort. "I will make certain you have your own sword. What should be done with Sir John?"

"Since he has seen fit to give your brothers all the information they wanted, I care not what happens to him. I do wish you would question Cecily though. Just to see if what we thought is true." He paused and shrugged. "Although, I would not be too harsh on her. Had it not been for their plotting and planning we never would have met."

"I will talk to Cecily." Then Marianne hissed. "And I will see to Sir John's demise myself."

Bryce grasped her hair and pulled her head back. "No. You will do whatever you can to protect yourself." He released her and nuzzled her neck. "We have a child to create and you need care for him above all else."

Marianne slipped a leg between his. "Are there other ways to...that we can...?"

Bryce laughed. "Many."

She rose up on her elbow and stared down at him. "Then we best hurry."

Rhian confronted her husband at the bottom of the steps leading up to the tower cell. "You cannot let Rhys do this."

"I have no choice."

"There is always a choice. What about this Sir John and Cecily? Could they possibly have something to do with Ashforde?"

Gareth shook his head. "I do not know, but it is possible. Perhaps I should find out."

"I would suggest you do so quickly then."

He stared down at his wife. "Aye, my liege."

Rhian smacked his arm. "You see to Sir John and I will pay a visit to Cecily of Glynnson."

Gareth nodded. "Before you do that, send Edgar out looking for Melwyn. See if he can determine Melwyn's opinion on the coming trial."

"And if Melwyn also thinks Rhys has overdone himself?"

"Then have Edgar try to talk him into coming back here. I may have a mission for both of them."

Morning had not yet broken when someone knocked on the door to the cell. Marianne and Bryce awoke in each other's arms, with a start. He kissed her forehead before calling out, "Enter."

Gareth strode into the cell and motioned for Marianne to join him. "Come, 'tis time to return to your chamber."

She hung back, clinging to Bryce's arm. "Not yet. There are still hours before morning arrives."

"I know. But Rhys might return early and I'll not have him discover you here."

Bryce rose, pulling her up with him. He gathered her against his chest, holding her tightly and whispered, "I love you, Marianne. If there truly is an afterlife, I will await you there."

She held his face between her hands and pulled his lips to hers. She kissed him fiercely, trying to fit a lifetime of kisses into a single one.

Gareth cleared his throat. "Please. Do not make this any harder than it is."

Bryce groaned against her mouth, then grasped her shoulders and pushed her away. "Go."

She looked up at him one last time. "I will always love you."

Gareth reached out and took her wrist. "Please, Marianne."

She let him drag her out of the chamber, holding back her tears until he closed and locked the cell door. Once they headed down the stairs, she nearly fell from the sobs racking her body.

Gareth picked her up in his arms and carried her back to her chamber. He kicked the door closed behind them and put her on her feet. Holding her shoulders, he shook her, "Are you a Faucon or not?"

Stunned and already weak from grief, she pulled away from him. "No. I am not a Faucon any longer. In my heart I am Marianne of Ashforde."

"Good. Then if you wish to truly be this Marianne of Ashforde, you might be more concerned about saving your husband than drowning in your premature tears."

A tiny glimmer of renewed hope flared to life. "And how do you suggest I do that?"

Lyonesse, Marguerite and Rhian walked out of her alcove, dragging Cecily of Glynnson behind them. They released her and she fell to the floor at Marianne's feet.

At first speechless, Marianne looked at each of the wives and to Gareth before she stared down at Cecily. "Why are you here?"

Cecily pointed at Lyonesse. "Because she hauled me from my bed."

"No." Marianne grasped Cecily's hair. "Why did you come to Faucon?"

"To see my betrothed."

Marianne knew she had not the time to play this game. She crossed the room to her chest and pulled out her sword. Unsheathing it as she went back to where Cecily sat wide-eyed on the floor.

She placed the tip of the sword to the woman's throat and pressed slightly. "Bryce of Ashforde is not your betrothed, nor has he ever been. He did not sign the last document and the two of you never spoke any words of promise." She twisted the blade a hair. "So, why are you here? How did you know Bryce would be here?"

Cecily visibly swallowed. "It was all his idea."

"Whose?"

"Sir John's."

Marianne doubted if that was completely true, but at least she was now getting somewhere. "His idea to do what?"

"To destroy Ashforde and place the blame on Faucon."

"Why?"

Cecily sobbed. "Because we love each other."

"What does that have to do with anything?" Marianne had already guessed Cecily and Sir John were involved with each other. What she did not understand was the connection to Faucon.

"Sir John and I have been in love with each other for years. But when the empress pledged me to Ashforde, we had to come up with a way to ensure the wedding would never take place."

Cecily paused and Marianne urged, "Go on."

"Do you not see? We had no wealth between us. But if I married Ashforde, we could share his wealth."

"Once he was gone." Lyonesse tried to hurry the tale along.

"Yes."

Rhian asked, "Why Faucon?"

"Because one of them killed Sir John's brother."

Marianne sighed. "So this was an easy way to deal with two people at once."

Cecily nodded. "Until you messed things up."

"I?"

"When Ashforde devised the plan to have you kidnapped so he could rescue you, Sir John paid other men to kidnap you. But they were supposed to kill you."

Marianne shook her head. "I fail to follow your logic."

"John was to let it be known that your death was at Ashforde's hands."

Something was not right. Neither Sir John nor Cecily seemed quick enough to devise this plan between them. Marianne narrowed her eyes and shifted her sword. She now held the edge of the blade across Cecily's throat.

"Who really devised this plan?"

"John and I." When the sword wavered against her neck, Cecily cried out, "My father and the empress."

Gareth cursed. He took the sword from Marianne's hand and slid it in its scabbard.

She stepped away from Cecily with her own curse. "I have to go." Marianne looked to Gareth. "Can you get me out of Faucon?"

"We can do better than that." Rhian and Marguerite stepped forward. Lyonesse went back into the alcove and returned with a pair of braies, a vest of hardened leather and a long quilted gambeson. She pressed the armor against Marianne's chest. "Put this on first."

Marianne stepped into the braies, tying them snugly

around her waist. As she slipped her arms into the gambeson and leather hauberc, Gareth opened the door, giving Darius, Melwyn and Edgar admittance.

Melwyn's bushy eyebrows met over his dark eyes as he stared at her. "Sir John is dead."

"Hell!" Marianne shouted over Cecily's noisy sobs.

Darius smiled. "But we know where his friend Eustace headed."

Marianne had hoped Eustace went to Warehaven.

"He slipped away when I spotted Sir John at the docks." Darius handed Marianne a mailed coiffe and nasal helm. "The man went to The Lair."

Marianne could not have contained her yelp of glee if she'd tried. "Good."

Rhian twisted Marianne's braids together and stuffed them beneath the coiffe before dropping the helmet on her head. While she strapped it tightly in place, she asked, "I assume you know who and where that is?"

"Aye." Marianne nodded. "It is Jared of Warehaven, the Dragon."

Rhian knelt before her and tapped Gareth's leg. "Give me your dagger." She took the short blade and slit the skirt of Marianne's bliaut and chemise. "Turn around." She then did the same with the back.

Melwyn muttered beneath his breath as he laced mailed chauces to her legs. "If we live through this day I will be surprised."

Edgar stepped behind Marianne and pulled the laces of her gambeson and hauberk tight before tying them off. "It seems that the last patrol spotted a large group of armed strangers entering Faucon's demesne lands."

Marguerite spun Marianne around and knotted the

sword belt about her waist. Her scabbard and sword hung at her left side.

Gareth grasped her shoulders and kissed her on the cheek. "Go with God, Marianne."

At the door of the chamber, Darius handed her a dagger that she shoved into her belt and a pair of leather gloves. "Be a good warrior and find an army to rescue your man."

Chapter Twenty

Uncertain if Gareth had had the time to give orders to the gate guards, Marianne, Edgar and Melwyn walked their saddled horses from the stable. They crept along the wall and out of the postern gate.

Once they gained the clearing between Faucon and the forest, they swung onto their beasts. Melwyn nodded toward the main road and Marianne took the lead, racing away from Faucon.

The night sky turned gray with the coming of dawn. Her hands shook with worry. Would they find Jared in time? She urged her horse faster along the road.

"They should be close," Edgar shouted from the rear.

Melwyn came alongside her. "Slow down and draw your weapon now."

"Now?" She'd learnt long ago that arguing with Melwyn would be futile. He would do more than ignore her, he would in all likelihood turn the horses around and head back to Faucon.

Marianne reined in her horse to a slower pace and

pulled her sword free from the scabbard. The added weight of the armor was unfamiliar to her, making her feel awkward.

Still at her side, Melwyn asked, "Can you swing the weapon?"

She tried. While she managed to keep a tight hold on the grip, her movements were stiff.

Rhys's captain reached over and grasped her upper arm. "Hold your arm out farther from your body. Now try again."

This time when she swung the sword, the bulk of her armor did not hinder the arc. But the movement of the horse beneath her did.

Edgar came up on the other side. "Relax your legs. Plant your feet and use the stirrups for support." He slapped the high back of her saddle. "Lean hard against the cantle, it will keep you in place."

Marianne looked from one man to the other. "Do you plan to do battle out here?"

When Melwyn's eyebrows disappeared beneath his helmet, Marianne let her legs go lax. She pushed down hard on the stirrups, making sure they would indeed support her weight. Then she shifted in the saddle, moving all the way back and pressing against the high padded cantle as Edgar had suggested.

Melwyn nodded. "Good. Now, arm up. Sword out."

She followed his order, satisfied that if need be, she stood a slim chance of defending herself. Marianne swallowed a misplaced smile. There was nothing at all amusing in this situation.

But how many women received last-minute battle instructions from their brothers' captains?

Melwyn raised his hand. The three of them stopped
at a curve in the road. The sound of approaching riders
grew louder. He leaned closer to Marianne. "How well
do you know this Warehaven?"

"I know that he is Bryce's brother in spirit, if not in
name."

"Good." The captain nodded toward the curve ahead.
"Because he should be arriving…just…about…now."

No sooner had the words left his mouth than Jared and
his men rounded the curve. Marianne rested her sword
across her legs and moved her horse forward. Melwyn
and Edgar fell into place directly behind her.

Jared reined in his horse and raised his hand,
stopping his men in their tracks. He stared at Marianne
and her companions. Then he leaned back in his saddle
a moment before shaking his head. "Let me guess.
Marianne?"

"Aye."

"What are you doing here? Where is Bryce? Who are
the men with you?"

She moved her horse closer. He did the same, meeting
her between the two groups of men. Marianne squared
her shoulders. "I need an army to rescue my beloved. I
would have yours in Ashforde's name."

Jared laughed, but sobered quickly. "Is it that bad?"

"Worse. If we stay here talking it may be too late."

He motioned his men to inch closer. Once they were
all within hearing, he unsheathed his weapon. He
grasped the blade and held the hilt toward her. "My men
and my own arm are yours to command."

Softly, Marianne said, "Thank you, Jared. I owe you
a debt I may never be able to repay." Louder, she said,

"Sheath your weapon, Dragon, and let us make haste for Faucon."

She spun her horse around and slid her weapon into the scabbard. Before she could spur the animal into movement, Melwyn grabbed her arm. "My lady?" He nodded toward Jared's men. "Your orders?"

"Oh." Marianne rolled her eyes to the ever-lightening sky before turning back to the men. She heard Jared's low laugh, but ignored him and said, "Follow me. We go to Faucon to rescue the Comte of Ashforde."

This time when she turned her horse toward Faucon, everyone fell into step behind her. Except for Jared. He rode at her side. "What has happened to make a woman don overlarge armor and a weapon with the intent of stealing my men?"

Marianne swung her head around to look at him. Unfortunately, her nasal helmet had come loose and did not turn with her. The nose guard now covered one eye.

Jared couldn't control a smile as he reached out and righted her helmet. "If you had not already stolen Bryce's heart, I would pull you from that saddle to my lap, kiss you senseless and ride away—never to be seen again."

To her own surprise she admitted, "If my heart and soul did not already belong to another, I might ride away with you willingly."

He squeezed her gloved hand a moment before sitting upright. "Now, tell me what has happened."

Rhys rode between the twin gate towers of Faucon and headed straight for the practice field. As much as he longed to see his wife, he would not do so until after this combat with Ashforde was over.

Lyonesse had already begged him not to go through with this. She had even used her tears against him, knowing how powerless they made him feel. That was the reason he'd spent the night away from the keep.

What was truly sad was that were it not for the anarchy, this war over the crown, he and Ashforde would be allies, perhaps even brothers-by-marriage. For once he had actually met a man who might deserve his sister's hand in marriage.

Rhys spat. It was a shame Ashforde had to be on the wrong side of this war.

Marianne was going to be distraught. He did not doubt that she would hate him before this day ended. So be it. He had a duty to protect her and he never shirked his duty—not even when she disagreed with him.

He would simply have to look harder for a suitable husband. Someone who could take her mind off Ashforde.

Rhys entered the practice field and perused the rather smallish gathering. Thankfully, his orders had been followed and none of the women were present. However, he had expected to see more of the men in attendance.

"Rhys." Gareth approached.

"Who guards the women?"

"Melwyn and Edgar. I thought the task would be easier for them than any of the other men."

He agreed with his brother. The captains would not be swayed by the women's pleading and screaming, where some of the guards might.

"Ashforde is being readied?"

"Aye." Gareth looked up at him. "Are you certain this is what you wish to do?"

"Yes."

"There would be no shame in backing out. Surely you could find another punishment for the man."

"You too?" Rhys gritted his teeth. "Does anyone think the Comte of Faucon knows what he is doing?"

"I doubt not your sanity, Rhys, only your reasoning."

"Has marriage made you soft, Gareth?"

"Nay. You know that is not the case."

"I defend Marianne's honor. I defend King Stephen, *our* king."

Gareth raised his hand. "You need not explain. Ashforde serves the empress. Will it always be thus? This war cannot last forever, Rhys. Do you not pray that someday friends will not be forced to kill friends and that brothers will be permitted to lay down their weapons and gather as a family?"

"Of course I do." Rhys stared up at Faucon Keep. He would enjoy nothing more than to spend each day here, seeing to his fields, his falcons and his family. "Do you think I, too, am not tired of war? My heart aches at the thought of fighting men I once shared jokes and ale with. It sickens me to face men I knew as boys, knowing they now have families and lands of their own.

"Aye, Gareth, I wish for the day when I can sheath my sword for good. More than you can ever know, I wish for it to happen. But that day is not yet here."

"Enough." Gareth gripped Rhys's arm. "I am sorry to have questioned you."

Rhys laughed. "If it had not been you, it would have been someone else." He paused, shaking his head.

"Marianne is well-served by her brothers and their wives."

"And while we all serve her so well, who serves you?"

He recognized the guilt choking Gareth's words. "Fear not, brother. It is our way to defend and support the one most in need. I do not begrudge Marianne your support or your love. If I thought for one heartbeat that she would permit it, I, too, would hold her close."

Not a foolish man, Rhys knew that if he tried to hold Marianne close, she would let him. She would gladly embrace him with one hand and use the other to ram a dagger into his heart.

He sighed when a dark frown creased his brother's forehead. "Gareth, if I die this day, I know your grief will be real. I have no doubt that your love for me is true. Set aside your guilt and see to Marianne."

Gareth stepped back from the horse and looked at the field. If Rhys had the slightest hint of the guilt all of them now bore, he would gut each and every one of them.

They had all worried about Marianne. Never once did they give a thought to what this act of treason would do to Rhys.

He opened his mouth, and then snapped it closed.

Rhys asked, "Is there something else on your mind?"

"No." Gareth's self-hatred grew until it nearly choked him. He cleared his throat. "Only that your lady wife bids you have a care."

"That is all? Have a care?"

"Well, she did add something about killing you if you lost."

"Ah," A smile lit Rhys's face. "Now that sounds more like Lyonesse."

* * *

Bryce paced his small cell. His chain mail clinked with each step. He reached down and made certain his sword slid easily from the scabbard hanging at his side.

True to her word, Marianne had somehow seen to it that he had the use of his own weapon. For that he was grateful.

Now, if someone could end this nerve-racking wait. The sun had risen. If this was Faucon's way of cutting at his nerves, it worked.

Heavy footsteps ascended the stairs. Bryce stopped his pacing. The locking bar scraped against the door as it was lifted free. Two guards with drawn swords opened the door. One man silently waved him forward with his weapon.

This, too, grated on him. Why was his rank not afforded any measure of decency? He was no longer a nameless mercenary used to being treated as less than a dog.

Regardless of which crown he served, he was the Comte of Ashforde. Not some scurrilous knave willing to be so ill used.

His honor alone would have kept him within Faucon's walls. There'd been no need to cage him in a bare cell. And how dare Faucon challenge him to this trial by combat? Who did he think he was to so flaunt convention? Faucon was not his liege, nor did he wear a crown.

Each step down the stairs, through the great hall and across the bailey fueled his anger. Dear God, he did not wish to die. Not like this. And not when he had such a reason to live.

Bryce fisted his hands. Now that the moment was nigh, how could he let Faucon run a blade through his heart?

When they reached the practice field, Gareth met

him. "Marianne asked that I give you this." He handed Bryce a package.

Pulling his gloves off with his teeth, Bryce tore the ribbon from the cloth-wrapped bundle and pulled out a blue silk tunic. A note was attached. "I had not the time to stitch this for you, my love. So, I used what paint and dye was available. It is crudely formed, but was designed by my heart and soul." Bryce held up the garment and swallowed at the tangible evidence of her love.

Emblazoned on the chest was an ash tree. His gaze was drawn to an uppermost branch—where a falcon stood guard.

Gareth whistled softly. "Put it on."

Bryce handed Marianne's brother his gloves and the ribbon. He then removed his belt and pulled his own tunic over his head. The blue one slid easily down over his mail. Once his belt was back around his waist, Gareth held up the leaf-green ribbon. "Hold your arm out."

He stepped closer and tied the ribbon around Bryce's arm. "Stall for time."

"What?"

"Do not kill Rhys and do not let him kill you. Stall. As long as you can."

Before Bryce could ask, or Gareth could explain, Rhys entered the field.

Once at the center, the comte unsheathed his sword. "Are you ready to die, Ashforde?"

Bryce shot a look toward Gareth, and then he joined Faucon on the field. His sword hissed as he pulled it from the scabbard. He held it with one hand and beckoned Faucon forward with the other. "Come, let us see what you're made of, Faucon."

Gareth sighed in resignation before he said, "They could be allies if given the chance."

"Nay." Darius shook his head. "They could be brothers."

Gareth looked briefly to the wall. Darius's man Osbert had taken up his position at the main tower. He would send them a signal when Marianne was in sight.

His attention was drawn back to the field by a groan from Darius. "What?" He immediately saw Bryce on the ground. Thankfully, Ashforde rolled clear and jumped to his feet before Rhys planted his sword through flesh and muscle.

Gareth nudged Darius. "What do you think makes Glynnson appear so pleased?" The man wore a misplaced expression of pure satisfaction.

"I am not certain. Why do we not join him?"

The two men walked farther down the line and stood behind Glynnson. Even though they already knew Glynnson had been involved in the plot against Bryce and Rhys, they wanted to know more. At the first opportunity, Gareth had every intention of questioning the man.

Gareth edged alongside Glynnson and rested his forearms on the wooden top rail of the jousting list. He said nothing, but it was obvious his presence made the older man nervous. His smile disappeared. Sweat beaded on his brow and he shuffled as if to move away.

Darius moved in closer behind him. "Do not make a scene." He kept his voice low. "Stay and enjoy the fight. Then we shall talk." Glynnson's throat worked, but he said nothing.

Gareth motioned one of Faucon's guards forward and whispered, "Keep this man company. Do not let him out of your sight. I wish to speak with him after the fight."

"Aye, sir." The guard moved to Glynnson's other side.

Certain their chance to question Glynnson would come, Darius and Gareth turned their full attention to the ongoing fight.

The men on the field fought back and forth down the practice ground. Using broadswords in this manner would tire them quickly. Gareth was impressed that their swings were still true. He noticed not even the slightest hesitation.

What he did notice was that neither man spoke. They'd both fallen silent in their single-minded focus on the battle. He watched Bryce. Marianne's man was a good match for Rhys.

They were so well matched that the winner of this battle would be due to a mistake on the loser's part. It would have nothing to do with who had the greater strength or skill.

Each time Bryce gained the upper hand, Rhys was able to push himself free. It was the same when Rhys gained the upper hand.

Maybe he'd not needed to tell Ashforde to stall.

Rhys spun away from Bryce's lunged thrust. The comte tripped and landed on his knees. Gareth held his breath. He heard Darius's loud intake of breath.

Bryce stepped back. "Surely you do not tire this easily?"

"Tire?" Rhys stood with a shout of rage. "Never."

Both Gareth and Darius breathed a sigh of relief. Bryce had given up his first chance to kill his opponent.

Rhys barreled toward Ashforde. He rushed him with his sword held out. To Gareth's amazement, Bryce didn't flinch. He slid the blade of his weapon along Faucon's until the cross guards locked. He then leaned into his shove and spun Rhys around, slamming the comte's back against the quintain post.

Obviously winded, Rhys shook his head. Again, Ashforde stepped back.

Darius whistled. "He needs to teach me that move."

"I am not certain, but I think it requires more desperation than brains." Gareth knew he'd not have the patience to slide his weapon against an opponent's in that manner. It would put him too close to the enemy. And one misstep could end badly.

He glanced up at the tower and nudged Darius. Sir Osbert was leaning over the wall, peering out across the clearing.

Within a matter of heartbeats, the captain turned and nodded to Darius and Gareth. Both men started counting. That was the plan. Count to twenty, and then give the signal of an attack.

Gareth wondered if Darius held his breath, too. At a count of fifteen, Darius pushed past Glynnson and the Faucon guard to stand at Gareth's side.

At the count of twenty, they both ducked under the wooden tourney list and stepped on to the field.

Their movements went undetected, as everyone's attention was drawn to the man on the wall shouting "To arms! Faucon, to arms!"

Gareth rushed and grabbed Bryce's sword arm. Darius went to Rhys's side.

Rhys cursed. "What the hell—?" He pointed at Bryce and ordered Gareth, "See that he is returned to his cell. We will finish this later. Then join me on the wall."

Without hesitation, Gareth did as ordered. He led Bryce back into the keep.

"What is happening?"

Gareth ignored Ashforde's question.

"Are you going to tell me what is afoot?" When Gareth again refused to answer, Bryce swore. "What the hell has Marianne done?"

At that, Gareth had to smile. He opened the door to the cell and waved Bryce inside. After closing the door and dropping the bar in place, he opened the small peephole and peered inside. "She does what she must, you fool."

He slid the square of wood back into place and headed down the stairs, with Bryce's shouts following him nearly to the great hall.

Rhys leaned against the wall and looked out at the clearing. A force of at least fifty men drew near.

At the moment they displayed no standard, so he had no way of knowing who approached Faucon in a manner that spoke of battle.

Gareth joined him. "Who comes?"

"I do not know. Where are Melwyn and Edgar?"

"I left them with the women."

Rhys narrowed his eyes. "Did you not think we would be better served if they joined us here?"

"Why? Do you expect to be attacked?"

The men in the clearing stopped. Then, they realigned their formation. Instead of two single columns, they stretched out to either side of their leader.

Rhys nodded. "I would say, yes, I expect to be attacked."

The group began to move toward Faucon once again. When they were half the distance to the keep, two riders raised their standards. The brilliant pennants unfurled in the breeze.

The two standard bearers rode closer, leaving the line of men to follow at a slower pace. Within a matter of heartbeats the spitting dragon of one standard came clearly into view. Alongside of it a nesting falcon fluttered.

Gareth watched Rhys closely. When the comte's eyes widened in recognition, Gareth stepped out of reach.

Darius did the same. But his move was to give Lyonesse, Marguerite and Rhian room to join them at the wall.

Lyonesse squared her shoulders and went to her husband's side. She placed a hand on his shoulder. "Hear her out, Rhys."

Marianne raised her hand, bringing the man at her side to a halt. She scanned the wall, looking for Rhys. He would be easy to find, since he'd be the one in an unreasonable rage.

"Hail, Faucon!" she shouted up at the wall.

Rhys leaned over and shouted back. "What brings you slinking to my wall with armed troops at your back?"

She drew in a breath and shouted, "I come to take possession of Comte Bryce of Ashforde."

"In whose name?"

"Marianne of Faucon."

Rhys tapped the hilt of his drawn sword on the wall. "Is this taking by force or ransom?"

Ransom? Was he still alive? Were they not too late? Marianne's breath caught. Jared nudged her with his foot. "Steady."

"Ransom."

"What have you to offer?"

Marianne slid from her saddle and walked closer to the wall. She looked up at the faces of her family for a moment before prostrating herself on the ground. "My heart."

Rhys cursed.

Jared cursed louder.

She held her breath, waiting for Rhys's reply. But no one made a sound. Marianne swallowed, forcing herself to wait.

Finally, when she thought she could stand the silence no longer, the gate opened wide enough to let one man walk out.

Strong, steady hands pulled her from the ground. "Marianne."

At the sound of Bryce's voice she threw herself into his arms. Unable to talk, she clung to him, taking comfort and strength in the safety of his embrace.

Rhys again leaned over the wall. "When you are finished, join us in the hall—unarmed."

Chapter Twenty-One

If Bryce did not know better, he would think his knees shook. Since he was not an old trembling woman that was not possible.

He untied Marianne's helmet and tossed it to the ground. "I am not certain if I should kiss you, or beat you."

"I care not what you do. Beat me until I can no longer move." She grasped his head and pulled him down for a kiss. "Kiss me until I can no longer breathe."

His lips hovered just over hers. "I am still debating."

Jared dismounted. He marched up to Bryce, snatched Marianne's helmet from the ground and then urged, "Kiss the woman. I am dying to see the inside of this keep."

Needing no further urging, Bryce claimed her lips with his own. It had only been a matter of hours since he'd last held her. But he had believed they would never see each other again. The knowledge that the threat of his death had lessened greatly made this kiss the sweetest he had ever had.

Gareth leaned over the wall. "Ahem. I would advise not making him wait overlong."

Bryce lifted his head. "There is your kiss. I will withhold the beating until later."

She laughed and grasped his hand. "Come. Bring your curious dragon and let us go speak with Rhys."

Melwyn and Edgar joined them. Melwyn told Jared, "I will have tents erected in the clearing for your men."

"And supplies?"

"Yes. Food and drink will be provided for the men and the horses."

Jared nodded. "Thank you." He turned and whistled at his horse. The animal turned about and headed back to the line of men.

"Speaking of men." Bryce looked at Jared. "Where did you obtain so many?"

"Twenty are mine, ten are yours, some are Faucon's and there are five or six mercenaries making up the rest." He glanced briefly back at the throng. "Rather regal is it not?"

"What do you mean ten are mine?"

Marianne tugged at Bryce's hand. "You can talk and walk at the same time. Let us go."

As the small group entered Faucon, Jared answered, "They simply showed up at Warehaven claiming to have been with the empress for these last months."

"Did they mention anything about the fire? What happened to them, who attacked Ashforde—anything?"

"No." Jared shook his head. "The empress ordered the ten men back to her court before the fire."

Marianne interrupted. "So why are they with you now?"

"They overheard talk of the fire at court. When their service was completed for the year, they headed toward

Ashforde to see what had happened and to offer assistance. Eustace ran into them and brought them to Warehaven."

"These men are loyal to Ashforde?" Edgar asked.

Jared shrugged. "They seem to prefer serving Ashforde over the empress."

"Seems mighty convenient that the empress ordered them away from Ashforde before the fire."

Bryce nodded at Melwyn's comment. "Aye, that is what I was thinking, too."

Marianne shook her head. "It is a shame that Sir John is no longer alive."

"What?" Bryce's shout reminded her that he did not know.

Melwyn cleared his throat. "I questioned him."

"Questioned him?" Jared looked over at Melwyn. "Sounds like a handy skill. I need you to speak to my man. He's far too easy on prisoners."

Bryce turned around and stopped. "Halt. Is there anything else I should know?" He stared at each of them one by one. "Marianne? Why in the name of heaven are you dressed as a man and where did you get that armor?"

Before she answered, he looked to Melwyn and Edgar. "And why were the two of you with Jared instead of standing on the wall alongside Faucon?"

Again, he moved on without waiting for an answer. "And you," his attention rested on Jared. "What are you doing at Faucon?"

A heavy silence fell on the group. Marianne sighed and then spoke up first. "Let me explain."

Bryce crossed his arms against his chest. "Please, do."

"The only way to stop Rhys was for me…us…my family." She paused. "Was for me to gather an army and attack Faucon. Lyonesse lent me the use of her leather armor. My brothers and their wives found the other pieces."

Edgar picked up the telling. "Strangers entering Faucon's lands were spotted and since we learned from Sir John that your other man Eustace had gone to Lord Warehaven, we assumed he led the strangers."

"Marianne assured us that Warehaven was your friend," Melwyn added. "Even so, we could not permit her to ride out alone."

"They taught me how to fight on horseback."

Bryce glared at her. "Good. We will find you a spot on the training grounds."

She ignored his sarcasm. "And when we found Jared, he graciously lent me the use of his men."

"How could I refuse the request from such a charming warrior?" Jared reached over, placed the helmet on Marianne's head and twisted it, putting the nosepiece over her one eye. "Be honest, Bryce, could you refuse this?"

It had all been too much. This day, this week, these last few months had been far too much for any one man. Bryce was in no mood for humor. He ignored Jared's question, instead focusing his attention on Marianne. "And now…" He took the helmet from her head before continuing, "Could you explain to me why you were prostrate at Faucon's wall?"

"When I offered ransom for your freedom over force, Rhys asked what I had to give."

Jared snorted, before he finished the explanation, "So she offered him her heart."

Bryce looked at the men. "This was your plan? To let her throw herself on the comte's mercy?"

"We had no plan at that point." Marianne shrugged. "It was all I could think of doing."

Bryce reached out and pulled her against his chest. "Your heart belongs to me."

"I know. And if he refused it, I would have given him my bride portion."

"Why did you not offer that first?"

"Because, we need it for Ashforde."

Bryce shook his head, before releasing her and resuming the walk across the bailey. "I must remember to beat you later."

Marianne was still laughing when they entered the keep. The sight of her three brothers standing shoulder to shoulder dampened her mirth. If they all lived to be a hundred, she would always find them an imposing sight when together.

The wives approached. Lyonesse took Marianne's hand. "Come. You need to change."

She looked from her brothers to Bryce. "What about—"

"Go." Rhys added in a milder tone, "He will be alive when you return."

When she still hesitated, Bryce tugged on the laces of her armor. "Leave us."

Marianne paced the floor of her chamber. Her head throbbed. It had been too long. She'd not only bathed and dressed, but she had eaten and tried to rest a while.

And still no one came for her. What were they doing to Bryce? Her mind conjured the most gruesome methods of torture, each one more horrific than the last.

Lyonesse, Marguerite and Rhian had ordered her to

remain in her chamber until someone came. The only reason she'd not tried to leave was because she wished not to anger her sisters-by-marriage. They had helped her far too much for her to disobey them now.

So, instead of disobeying them, she made herself sick with worry.

Her door opened, then closed. Marianne stopped pacing, folded her hands together before her and held her breath.

When Rhys walked into the chamber, she swallowed hard. He stopped just inside the room and stared at her. She met his steady gold-flecked gaze and fought the childish longing to throw herself into his arms.

The hard intensity of his stare made her nervous. When had that come about? What was this sudden worry that he would find her lacking?

"I am glad you are home and that you are safe, Marianne. Even if you will only be with us for a short time."

She took a step in his direction. "I am going somewhere?"

"Your husband-to-be wishes to leave before the weather turns hard."

She ignored the voice in her head telling her to act like an adult, and nearly flew toward him.

Rhys grasped her arms and held her away from him. "I am sorry I did not notice that you were no longer a child."

"If anyone should be sorry, it is I. Rhys, I never meant to hurt you or to dishonor you."

He pulled her against his chest. "Good Lord, no, Marianne, you did no such thing. You were a woman fighting to discover your place in this life by yourself. I cannot fault you for that."

"I could have gone about it in a less worrisome manner."

"Ack. You are a Faucon, we do nothing by halves."

That much was true. "Rhys, would you have truly killed Bryce?"

His chest shook with his wry laugh. "Do not repeat this, because I will deny it. Your Bryce could have killed me more than once, yet he did not. When his chance was clear, he stepped away. Would I have killed him? I am not certain I would have had the opportunity."

"Then I am thankful I interrupted your fight."

"Marianne, you might want to temper such rashness."

"Yes, I get the impression Bryce wants me to be a little less daring, too."

"It is a husband's way."

She pulled back and looked up at him. "What happens now?"

"You will remain here a month. If the two of you still seem a good match, you will marry here at Faucon and then be on your way to Ashforde."

"And Bryce knows this?"

"Of course he does." Rhys's eyebrows winged together. "He has also sworn not to share your bed until you are wed."

Marianne felt the fire race up her face. At the same time her heart fell to her toes. A month was a long time.

Rhys must have read her thoughts because he released her and laughed. "I have never heard of anyone dying from unfulfilled lust."

"There could be a first time."

He pushed her toward the door. "For once in your life, behave yourself."

* * *

Stars dotted the night sky. It had been a long day of discussing marriage plans and ideas for rebuilding Ashforde a bit quicker than Bryce had thought.

Gareth and Darius had questioned Glynnson. Between her, Bryce, Jared, her brothers and their captains, they were able to piece together what had transpired.

While it was true that Cecily and Sir John had been in love with each other, Marianne had been right. Neither of them were quick enough to plan everything on their own. In a way, they were pawns, much as Bryce had been.

Glynnson wanted Ashforde Keep. But he'd killed one of Stephen's men and had laid waste to the man's land. Stephen would have set his army on Glynnson had the man taken over Ashforde Keep.

The empress owed Glynnson for a favor he refused to name. Not even Melwyn could get that information from him. Between Glynnson and Matilda they hatched a plan to get Ashforde Keep into Cecily's hands.

Had Rhys seen fit to kill Bryce as they'd expected, then everything would have fallen into place. The betrothal document in Bryce's saddlebag would have contained a forged signature, which no one would be able to prove he'd not signed. That was what led Glynnson to Faucon—he needed that document. Because once Bryce was dead, the hereditary charter to Ashforde would have been give to Cecily.

Now, Glynnson and his family left Faucon with nothing but their lives.

Bryce still held the charter to Ashforde. Rhys had every intention of having that charter documented with King Stephen. He would vouch for Bryce as long as he swore not to attack his neighbors. It was a vow Bryce made willingly.

By the time the evening meal was served, Marianne had been ready to scream. She and Bryce had not had one moment alone. Now, she stared out the window in her chamber and saw him on the wall.

She quickly grabbed her hooded cloak and raced to join him on the wall.

Once there, she pulled the cloak tightly around her to ward off the chill and walked to his side.

"I am ready for my beating, my lord."

Bryce laughed softly and put his arm across her shoulders. "I thought for sure I would have to stand out here all night waiting for you to come keep me company."

"I would come to your chamber if I knew where it was."

"Oh, yes. Melwyn, Osbert and Edgar would enjoy that."

Marianne gasped. "You are not under guard."

"No. Fear not. I only share a chamber with them."

She shook her head. "Is this Rhys's idea of a joke?"

"I think it is his way of keeping us out of each other's bed for a month."

"I will talk to Lyonesse."

"No. A month is not that long, Marianne. We will live." He placed a kiss on the top of her head. "Just imagine how much we will need each other by then."

"I need you now."

Bryce turned to face her. He covered her hands with his own and lifted them to his chest. "My love, you already have me."

"And I'll not let you go. Ever."

"I would hope not." He released her hands and slid his arms around her, pulling her close. "I am counting on you to hold my heart as gently and thoroughly as I vow to hold yours."

"Always, my love. Always." Marianne turned her face up to his. "Kiss me, Bryce."

His lips were warm against hers. Warm with a promise of the future. A promise so true and strong that it sent her heart soaring.

When his heartbeat tapped in unison against her chest, Marianne knew without a doubt that for today and all of their tomorrows, they would indeed hold each other's heart gently and thoroughly.

* * * * *

Happily ever after is just the beginning....

Turn the page for a sneak preview of
DANCING ON SUNDAY AFTERNOONS
by
Linda Cardillo

Harlequin Everlasting—Every great love
has a story to tell.™
A brand-new line from Harlequin Books
launching this February!

Prologue

Giulia D'Orazio
1983

I had two husbands—Paolo and Salvatore.

Salvatore and I were married for thirty-two years. I still live in the house he bought for us; I still sleep in our bed. All around me are the signs of our life together. My bedroom window looks out over the garden he planted. In the middle of the city, he coaxed tomatoes, peppers, zucchini—even grapes for his wine—out of the ground. On weekends, he used to drive up to his cousin's farm in Waterbury and bring back manure. In the winter, he wrapped the peach tree and the fig tree with rags and black rubber hoses against the cold, his massive, coarse hands gentling those trees as if they were his fragile-skinned babies. My neighbor, Dominic Grazza, does that for me now. My boys have no time for the garden.

In the front of the house, Salvatore planted roses. The roses I take care of myself. They are giant, cream-colored, fragrant. In the afternoons, I like to sit out on the porch with my coffee, protected from the eyes of the neighborhood by that curtain of flowers.

Salvatore died in this house thirty-five years ago. In the last months, he lay on the sofa in the parlor so he could be in the middle of everything. Except for the two oldest boys, all the children were still at home and we ate together every evening. Salvatore could see the dining room table from the sofa, and he could hear everything that was said. "I'm not dead, yet," he told me. "I want to know what's going on."

When my first grandchild, Cara, was born, we brought her to him, and he held her on his chest, stroking her tiny head. Sometimes they fell asleep together.

Over on the radiator cover in the corner of the parlor is the portrait Salvatore and I had taken on our twenty-fifth anniversary. This brooch I'm wearing today, with the diamonds—I'm wearing it in the photograph also— Salvatore gave it to me that day. Upstairs on my dresser is a jewelry box filled with necklaces and bracelets and earrings. All from Salvatore.

I am surrounded by the things Salvatore gave me, or did for me. But, God forgive me, as I lie alone now in my bed, it is Paolo I remember.

Paolo left me nothing. Nothing, that is, that my family, especially my sisters, thought had any value. No house. No diamonds. Not even a photograph.

But after he was gone, and I could catch my breath from the pain, I knew that I still had something. In the middle of the night, I sat alone and held them in my hands, reading the words over and over until I heard his voice in my head. I had Paolo's letters.

* * * * *

Silhouette®

Romantic
SUSPENSE

Excitement, danger and passion guaranteed!

Same great authors and riveting editorial
you've come to know and love.

Look for our new name next month
as Silhouette Intimate Moments® becomes
Silhouette® Romantic Suspense.

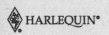

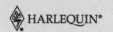

This February...

Catch NASCAR Superstar **Carl Edwards** *in*

SPEED DATING!

Kendall assesses risk for a living—so she's the last person you'd expect to see on the arm of a race-car driver who thrives on the unpredictable. But when a bizarre turn of events—and NASCAR hotshot Dylan Hargreave—inspire her to trade in her ever-so-structured existence for "life in the fast lane" she starts to feel she might be on to something!

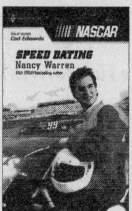

Collect all 4 debut novels in the Harlequin NASCAR series.

SPEED DATING
by *USA TODAY* bestselling author
Nancy Warren

THUNDERSTRUCK
by Roxanne St. Claire

HEARTS UNDER CAUTION
by Gina Wilkins

DANGER ZONE
by Debra Webb

On sale
February
2007

REQUEST YOUR FREE BOOKS!

Harlequin® Historical
Historical Romantic Adventure!

2 FREE NOVELS PLUS 2 FREE GIFTS!

YES! Please send me 2 FREE Harlequin® Historical novels and my 2 FREE gifts. After receiving them, if I don't wish to receive any more books, I can return the shipping statement marked "cancel." If I don't cancel, I will receive 6 brand-new novels every month and be billed just $4.69 per book in the U.S., or $5.24 per book in Canada, plus 25¢ shipping and handling per book and applicable taxes, if any*. That's a savings of close to 15% off the cover price! I understand that accepting the 2 free books and gifts places me under no obligation to buy anything. I can always return a shipment and cancel at any time. Even if I never buy another book from Harlequin, the two free books and gifts are mine to keep forever.

246 HDN EEWW   349 HDN EEW9

Name _____ (PLEASE PRINT) _____

Address _____ Apt. # _____

City _____ State/Prov. _____ Zip/Postal Code _____

Signature (if under 18, a parent or guardian must sign)

Mail to the **Harlequin Reader Service®:**
IN U.S.A.: P.O. Box 1867, Buffalo, NY 14240-1867
IN CANADA: P.O. Box 609, Fort Erie, Ontario L2A 5X3

Not valid to current Harlequin Historical subscribers.

Want to try two free books from another line?
Call 1-800-873-8635 or visit www.morefreebooks.com.

* Terms and prices subject to change without notice. NY residents add applicable sales tax. Canadian residents will be charged applicable provincial taxes and GST. This offer is limited to one order per household. All orders subject to approval. Credit or debit balances in a customer's account(s) may be offset by any other outstanding balance owed by or to the customer. Please allow 4 to 6 weeks for delivery.

Your Privacy: Harlequin is committed to protecting your privacy. Our Privacy Policy is available online at www.eHarlequin.com or upon request from the Reader Service. From time to time we make our lists of customers available to reputable firms who may have a product or service of interest to you. If you would prefer we not share your name and address, please check here. ☐

HARLEQUIN® *Romance*®

What a month!

In February watch for

Rancher and Protector
Part of the Western Weddings miniseries
BY JUDY CHRISTENBERRY

The Boss's Pregnancy Proposal
BY RAYE MORGAN

Also in February, expect
MORE of what you love
as the Harlequin Romance line
increases to six titles per month.

COMING NEXT MONTH FROM

HARLEQUIN®
HISTORICAL

- **THE LAWMAN'S BRIDE**
  by **Cheryl St.John**
  (Western)
  The last thing Sophie Hollis wants in her life is a lawman—with a
  past like hers, it can only lead to trouble. But Clay Connor won't
  take no for an answer.

- **A SCANDALOUS MISTRESS**
  by **Juliet Landon**
  (Regency)
  Scandal followed Lady Amelie Chester. Especially when she
  falsely confessed to an intimate relationship with Nicholas,
  Lord Elyot! Enchanted and intrigued, Nicholas was quick to
  take *every* advantage of the situation....

- **WARRIOR OR WIFE**
  by **Lyn Randal**
  (Roman)
  Deserted by her lover, high-born Lelia becomes Leda—the
  gladiator! When her soldier returns to claim her, Lelia must choose
  between the danger of the arena and the more frightening prospect
  of giving her heart.

- **ASHBLANE'S LADY**
  by **Sophia James**
  (Medieval)
  Alexander Ullyot, Laird of Ashblane, should have had no
  compunction about using the beautiful Madeleine for his own
  ends—but he desired her. Was Alex in danger of falling for the
  woman who was his means of revenge...?